CH00925937

THE OTHER
HARLOW GIRL

LYNN MESSINA

potatoworks press
greenwich village

CHAPTER ONE

As Miss Lavinia Harlow prided herself on possessing faultless good manners, she considered soaking a gentleman with an exploding garden hose to be not only a significant breach in social etiquette but a deeply mortifying miscalculation as well.

With a horrified gasp, she dropped what little remained of the hose to the conservatory floor and raised an appalled hand to her mouth as droplets fell from the soggy stranger's impeccably cut bottle-green waistcoat. Bravely moving her gaze upward, she discovered everything about the gentleman was impeccable: His shoulders were reassuringly broad but not robust, his jaw was agreeably firm but not obstinate, his nose was pleasingly patrician but not aquiline. The only thing about him that did not fall in line were his eyes, which were a remarkable shade of aquamarine—not quite blue, not quite green, wholly breathtaking. The color was so stunning, it made her own cornflower blue seem insipid by comparison, an inconsideration Vinnie thought was the height of rudeness.

"I beg your pardon," the gentleman drawled in a fine baritone.

He bowed slightly, and Vinnie realized that his composure was just as faultless as the rest of him. If the water dripping into his inappropriately beautiful eyes caused him

1

the least discomfort, he gave no indication. Indeed, he stood drenched in the Duke of Trent's conservatory with the same bland indifference as he would completely dry in his grace's drawing room.

That he had the excellent good breeding not to let his displeasure show irritated Vinnie further. Knowing she was in the wrong was uncomfortable; not being taken to task for it was unbearable.

If only he had the consideration to vent his spleen, Vinnie thought, then she could be justifiably annoyed at him for overreacting to what was merely an unfortunate accident.

Vinnie knew full well that it was *she* who should be begging *his* pardon, but she'd never doused anyone before, let alone a personage so refined and handsome as the gentleman standing before her, and she was quite at a loss as to how to proceed. Reasonable options occurred to her—ring for a servant to help him remove his topcoat, provide him with a cloth so that he may dry his hair—but for some reason she couldn't put any of these plans into action. All she could do was stare in horror as water dripped from his nose.

The situation was intolerable. She had to do something immediately.

"Turpentine," she said with unexpected vehemence.

At this inexplicable communication, the gentleman raised one eyebrow. "Turpentine?" he repeated mildly.

For a moment, Vinnie was transfixed by the perfect elegance of his eyebrows. They were so dark as to be black, and the contrast between them and his aquamarine eyes was as unsettling as the eye color itself. His hair, cut a little longer than fashionable and just a shade lighter, intensified the effect.

Where was I?

"Yes, turpentine," she repeated more calmly. "I'm working to improve the flexibility of the garden hose. You see, the modern garden hose is typically made of leather stitched together, which works well enough, but its utility is limited by the poor elasticity of the material, which makes it burst rather than stretch. In 1791, however, a shoe manufacturer named Samuel Brill patented a method by which he combined Indian-rubber and turpentine to make the leather of his shoes impervious to rain and puddles, and I thought that perhaps a variation on his method could be applied to the garden hose to improve its elastication."

Even as she made her remarkable speech, Vinnie knew her behavior was beyond the pale. One didn't talk at length on an obscure topic of no interest to one's listener at the best of times. To do so when one's audience was miserably wet was insupportable. And yet she couldn't seem to stop herself.

"I have made six formulations so far," she explained, "and this latest was the most promising. Indeed, it outscored its predecessors in all five categories, including ability to withstand increased water pressure, which is, of course, the most important measure. Admittedly, my technique is primitive, since I use a screw pump, which dates back to the ancient Egyptians. Archimedes, as you know, invented—"

Vinnie broke off midsentence when she noticed the bored expression on the man's face. It was that look of utter ennui that finally gave Vinnie the self-possession to stop her aimless chatter and to say something sensible.

"I do apologize," she exclaimed in a breathless rush, more embarrassed than she'd ever been before. It was one thing for a device like a garden hose to malfunction; that was a work in progress and could be improved upon with time and effort. But her inability to work properly could not so easily be fixed, and she knew it. She'd been like this her whole life—either as quiet as a church mouse or as chirpy as a magpie. For her, there no midway point between a lack of conversation and too much of the wrong kind. This defect explained why she'd never caught on with the members of the *ton*, despite being reasonably dowried and passably pretty. She'd managed to attach only one *parti* in her twenty-four years, and he turned out to be a traitorous spy who tried to end her sister. Instead, Vinnie had ended him.

And she knew if *that* story ever got out, it would be the end of her social career, such as it was.

"I've behaved atrociously. First, my hose explodes on you and then I compound the error by rambling on about inconsequential things," Vinnie said, struggling for calm. Looking at him made sense harder to come by so she looked away. She reached for the bell tug to summon a footman, then rummaged through the side cabinet for something with which to dry him. She found an old cloth that was more rag than cloth and was sensible enough not to offer it to him. Clutching it anxiously in her fingers, she turned back to him and smiled with some effort. "I do hope you can forgive me."

"Of course," the gentleman rushed to assure her. "No doubt it's my fault for startling you."

The suggestion was so absurd—not just the scientific inevitability of increased water pressure and stiff leather but also the obviousness of the lie—that Vinnie burst into laughter. As if a dam had broken, she let free a torrent of giggles so intense it brought tears to her eyes. She knew this unrestrained amusement was a social faux pas as bad as the soaking and the babbling, but she didn't care. There was something so liberating about sincerely felt mirth.

As the laughter subsided, Vinnie dabbed the tears from her cheeks with the worn cloth in her hand. Then she looked back up at the gentleman with her brightest, most genuine smile, intending to thank him for his generous description of the situation, but the look of annoyance on his face stopped her. With an abrupt hand, he swept his wet black hair back from his forehead, causing fresh droplets to course down his nose. It was the first indication that he was less than comfortable in his saturated state.

Vinnie felt a new wave of embarrassment—how all too brief that moment of liberation had been!—but refused to let herself be ruled by it. Instead, she straightened her shoulders and called upon the great good sense for which she was famous. Everyone knew Miss Lavinia Harlow was not given to frivolity. She was a capable young woman who was often sought out for practical reasons: advice on how to fix a drainage system, a partner to fill out a country dance. She vowed to apply her levelheadedness to the situation, and just as she was about to assure her company that she would have him dry and drinking tea in no time, a footman entered the room.

"Ah, Tupper, there you are," she said, greatly relieved. Finally, the end of this appalling episode was in sight. "As you can see, this gentleman is in need of assistance. I'm afraid my garden hose experiment went sadly awry just as—"

She broke off as she realized she had no idea who the gentleman was or what business he had in the Duke of Trent's conservatory. Should she pause now for introductions or brazen it out? She knew the former was the correct course of action, for her governess had impressed upon her that it was never too late to do the right thing, but she was loath to draw attention to the fact that she had previously done the wrong thing. Perhaps the lack of introduction had escaped the gentleman's notice. He had been soaked by a cold rush of water, after all. Something like that tended to shift one's focus.

Brazening it would be.

"And this poor gentleman was the unfortunate victim of my scheme," she explained. "Please escort him to the red bedroom." Why she specified the red room when the London town house didn't any have such accommodation, she had no idea, other than a desire to appear in control of the situation. She knew Tupper to be an intelligent and able young man and was confident he would devise a solution that wouldn't make her look like a complete ninnyhammer. "I'm sure the duke's valet wouldn't mind arranging for some clothes to be lent as a temporary measure. The two gentlemen seem to be of the same size, though I think perhaps the duke might have the advantage of a few inches. Additionally, tell Mrs. Wellburger"—actually, the housekeeper's name was Mrs. Crenshaw but correcting herself now would make her appear foolish—"to send up tea and a light collation of cheese and meats. And lastly, please make my apologies to Caruthers for the mess caused by my unsuccessful garden hose experiment and leave a cutting of the *Bletia purpurae* in his room as a thank-you for his prompt attention to this matter."

It went without saying that Tupper didn't know a *Bletia purpurae* from a *Cattleya skinneri*—or, for that matter, a *Rosa moschata*, which was but a common garden rose—and she would have to clarify that later, lest he unwittingly damaged one of the duke's favorite orchids. For now, however, she spoke with authority, confident that her audience knew she was competent and in charge.

Vinnie forced herself to look once more at the man with the unsettling aquamarine eyes whose name she didn't know and curtsied. The whole ordeal had left her a little weak in the knees, which explained why she dipped far lower in her curtsy than was proper for a personage of nonroyal blood. If she had an ounce of room left in her body for more embarrassment, she'd be horrified that the unknown gentleman probably now thought that she thought he was the prince regent himself. But she didn't have the room, so she simply straightened her shoulders and smiled politely. "I'm sure Tupper has everything well in hand, so I will take my leave of you. I apologize again for the mishap and appreciate your understanding. Good day, sir," she said, meaning *good riddance,* and swept out of the room, determined to never think of him again.

The Duchess of Trent, formerly Miss Emma Harlow and still currently the Harlow Hoyden, laughed at the disgruntled look on her sister's face.

"I'm sorry, my dear, but I simply don't keep track of the comings and goings of everyone in this town house. I don't even know where my own husband is, let alone anyone else's," she said, closing the book in her lap and straightening her legs, which were curled under her in the armchair. Prior to Vinnie's interruption, she'd been employed in the very un-hoydenish activity of reading quietly in her study while snacking on tea cakes. The room was large and cheerful, with dappled yellow flowers on the walls, a welcoming settee and oodles of bright sunlight pouring in through the windows. It was all a lady could desire in a study, yet Emma had been quite vexed when Trent had insisted she take it. She'd wanted something small and simple, a bare room with a fireplace and an armchair and perhaps a table on which to rest her teacup, preferably in the servant's quarters or in the cellars. The problem with a large and cheerful study with a welcoming settee was that people felt welcomed.

Her sister didn't count as people, of course. She never minded a visit from Vinnie, and some of her happiest moments in the London house had been spent in this very room reading while Vinnie worked on her horticultural text at the desk near the east-facing window.

"I didn't say he was married," Vinnie announced, plopping down on the settee, which her sister noted with fascination. Vinnie never plopped. She always lowered herself gently—onto chairs, benches, sofas, picnic blankets. Of course she did. Vinnie was the perfect lady, the pattern card of how a young miss should deport herself among the *ton*.

Emma didn't know how she did it. Whenever she herself tried to abide by the constricts of society, she was inevitably undone by impatience or annoyance or boredom or a general impishness that could never quite be tamped down. It had, she admitted, been easier to stay out of trouble in the six months she'd been married to the duke, but that was because they'd been rusticating in the country for four of them. It was much harder to break the rules when there were so few of them.

"I said he was rude and awful and pompous and quite full of himself and insufferable, but I never said a word about his marital status," Vinnie replied in a huff. "I wouldn't presume to know it. As I mentioned, I don't even know his name."

Emma laid the book on the table next to her, piled several tea cakes onto a plate and plopped onto the settee.

"Here," she said, handing her sister the generous serving.

Vinnie accepted the dish with a quizzical look. "Why are you feeding me?"

"You must be hungry," she explained.

"I must?"

"You always get out of sorts when you're hungry."

"I'm not out of sorts. I'm merely expressing my displeasure over an extremely disagreeable experience," she said reasonably.

As her sister stared down at the tea cakes, Emma leaned over and wiped her cheek with a cloth.

"What are you doing now?" Vinnie asked.

"There's a streak of dirt on your cheek. In fact, there are several."

"What?" she asked, dropping the plate onto the settee as both hands flew to her cheeks. "Where?"

Emma laughed. "They're just small streaks, and I think they show you to advantage. You look like a proper English lady enjoying a genteel afternoon in her garden."

"Oh, that stupid cloth!" Vinnie said angrily, imagining how absurd she must have looked issuing orders to Tupper with dirt stains on her face like a chimney sweep or a climbing boy. "I laughed so hard, I cried and then I dabbed at my tears with one of the cloths from the side cabinet where sundry supplies are kept. I should have known better. I *did* know better, which was why the awful rag was still in my hands."

"But I thought the gentleman made you angry," Emma said, reordering the scattered cakes on the dish and brushing the crumbs off the cushion.

"He did. Exceedingly angry. And then he said something that made me laugh uncontrollably," she explained.

"Quite a range of emotions," Emma observed and pressed the plate of tea cakes on her again. "No wonder you're hungry."

Lavinia was about to assure her for the second time that she wasn't hungry—it wasn't all that long since she'd had lunch—when Jane, the Dowager Duchess of Trent and

Emma's mother-in-law, entered the room.

"Ah, there you are, my dear," she said with a delighted smile, as she directed the footman to lay an armful of ledgers on the table. "That will be all, Jepson. Thank you."

Having the Harlow Hoyden as a daughter-in-law should have appalled the dowager duchess above all else, especially when she'd gone through the trouble of picking out the wonderfully proper Miss Portia Hedgley for her only son. But in fact Emma presented Jane with the one thing she loved more than propriety: a rehabilitation project. To her, Emma was like a provincial drawing room decorated in the outlandish Oriental style of the Prince's Pavilion in Brighton. All she needed was someone with excellent taste to take her in hand and replace all those garish fixtures with good, old-fashioned English furniture. The dowager, of course, had the credentials: She was respected by her peers, feared by her juniors and generally held in high regard by her relations. If the Harlow Hoyden had landed in any other family in the kingdom, the stock of her new relations would have gone down. Of that, Jane was certain. But since the Hoyden had had the very good sense to land in *her* family, the stock of her new relations was sure to rise. The Dowager Duchess of Trent would do everything in her power to ensure it. The truth was, she had been waiting her whole life to stand on her consequence and was almost grateful to Emma for giving her the opportunity.

"Menus," the dowager said now with sincere and surprising relish.

Vinnie, perceiving immediately the discussion to be had, stood up and offered the older woman her seat. "Here, ma'am, let me."

"Thank you, Lavinia," she said. "You are a dear."

Emma also understood what was in store—a long, boring afternoon of discussing menus for the ball the duchess was determined to throw on her and Trent's behalf—but she made a feeble attempt to evade it anyway. "No, thank you, ma'am. I've already had lunch, and I believe Alex and I are dining out tonight."

Well used to Emma by now, the dowager merely laughed and reached for one of the books that Vinnie held out. "The first course is the most important course to be served because it sets the tone for the entire meal," she wisely intoned. "Make a misstep at the very beginning and your guests will be grousing about the grouse while devouring the dish, and there is nothing, I assure you, that brings on indigestion faster. So we must deliberate carefully for as long as possible to make sure we arrive at the correct decision. Needless to say, of course, all decisions will be contingent upon your choice of dress."

In actuality, however, the connection between Emma's dress and the first course of the meal needed not only to be said, but expounded on at some length as well, as neither of the Harlow sisters could conceive what one had to do with the other and communicated this fact over the dowager's head with raised eyebrows and furrowed foreheads.

"Now here is the menu for the ball Alex's father and I hosted when we were first married," she said, handing Emma a sheet of parchment that was yellowed at the edges. "You'll see we had oysters, which were *tres fashionable* at the time but which I think are garish now. Ah, the folly of youth. And here is the menu for the second ball we hosted. It was a Christmas affair."

As the dowager and her duke had plighted their troth to each other more than three decades ago, Emma imagined endless hours of reviewing menus with no decisions made for the first course, let alone the whole meal. She couldn't believe this was how she would spend her afternoon.

She looked to Vinnie for sympathy, but her sister was no help. The other Harlow miss had not only an eye for detail but a genuine appreciation of it as well. She loved charts and evaluating data, and Emma could well imagine her graphing the grouse and foie gras on X and Y axes.

The only thing that could make the afternoon worse was a visit from her sister-in-law, whose opinion of her brother's marriage had not been as sanguine as her mother's, and Emma had no sooner had the thought than the woman in question appeared in the doorway.

"Mama, I've been looking for you everywhere," Louisa said in scolding tones as she stepped into the room, which she could easily accomplish because there was still so much space left, despite the crowd already gathered. She settled herself into the armchair to the left of the settee, a piece of furniture that Emma had particularly protested when Trent had it installed. One armchair and a settee was company. Two armchairs and a settee was a party.

"I was just at the milliner and Letitia Hawkins-Bonds was there ordering the most horrid chartreuse-and-pink organdy hat with a purple plume," she said, launching immediately into the purpose of her visit. "She swears anyone who is anyone in Paris is wearing it, but I can't credit such an absurdity, even for foreigners, and if it were true, I'd insist on chopping off my own head with a guillotine rather than laying that atrocity upon it. She said—Letitia Hawkins-Bonds, that is—that Mrs. Delano is having a little soiree on the same evening as our ball. Ordinarily, I'd be offended at the obvious slight, as invitations for our ball went out two weeks ago and the event is well established. However, Mrs. Delano is godmother to Miss Hedgley and is no doubt throwing the party to spare her dear goddaughter the humiliation of attending our ball or, worse, the humiliation of not attending our ball on a flimsy pretext. With all this in mind, I do think the soiree is but an act of kindness and it would hardly be appropriate for us to cavil at it."

The dowager, who had been on the verge of presenting the menu for Louisa's coming-out ball for several minutes, scowled at her daughter. "If we need not cavil, then we need not discuss it. As I was saying—"

"Yes, Mama, but I am more sensible of the insult done to Miss Hedgley, given the way my brother quite threw her over, and can't help but wish we could come to some sort of detente with her family," she said, with a hint of genuine tragedy in her voice. It was harder to say for whom she felt more sorry: herself or Miss Hedgley.

"I have an excellent solution," Emma said, with a devilish grin her sister-in-law was not sensible enough to recognize.

"Really?" Louisa asked snidely in a tone that implied her brother's wife had few ideas at all, let alone any excellent ones. "Do tell."

"I shall divorce Alex and go to the soiree myself," Emma offered. "It sounds like a very pleasant gathering and as a guest I will not be consulted on the menu. A happy resolution all around."

"Unacceptable, imp," said her husband, who stood at the entrance with an ineffable twinkle in his warm brown eyes. "If I have to go the ball, then you have to go to the ball."

Emma grinned back at him. "Well now, the gang's all here," she said with a pointed look at the crowded room.

He understood her meaning as clearly as if she'd said *I told you so* and crossed one black Hessian over the other as he leaned against the door's frame. "I will not have the servants discomforted, not even for you, my love," he announced to the confusion of his mother and sister.

But Vinnie knew them both well enough to follow the conversation, and she immediately applauded his good sense. "We tried it at Crescent House and had lumpy hollandaise sauce for a week."

The dowager, who knew all about the dangers of lumpy sauces—and was happy to pontificate on the great béarnaise disaster of '09 if her family would only let her get to the ball she threw that year—harrumphed at these absurdities. "I have no idea what you're talking about, and I'm sure I don't want to know. The ball is in one week, and we've yet to settle on a menu. As you all know, I'm a temperate soul not given to melodrama, but the situation is about to become dire and I do not appreciate the frivolity with which you are treating the matter."

"I am never frivolous," protested Louisa.

"No, I know, dear," said her mother with what may have been a hint of disappointment.

"I apologize, Mother, for interrupting," said Trent. "It was not my intention to upset your planning, as I'm quite aware of the honor you do me and Emma in hosting this affair. I realize the timing grows crucial, but I don't doubt for a moment that you will bring it off without a hitch." At this officious speech, his wife stuck out her tongue at him and he bit back a grin, lest his mother accuse him of frivolity again. "I'm only here because Felix has returned from his travels and I thought you might want to say hello. He's practically family so I felt certain you wouldn't want to stand on ceremony."

In an instant, the dowager's demeanor changed and her moue of annoyance became a smile of delight. "Felix is here?"

The duke nodded. "He returned last night and barely paused to wipe off his travel dust before paying us a call."

Even Louisa seemed to perk up at this news. "That's above all things wonderful. Where is he?"

"He'll be along in a moment. He is greeting Mrs. Crenshaw, whom he seems unduly happy to see is still with us. I suppose he thought she had been pensioned off. Ah, here he is," said Trent eagerly. To his surprise, he found he couldn't wait another moment to introduce his oldest and best friend to his wife. "Felix Dryden, Marquess of Huntly, I'd like you to meet Emma, Duchess of Trent." He rarely spoke with such pomp and circumstance and even now meant the recitation of her title more of a joke on himself than a proper introduction. And yet nobody could mistake the pride in his voice.

Emma, as bold as ever, stood up and offered her hand to the handsome peer, who appeared momentarily put off by her audacious behavior. He stared at her, then her hand, seemingly not quite sure what to do with either. Then, as if figuring out the answer to a great puzzle, he took her hand and gave it a hearty shake. "It's a great pleasure to meet the woman who has made my friend so happy. Truly, I never expected to see the Duke of Trent relishing married life. It's a sight to behold."

"I assure you," Emma said with a laugh, "I didn't expect it myself. Like all good hoydens, I had quite resolved to never marry."

"Well, I'm very glad you relented."

"I am, too," said Emma, as if it were still a surprise.

"And this," said Trent, gesturing toward Vinnie on the footstool at his mother's elbow, "is my very dear sister-in-law, Miss Lavinia Harlow."

Entirely nonplussed by the awfulness of the situation—how could he be here now when she'd said good-bye to him hours before?—Vinnie kept her eyes trained on the menu the dowager was holding. Was it from a ball in 1802? Or did that say 1807? She couldn't quite tell, for her eyes had suddenly blurred. And the heat was unbearable. Her cheeks felt as if two dozen suns were shining directly on them.

She had never been more embarrassed in her entire life—and that was saying a lot, as the entire episode earlier that day had been one long descent into the valley of mortification.

Fret as she would, there was nothing she could do now. She was trapped, and Lavinia Harlow, never a hoyden but certainly not a coward, raised her head to stare into the unsettling aquamarine eyes of her brother-in-law's dearest friend.

She was prepared for it, she knew exactly what to expect, and yet it was still a shock.

CHAPTER TWO

Felix Horatio Dryden, sixth Marquess of Huntly and eighth Earl of Revesby, needed only three things in life: a warm meal, dry clothes and a soft place to lay his head at night. He'd learned this fact about himself while on a Royal Navy expedition onboard the HMS *Triton,* which had supplied these requirements for the last one year, ten months and twenty-one days, and it had come as a revelation for a man who had been raised with so much abundance.

He hadn't gone on a voyage to the South Seas looking for Spartan austerity—his goal had been new flora, which he had achieved in spades—but he'd returned to London determined to retain a simple existence. His life before the expedition had a certain floridness that embarrassed him now. An entire village on Tarawa could be constructed from his waistcoats alone—a bright, colorful, perfectly absurd village, yes, but a village nonetheless.

It was with this new aesthetic in mind that he'd gotten dressed that morning. He knew, being back in the metropolis, he could no longer get away with the casual comfort of an islander, but he'd done the best he could, to the displeasure of his valet. Petrie, who had accompanied the marquess on the trip, along with two other servants, had borne the indignity of discarded cravats and rolled-up pantaloons only on the understanding that such improvisions were temporary. That the marquess planned to continue his island habits in London was a horror that had not occurred to the little Welshman.

Having won an argument with his valet, something he rarely accomplished, and eager to see the duke and his family after the long absence, Huntly had walked to Grosvenor Square in the best of good moods. He greeted everyone he passed with a tip of his hat, even Lord Marshall, who had dunned him out of fifty pounds in a specious bet about the mating habits of the great auk on the eve of his departure, and when Caruthers opened the door with his customary scowl, Huntly felt a contented peace descend. Nothing has changed, he thought with satisfaction and relief.

The duke was out and the dowager indisposed—this, too, was a familiar circumstance—and the marquess, who had run tame in the house since he was in leading strings, did what he always did: visited Trent's magnificent conservatory.

He assumed the room would be empty. Only a few servants were entrusted with the care of the precious flowers, and they typically did their watering first thing in the morning, when the east sun was at its strongest. He thought to pass a quiet hour inspecting Alex's impressive collection of orchids. As a botanist, Huntly knew all about flowers— he could identify phylum, genus, species at a glance—but he didn't have the duke's skill in raising them. He expected to be awed and humbled, as always, by what his friend had managed to bring to life.

What he didn't expect was a rain shower. No, not a rain shower, he thought, a cloud burst. He'd supposed, ensconced as he was in the duke's magnificent *indoor* conservatory, that he was safe from the unpredictable forces of nature. And yet he had no sooner set foot in the room than he'd been accosted by a wall of cold water. It happened so quickly and with so much force that all he could do was lament the loss of yet another dry shirt.

The effect was so similar to what he had experienced

on his travels that it took him a full sixty seconds to realize he wasn't in a subtropical jungle many thousands of miles from England. His inability to understand what had happened did not put him at a disadvantage because the architect of his misfortune—a pretty blond woman with a trim figure and blue eyes—seemed equally dumbfounded. She stared at him for so long and with such intensity that he began to fear he'd sprouted a second head in the rainstorm.

He tilted his head forward to confirm that there was still only one there—not that a second brainbox would necessarily be amiss—and begged her pardon. Although he couldn't discern her purpose, he'd clearly interrupted a delicate operation.

This attention to the gallantries elicited no response, and Huntly began to fear that the lady didn't have all her faculties. He tried to remember if the duke had a cousin who had suffered a fall from a horse or some equally debilitating accident. And then the woman made her astonishing exclamation: turpentine!

Huntly, who accounted himself quite knowledgeable of many subjects, had absolutely no idea what she was talking about. Turpentine?

Fortunately—or, rather, unfortunately, depending on one's capacity for precise detail on esoteric topics—the woman explained. As she talked, the marquess wished for a miraculous rescue and darted his eyes toward the door in hopes of seeing Caruthers or the duke magically materialize there.

His luck was as soggy as he was, however, and for several minutes he suffered a lecture on the screw pump, which, no, he hadn't known was invented by Archimedes, thank you very much. And, frankly, he didn't see why he should have to know it now. Thirty-one years of ignorance of this fact had in no way impeded the pleasure of his existence.

The woman finally recalled herself and did the proper with an apology for not only the accident but the overlong explanation as well. Huntly appreciated her effort and did the proper right back in hopes that an exchange of polite nothings would bring the episode to a close. But no! Instead, the woman did a second very astonishing thing and broke into hysterics, laughing so hard that tears trailed down her cheeks, which she wiped at with a cloth so filthy it left fat streaks of dirt behind.

At this point, Felix decided the woman was an escapee from Bedlam and waited for a pair of orderlies to carry her away. Instead, a footman named Tupper appeared to carry *him* away, which he didn't object to in the least. He was happy to go to Bedlam himself if it meant ending this interview, especially as Tupper's ready response to her orders indicated that she in fact belonged in the house.

With a heavy heart, the marquess realized that much had in fact changed while he was gone. There was now a red room amid the tastefully appointed blue bedrooms on the second floor, and beloved Mrs. Crenshaw, for whom he'd brought back a beautiful carved parakeet, had been replaced by a creature called Mrs. Wellburger. Most troubling of all was the introduction into the household of this awful woman who had the temerity to call him short. He was not short and could in fact go inch to inch against the duke.

Who the devil was she?

Huntly was trying to reconcile all these changes when Tupper said the words that stuck pure terror in the marquess's heart: *the duke's wife.*

Impossible, thought Huntly, as he followed Tupper up the stairs. Absolutely impossible. He knew the duke's mother and sister were always scheming to bring him about. Every season, they settled on one green miss from a respectable family who would produce fine-looking grandchildren and threw her at his head. But Trent had fine reflexes and always managed to duck in time. There was no way his mother had finally succeeded, certainly not with the latest contender, if he remembered correctly. Trent would never go for a milk-and-water miss like Portia Hedgley.

But there was no doubt about it: Tupper had definitely said *the duke's wife,* and there was no getting around the fact that there was a young, missish and remarkably bizarre woman installed in the house.

The duke's wife?

Surely not. The Duke of Trent was far too smart and sophisticated to fall for a quiz like she. There had to be a mistake, Huntly told himself as he got to the top step. Then he looked up and there was the man himself standing at the end of the hall: Alexander Keswick.

"Alex, old man," he said, a huge grin splitting his face in half, "this good fellow here is trying to gammon me into believing you got married."

Tupper immediately began to stammer, and the duke raised a hand to calm him. "Don't worry about it, Tupper. You can go. I'll take it from here."

Happy to be dismissed, Tupper bowed and scurried down the stairs.

"I'll thank you not to tease my staff, Felix," the duke said, as he strode across the hallway to envelop his friend in a hug. He noticed immediately that the marquess was wet and stepped back to examine him with interest. "What you do? Swim all the way from Oceania?"

"Ha!" Huntly said, greatly relieved that his friend seemed unaltered despite all the changes around him. "We got in last night. I haven't even unpacked yet. You were my first stop. But, come on, tell me this Banbury tale isn't true. You're not married, are you?"

Trent laughed and led his friend to his quarters to lend him dry clothes. Morrow was in the dressing room ironing a cravat for that night's dinner engagement, and he looked up, surprised to see the duke back so soon. "The marquess seems to have had a mishap, the nature of which I'm not still not clear. Please provide him with some temporary provisions and send one of the footmen to his address to get a change of clothes."

"Very good, your grace," he said, disappearing into the hall to pass on the message.

Alex offered to help Felix peel off his wet topcoat and

confirmed that the report of his marriage was indeed accurate. "By special license not six months ago," he said, when the offending coat was finally removed and tossed over a chair. "I started to put it in a letter and decided I would much rather confess my weakness in person. Your timing is impeccable, for the dowager is throwing a ball for us next week. She is determined to put a brave face on my marriage."

"A brave face? I do not understand," Huntly said.

"I married Emma Harlow," he said simply, as if it explained everything.

But it explained nothing to Huntly, who furrowed his brow as if trying to recall why that name was familiar to him. Had they met at the duke's stately family seat, Pembroke Hall? At Almack's during one of his rare visits? Did she have her come out the year he left?

The duke saw his confusion and sought to help his memory. "The Harlow Hoyden."

"You're joking," Huntly said, although even as he uttered the words, he knew it was not a joke. The woman in the conservatory—the confused, bizarre, entirely daft woman—fit the description of a *hoyden* to a T.

"She's an absolute scapegrace and she has an absurd amount of confidence in her own abilities, but she's kind and she's clever and she makes me laugh and every time I'm away from her I want to be with her. It's really a rather dreadful state of affairs," the duke confessed with the brightest smile his friend had ever seen on his face, "and I'm sorry you have to see me like this."

"I'm not, old man," Felix said with an honesty that surprised him. Yes, he was horrified that the duke had aligned himself with such a quiz. He'd always imagined him with someone as elegant and sophisticated as he was. But he couldn't deny his friend's happiness and he couldn't deny the appeal of a woman who didn't fit the typical mold. After years and years of insipid misses, it was little wonder the Duke of Trent would fall for a hoyden who would invent her own watering hose. It was obvious she shared his gardening bent.

Of course, the marquess thought, realizing this was the last piece of the puzzle, the duke could never be happy with a woman who didn't raise orchids, as the cultivation of flowers was a significant part of his life.

Even a man like Huntly, who had cleverly sidestepped the parson's mousetrap on more than one occasion, knew common interests were a vitally important component of a successful marriage. He was not entirely averse to wedded bliss, of course. He simply did not feel that it suited him at this juncture, for he relished his freedom and could not in all good conscience have sailed away for years at a time if he'd had a wife and children at home. Although he believed his decision not to abandon a family for the high seas showed maturity and consideration, the mamas of unattached daughters found his scrupulousness officious, if not downright treasonous. As far as they were concerned, any marquess possessed of a large fortune owed it to king and country to remain in the country.

Knowing he was a prime catch, Huntly had limited his flirtations to bachelor fare and had had a black-haired Cyprian in keeping at the time of his departure. A man of considerable address, he didn't doubt he could pick up his liaison with the lovely Titania—or, indeed, any of his former paramours—at the exact spot where he'd dropped it, but he found the idea oddly unappealing. During his many months at sea, he'd thought of her only once, when the ship's doctor quoted a scene from *A Midsummer Night's Dream,* and although he had little experience with romance—and even less with love—he suspected one should think about the object of one's affection at least twice in as many years.

Trent's valet returned with a tray of cheese and meats, which had been pressed upon him by Tupper, and assured the marquess that his own garments would be up directly. In the meantime, Morrow provided him with a dressing gown rather than lend him a full set of the duke's clothes. By the time he had him properly dressed, he would have to undress him to dress him properly again.

The two friends removed to the sitting room, where a bottle of wine and two glasses had already been set up. "Perfect," said the duke with satisfaction. "Now sit down and tell me all about your travels."

"I'd rather hear the story of your courtship," Huntly said, but he complied with the duke's request and devoted a good deal of the afternoon to entertaining Trent with various misadventures at sea.

"And of course the boat sunk," the marquess said as Trent laughed at the image of his elegant friend being toppled by an overlarge bird with a beak the size of a gentleman's shoe. "We were in the shallows so nobody suffered any ill effects, except I was wearing my last dry shirt because of the rainstorm the night before. I had nothing to change into save Lord Swarthmore's riding cape, which was made for a British winter, not a tropical summer, and I was bundled so tightly I thought for sure I would develop some frightful ague that would carry away my nose or some other appendage like poor Lord Elgin. But we achieved our goal and indeed confirmed that the auk we had discovered was of an unknown species. I do not know how it will be officially classified, but I suggested it should be called *Gigas dolors in asinum*, which translates as the giant pain-in-the-arse auk," he concluded with deep satisfaction.

"Clearly, it was a remarkably successful expedition," Trent observed. "When do you set out again?"

"When I think of all the estate business that has piled up in my absence, I'm sorely tempted to hop on the first freighter out of London," Huntly confessed with a rueful laugh. "But I will steadfastly resist the urge, for I am enjoying the novel sensation of being back on dry land. Or," he added with a wry grin, "perhaps I should say *was*, as the land in this particular spot is rather soggy. To be completely candid, I find I'm eager to enjoy the simple life of a London gentleman. Do you know, I'm actually looking forward to sitting in the bow window at White's and watching the dandies parade by in their fine plumage."

The duke smiled. "From your description, I gather you've been watching a parade of fine plumage for two years."

"Ah, but with a glass of fine claret in my hand. Trust me, my friend, that will make all the difference. Now tell me about yourself. How did you meet the Harlow Hoyden?"

Few knew the truth of his and Emma's courtship, which was by all accounts scandalous, from the moment she asked him to seduce her sister to the moment she herself seduced him in an inn in Dover, and Trent gave his friend a version that was less edited than the story generally known but one that still concealed most of the truth. Although there were state secrets at stake, he couldn't bring himself to elide the part where Emma saved England from possible invasion by chasing down a French spy. He left out many of the damning details, such as the fact that the spy in question happened to be her sister's fiancé, who had only proposed to the girl in order to gain access to her brother's secret documents.

"The devil you say!" Huntly exclaimed when the duke described the scene that still haunted him: arriving at a country shack on the outskirts of Dover to find the villain with his fingers wrapped around Emma's neck.

"Keep in mind, however, that she would not have been in such a vulnerable position had I not interfered at the inn earlier that day," Trent was quick to point out. "She had everything well in hand."

The pride in his voice caused the last of the marquess's prejudices to melt away. Obviously, the alarming discombobulation in the conservatory had been an anomaly for Trent's very capable bride.

"I find it beyond insufferable that while I was off in the South Seas discovering new species, battling the elements and generally having the thrilling adventure of a lifetime, you managed to save Merry Olde England from invasion and nab a heroine for a wife. You were always competitive, old man, but even for you that was poorly done."

Trent sat back in his chair with a grin that could only be described as triumphant. "I can't apologize. I never expected it to happen, I never thought it could, and the way it worked out is enough to make a cynical man believe in fate."

Just then Morrow entered with the marquess's change of clothes, and the tête-à-tête gave way to grooming.

And a good thing, too, thought Huntly, who, though genuinely pleased for his friend, felt oddly aggrieved by the duke's happiness. The marquess had spent two years doing exactly what he wanted—exploring the world, living free, waking up each day to the wholly unknown—and yet Trent had managed to make him feel as though he'd missed out on something.

Very poorly done indeed.

"Morrow," said the duke as his valet helped the marquess into his dry topcoat, "do you know where my wife is?"

"She is in her study discussing menus with your mother, I believe."

"Her study?" Huntly asked.

"Her one request upon moving into this town house was a private room exclusively her own. She uses it mostly for reading but also to hide from my mother, though with little success. My mother's sense of courtesy does not extend to closed doors," the duke explained. "Much to Emma's disgust, I gave her the front parlor. She had picked out a closet in the lower quarters—the one next to the pantry where the linens are kept—because it was large enough for only one person, but I couldn't possibly do such a bad turn to the servants as to have their mistress constantly in their midst."

Clearly, Morrow perceived this horror, for he shuddered at these words and uttered a heartfelt thank you to his grace.

Huntly, who knew all too well the importance of keeping one's domestics happy—you couldn't ask your valet to tie a Windfall on a bobbing ship and not know his needs came before your own—laughed in appreciation.

"I'm relieved to see that not everything has changed while I was away," he said, as the valet stood back to admire his handiwork. Morrow was inclined to improve upon the cravat, but the marquess assured him it was already a work of art. "Now let's go greet the dowager. I own, I'm unduly excited to see her again."

But as eager as he was to see the duke's mother, he happily spared several minutes in his delight at encountering Mrs. Crenshaw in the drawing room clearing a tray. If the housekeeper was taken aback by his enthusiasm, she didn't let on and cheerfully answered his questions. She even asked a few of her own.

"I have a souvenir for you," he said to the woman who had always been like a kindly aunt to him. "Please don't let me forget."

Mrs. Crenshaw was far too old and sensible to giggle like a schoolgirl, but she was still capable of a chortle or two. "Yes, my lord."

"Good. Now I must go meet his grace's bride."

"She's a dear girl," Mrs. Crenshaw said warmly.

"I'm glad to hear it."

Emma's study (née the front parlor) was only a few steps down the hall, and as he approached the room he resolved to put his earlier encounter with her behind him. If she didn't mention it, he certainly would not be so ungentlemanly as to do so himself. He would follow her lead and be everything that was warm and welcoming, and it would be easy, he knew, for he was determined to like her no matter what.

"Ah, there he is," said the duke.

Huntly saw her the moment he entered the room. She was impossible to miss, perched on the footstool at the dowager's elbow, her head tilted down. Now that he wasn't sopping wet or struggling to maintain his dignity, he could admire her smooth blond hair and the delicate column of her neck. That she didn't look up when the duke said her name didn't surprise him—he knew her to be a bizarre woman and given to queer starts.

What did surprise him—and surprise him hugely—was that another woman, this one also with smooth blond curls and a delicate column of a neck, presented herself to him with an outstretched hand. For a moment, he stared at her hand as if he'd never seen one before—and, in a way, he hadn't because this hand belonged to Trent's wife and the hands he had seen earlier belonged to her twin.

But of course! he thought, gratefully grasping Emma's hand. It all made sense now. *This* was the Incomparable Trent had fallen for, the bold hoyden who had captured a spy and saved England from invasion. How absurd to think the awkward girl with the exploding garden hose and turpentine solutions could have won the duke's heart. He knew his friend had sophisticated tastes and would never fall for anything less than an Original.

Much relieved, he thanked the new duchess for making his friend so very happy. "Truly, I never expected to see the Duke of Trent relishing married life. It's a sight to behold."

Emma laughed, revealing a dimple, and Huntly tried to recall if he had seen the same one on her sister when she'd laughed like a bedlamite in the conservatory. He thought not, otherwise he would have noticed how becoming it was.

"I assure you," Emma said. "I didn't expect it myself. Like all good hoydens, I had quite resolved to never marry."

"Well, I'm very glad you relented," he said with all sincerity, confident now that his friend's happiness would last.

"I am, too," said Emma.

"And this," the duke said, reclaiming his attention, "is my very dear sister-in-law, Miss Lavinia Harlow."

The warmth in his friend's voice was apparent, and Huntly, still feeling relieved, as if he himself had dodged a bullet, not just his friend, resolved to treat this madwoman with every consideration, despite any and all provocation. Clearly, the duke held her in affection.

Abruptly, as if almost against her will, Lavinia Harlow raised her eyes to his and the marquess felt an inexplicable jolt. No, he assured himself, not a jolt. Merely a fissure of surprise at the intensity of her gaze. How could her eyes be so like her sister's and yet so completely different?

Lavinia stood, dipped her head and curtsied. "It's a pleasure to meet you, my lord."

He bowed over her hand. "The pleasure is all mine."

The exchange was everything that was polite and proper, and yet something about it felt wrong to Huntly. But he couldn't say what and before he even had a chance to puzzle it out, the dowager claimed his attention with a hug.

"It is very good to see you, m'boy," she said softly.

"And you, ma'am," he said, delighted to see she was as stout as ever. No dwindling into a frail old lady for the Dowager Duchess of Trent.

"You won't do that again, will you," she asked, "scampering off to parts unknown to chase exotic species? This is England. We have more than enough exotic things to entertain you."

For some reason, his eyes darted to Lavinia at the words *exotic things*. "I can't make any promises, ma'am, but I'm certainly not going anywhere for a long while."

"Good. Good," she said, sitting down again. "Then you'll be here for the ball. Trent will need all the support he can muster if he's going to squeak by with the Harlow Hoyden as his wife."

As nobody took offense at this comment, Huntly assumed it was meant good-naturedly. He turned to Louisa, who had stood as soon as he entered. He kissed her cheek. "How are you, my dear?" he asked.

"Bearing up as well as can be expected under the threat of looming social ostracism," she said with a smile, as if happily resigned to her inevitable fate. Over her head, he saw Trent roll his eyes at his duchess.

"And Charles and the children?"

"Very well. Little Chloe just sewed the most charming sampler, and Joseph knows his fives multiplication tables."

Well familiar with her grandchildren's accomplishments, the dowager prevented further recitation of them with an order to Huntly to sit down. "I do not doubt that you have a hundred things to do, m'boy, now that you've returned, but you are staying right here and telling us all about your travels. Emma, be a dear and ring for tea."

Ever compliant, her daughter-in-law jumped to her feet, darted to the door, took a deep breath and opened her mouth to call for Caruthers, as was her habit.

"I said ring for tea," the dowager drawled, "not to make my ears ring."

With a sigh, Emma leaned over to tug the bell pull and said in a stage whisper to her husband, "One chair. Wooden floor. Perhaps some linens."

The dowager ignored these antics. "I read your dispatch that was printed last year in *The Times* about the Arcadia anomaly—"

"*Acacia anomala,*" he interjected.

"—and thought it was unspeakably rude of you to waste our time with a lot of nonsense about foreign trees when we already have so much good, stout English foliage right here. Now do tell us how you got on without a valet for more than two years. Did you learn how to tie your own cravat?"

Huntly shuddered as if horrified by the thought. "I traveled with my valet, your grace. I'm a naturalist, not a heathen."

"Did you get dreadfully brown like the natives?" Louisa asked.

Having been away for nearly two years, the Marquess of Huntly did indeed have a startling number of things to do, which his secretary would be the first one to tell him—if he had a secretary. But he'd known when he'd left the house that morning how he was going to spend the day. He would not spend it at the bank reviewing his accounts or with the steward examining the rents or with the solicitor answering complaints from tenants. No, he would spend his first day back with his adoptive family and return to the business of being a responsible landowner and caretaker of a large estate tomorrow. For now, he was content to sit in his best friend's wife's study (which, he had to admit, was far more comfortable now than when it had been the front parlor) and talk about his years at sea.

It was good to be home.

CHAPTER THREE

Dismissed!

Sixteen hours and twenty-three minutes later, Vinnie was still smarting from the casual indifference with which the Marquess of Huntly had treated her the day before—as if they'd never met, as if the incident in the conservatory had never happened, as if they were *complete strangers.*

Raising her head to look him squarely in the eyes had taken all her courage, but she'd mustered it because that's what a proper young lady did: She faced challenges directly. She didn't hide from them, even if her heart was pounding and her ears were ringing and she wanted nothing more than to sink into the carpet.

No, she acquitted herself with bravery and equanimity, especially if she was a Harlow.

The Harlow girls were made of the stern stuff.

And what did she get for her pluck? A polite greeting and a calm dismissal. She'd known, of course, that Huntly would not linger over the episode. He had far too much breeding to embarrass a lady, but she'd thought for sure she would see some hint of recognition or spark of awareness in his unsettling blue-green gaze. Instead, she'd been treated with the cool disinterest of a handsome peer meeting the inconsequential spinster sister of his best friend's wife.

She had suffered that slight before and would no doubt suffer it again, but somehow experiencing it from the gentleman whom she had recently soaked with an exploding garden hose made it altogether unbearable.

Interestingly, her status had never annoyed her before. With customary pragmatism, she accepted that the *ton* must believe she was in mourning for her recently deceased fiancé, Sir Waldo Windbourne, a seemingly respectable if dull baronet who turned out to be a murderous spy for France. An extraordinarily banal little man, he had been motivated by the usual cause (unsettled gambling debts), and somehow the sad predictability of his situation gave her a further disgust of him. That her opinion of him could sink any lower was a considerable achievement, given that he had tried to kill her sister on two separate occasions.

The truth about Windbourne could never be revealed for many reasons, the two most pressing of which were it would endanger her brother, Roger, who was a spy for England, and it would brand her a murderess. The fact that she had acted in defense, first of her sister and then of herself, would do little to mitigate the fact that she had taken a life. There was nothing less decorous than a lethal female. For the sake of propriety, then, she had to pretend to wear the willow for the man she'd shot in the dead of night at point-blank range as he tried to gut her with a fish knife.

Vinnie, whose lack of artifice made the pretense difficult, found having to pay tribute to a blackguard altogether infuriating, but she refused to dwell on the injustice. As a matter of principle, she refused to dwell on anything pertaining to her treacherous former fiancé, and if there were moments when an uncustomary horror crept in, when she could feel her finger twitch on the trigger even though there was no gun in her hand, she simply called to mind Emma's glowing smile on her wedding day to banish them.

She felt no remorse for her action, but if she did, she would gladly accept it to see her sister alive and happy.

Because the pretense was so difficult for her, Vinnie welcomed the custom that excluded her from the social whirl and gladly sat out *ton* events. The story that had gotten out about Sir Windbourne's death, devised by Emma to posthumously humiliate him and whispered by her in the ear of that great gossip Lady Fellingham—*entre nous, n'est c'est pas?*—had inadvertently made her situation worse by turning her into an object of pity. Poor Miss Lavinia Harlow, widowed before married by a vain fool of a man who suffocated himself by overtightening the stays of his corset.

Yet being the target of such utterly absurd chatter had not discomforted Vinnie as much as Huntly's easy dismissal. She had enough sense to realize her anger was somewhat unfair, but that did little to temper it.

"I'm sure the eggs will apologize," Emma said, as she entered the dining room, where Vinnie sat by herself, staring down at a white porcelain plate with a cross expression.

Startled out of her reverie, Vinnie looked up at her sister. "Excuse me?"

Emma took the seat next to her as Tupper laid a newspaper and a fresh pot of tea on the table. "If you explain to the eggs what they have done to offend you, I'm sure they'll apologize. You know how eggs are—such chickens."

"Very funny, your grace," Vinnie said, reaching for the teapot to replenish her cup and belatedly realizing it was already full. She touched the side and, observing it was cool, wondered how long she'd been sitting there.

Tupper immediately mopped up the small spill with a cloth, spirited away the tepid brew and placed a fresh cup in front of her.

Dipping her head in gratitude at the efficient footman, Emma unfolded her table napkin. "What has you so blue-deviled?"

"Lord Huntly," she stated.

"Lord Huntly?"

Vinnie nodded firmly as she picked up her fork to eat her eggs. "I found him to be very rude."

Emma wrinkled her forehead in surprise. "Lord Huntly, the marquess?"

"Yes, he was the height of inconsideration," she said, tasting the eggs, which were also disagreeably chilled.

"The Lord Huntly who was here yesterday?" Emma asked. "Spent the last two years on a ship studying foreign flora? Alex's oldest friend? *That* Lord Huntly?"

Vinnie did not appreciate her sister's attempt at humor any more than she did the cold eggs, and as she considered a breakfast roll, she said with a hint of condescension, "You were no doubt partial to him because of your husband's fondness, but I found his treatment of me very shabby indeed."

Not at all offended by the implied corruption of her judgment, Emma examined her sister over a cup of tea. "How so?"

"He did not have the courtesy to acknowledge the episode in the conservatory," she said as the ever-observant Tupper replaced her plate of eggs with a freshly made batch.

"You mean the episode wherein you soaked him with water from an improvised garden hose and then proceeded to laugh uncontrollably while dabbing your face with a filthy cloth?" Emma asked mildly.

"I concede that the events do not show me to an advantage, but when two people have been through an experience together, it's customary for the one person to indicate some awareness of that experience to the other person," Vinnie said, as if reciting a passage from *Mrs. Marshall's Guide to Proper Etiquette and Social Obligations.*

The duchess, who had never been a pattern card of proper etiquette or social obligation, was not familiar with this rule. "And Lord Huntly made no such intimation to you?"

"No, he did not. He treated me with as much respect and attention as he would an old family retainer," she explained, taking a bite of a well-buttered breakfast roll, which was, she decided, a little dry. She dropped it onto her plate with a sigh.

For an extended moment, Emma considered her sister

silently, weighing the sigh and the discarded roll and the unexpected charges leveled at yesterday's guest. Then she said, "Now that I think about it, you are correct. Lord Huntly's manners definitely left something to be desired. Did you observe how he corrected the dowager when she mistakenly called the specimen he wrote about for *The Times* the Arcadia anomaly?"

"I did, yes," Vinnie said with asperity. "A more gracious gentleman would not have remarked upon the error."

"And not a word of apology for missing my wedding," Emma added, managing to sound genuinely aggrieved that a man who had been out of the country had been unable to attend an event to which he wasn't invited.

Vinnie nodded. "He is a truly awful man."

"Without question, one of the worst I've ever met," she said with a frown of censure, though her eyes twinkled with amusement.

Abruptly, Vinnie threw her napkin on the table and stood up. "If you'll excuse me, my dear, talk of the wretched Lord Huntly has quite destroyed my appetite."

"Of course I understand. It's a wonder I can eat anything at all myself," she said, scooping a spoonful of scrambled eggs into her mouth.

Vinnie thanked her for her sensibility and, feeling quite out of sorts, went to the conservatory to finish the project she had started the day before: repotting an *Aerides huttoni* that Mr. Berry of the British Horticultural Society had sent as a thank-you for her hard work in writing an introductory manual to drainage systems. Although he had in fact requested the pamphlet from her, an indication, she thought, of his faith in her ability to produce a useful document, he'd seemed taken aback by the level of detail and good sense it contained. In exchange, he had given her the lovely orchid, with its cascade of rose-purple blossoms.

As beautiful as the flower was—and it was certainly one of the most striking in her collection—she would much rather have been given the opportunity to write an advanced manual to drainage systems. Working on the booklet had been nicely engrossing, particularly during the four months she was buried in the country with her brother. Without question, Vinnie loved her brother, Roger, and his wife, Sarah, and she adored her nephews, a trio of endearing scapegraces who could reliably be found with a surfeit of mud or chocolate on their faces. But the months in London that spring—during Emma's courtship of the duke and her own disastrous engagement to Windbourne—had altered her in some fundamental way. No longer content to toil in isolation on her beloved flowers, she now craved the company of like-minded fellows. The hours she'd spent with the duke arguing and discussing growing methods and soil composition and drainage pumps had been some of the most satisfying of her life.

She thought of seeking out the duke to ask his opinion about how best to repot the huttoni, but she didn't want to intrude on his time with Emma. They had been married only six months and were still very much in the honeymoon period, a fact that delighted Vinnie, as she considered bringing off the match to be her finest achievement. No doubt, the pair of them would still be smarting from imagined slights and petty offenses if she hadn't stepped in and forced them to clear the air.

Recalling the scene in which she finally convinced Alex that Emma loved him—in the small back room of a ramshackle inn where his cawker of a cousin complained about being confined to bed rest after having the decidedly poor judgment to get himself shot—made her smile. But it did nothing to alleviate her mood, which grew darker by the moment, and, in a spark of unprecedented impulsiveness, she ran into her room to change into a walking dress. Miss Lavinia Harlow was going out.

Emma was still staring after Vinnie when the duke entered the room a few minutes later. Dressed simply in fawn-colored pantaloons and riding boots, he had spent the last two hours examining the accounts with his estate agent and would no doubt spend the next two hours in the same repose.

"What has you looking so thoughtful?" he asked, taking the chair recently vacated by Vinnie. Tupper stepped forward to lay a new place, but Trent forestalled him with a hand. "Just tea for me. Thank you."

"How is the estimable Mr. Colson?" Emma asked with a brisk nod at Tupper, who refilled her cup as well. Then she buttered another roll.

"Cross with me, as always, for being unduly generous with the tradesmen. He seems personally affronted by my paying them on time, a fact I find puzzling, as I understand his father was a grocer."

"Perhaps you are depriving him of the pleasure of grumbling over how terribly his employer treats the tradesmen with the other estate agents. Your decency is probably an embarrassment to him," she suggested reasonably. Her own parents never paid a whole bill when they could pay an insignificant fraction of it. "I'm happy to help out with the bookkeeping. I'm a passably tolerable mathematician. I can say that without sounding like I'm bragging because that's exactly how my governess described me to Roger once."

"I don't doubt your math skills are excellent, but it's my responsibility and I won't burden you with it," he said.

Emma shook her head, reached for his hand and kissed it. "Isn't that the point of marriage—to share the burdens?" she asked before promptly returning her attention to the breakfast roll.

She glanced away so quickly she didn't notice the arrested look on the duke's face. Even after six months of marriage, his wife's habit of careless affection still took his breath away. For years he'd believed intimacy was two writhing bodies in a house in Chelsea, and it stunned him to realize it was actually a peck on the cheek when he least expected it.

"Besides, it would provide me with an excuse to avoid planning the ball," Emma added. "I don't know why your mother cares so much whether we should serve turtle soup during the first course. Moreover, I don't know why she cares what *I* think. I'm far more notorious for releasing turtles than eating them."

Trent tilted his head. "When was that again?"

"Two years ago. Lord Ashby's house party in Dorset," she said matter-of-factly. "His appalling children were using the turtles for target practice. I'm all for improving one's shot, but I think it should be a fair fight. I'm sure nobody would have noticed they were missing if a silly housemaid hadn't found one of the turtles in my shoe and started screaming."

"And therein lies the flaw in your plan: Never put a purloined turtle in a shoe," the duke said logically.

Emma grinned. "There wasn't a plan. It was a crime of opportunity, and after I had the turtles in my possession, I realized I needed to change into my boots to bring them out to the pond, for it had been raining and the fields were muddy. I'd put them down for only a moment. I must say, for a turtle, they moved with impressive speed and I had to constrain them somehow."

Her tone—equal parts disgruntled and admiring—made the duke laugh. "I'm sure if you told the dowager that you trusted her decisions implicitly, she would excuse you from the planning."

"Shame on you, your grace," she said, dimpling. "You don't think I tried excessive flattery weeks ago and many times since? Your mother is not content merely to reform me. I must share in the reformation. I believe my active involvement is part of the process of character reformation."

Trent, taking a cue from his wife, reached for her hand and raised it to his lips. "I'm sorry. Will you mind very much being a reformed character?"

Emma grasped his other hand and leaned forward. "How can I mind being a reformed character for you when you are willing to be an outcast for me?" she asked softly.

This sentiment so overwhelmed the duke that he tugged her close and kissed her with passion not appropriate to the breakfast parlor. Displaying emotion in the middle of the day or in front of the servants was also something he'd never done, despite all that writhing in Chelsea.

With regret, Trent pulled away, keenly aware that the interminable two hours yet to be spent with Colson had just become somehow more interminable. He could put the estate agent off, of course—Colson served at his pleasure and would never cavil at the treatment—but the duke's sense of obligation ran deep and he knew it was far better to get unpleasant tasks over with than to postpone them indefinitely.

Emma sat back with a happy sigh. "Anyway, it probably won't take."

"What won't?" he asked, confused. Had he missed something?

Emma laughed, delighted that she could make him lose the thread of the conversation. It was only fair, she thought, as he could do the same to her. "My reformation. I was woolgathering during our very important discussion of menus yesterday. It wasn't intentional. I was determined to pay attention and truly meant to listen, but it was simply too tedious for any sane human being. Three decades of extravagant dinners reduced to facts and figures. Vinnie, of course, was interested. At first, I thought she was mocking of your mother by asking so many questions about inconsequential details, but then I realized her curiosity was sincere."

"Your sister has an orderly mind and a prodigious talent for simplifying complicated sets of data," he said, thinking of the many useful graphs and charts in her drainage pamphlet. Concepts that had eluded him for years had suddenly become clear as he examined the illustrations.

Recalling her sister's talents and interests, Emma said, "Huntly, by the way."

The duke knew that this time his confusion had nothing to do with the addling effects of his wife's charms and everything to do with her penchant for non sequitur. "Huntly?"

Emma nodded. "Previously, you asked what had me looking so thoughtful. The answer is the Marquess of Huntly."

Without question, Trent wanted Emma to like the marquess; he was one of his intimates and considered by all members to be one of the family. But there was something in her tone, a certain arch knowingness, that made him realize there was much more afoot here than mere liking.

"What about Huntly?" he asked, unable to keep the suspicion out of his voice.

"It's the most remarkable thing: Vinnie doesn't like him," she explained.

Trent felt certain his wife exaggerated. Vinnie was far too sensible to dislike someone she barely knew. "I find that very unlikely, but even if it's true, there's nothing remarkable about it. Disappointing, yes, as he is a good man and an excellent botanist, and I think he and Vinnie would have much in common."

"But it *is* remarkable. Think of it. Vinnie never dislikes anyone. She was engaged to the most insufferable bore in the kingdom for more than a month and excused even his most ill-mannered behavior. My sister has the disheartening habit of looking for the good in everyone. She never says an unkind word about anyone, whatever the provocation and I assure you, Windbag gave her lots. And yet," she announced with relish, "moments ago she sat in that very chair and called Lord Huntly rude, inconsiderate and awful."

The duke had to concede the oddness of such behavior. "But I'm sure you misunderstand the matter. Vinnie met the marquess only briefly yesterday and spoke but a few words to him. She would never form a personal dislike based on such insubstantial evidence."

"Ah, but that wasn't their first meeting," she said, savoring the look of surprise on her husband's face. "They met a few hours earlier in the conservatory."

Trent nodded, as it made sense that Huntly would have been eager to examine the duke's orchids after so much time away. "The turpentine?"

"Alas, yes. Another imperfect formula, another exploding hose," she said with a grin. "Apparently, it burst just as the marquess entered the room and sopped him quite thoroughly."

Immediately, Trent's lips began to twitch, as he imagined Huntly standing in the conservatory with water dripping from his ears. The wet welcome was hardly the triumphant homecoming his friend had been expecting. "So that's why Felix's clothes were all wet. He wouldn't explain."

Emma nodded. "Precisely. Lord Huntly's response to the mishap has been everything that's gracious and correct. And despite his impeccable behavior, Vinnie has taken an aversion to him."

The duke understood now why she thought her sister's reaction was remarkable. There was definitely something notable in the way Vinnie seemed to have taken a pet over a harmless encounter. "I'm sure your sister's unusual reaction stems from embarrassment. No doubt she is deeply mortified and would choose to keep her distance from the witness to her humiliation."

"Of course," Emma said agreeably, reaching for another breakfast roll. "I'm sure you're right. Her dignity did indeed take quite a pummeling."

Although Trent believed this to be true, he didn't for a moment think that his wife believed it, as well. There had been far too much archness in her tone earlier for easy assent now. No, his wife was up to something and merely telling him what she thought he wanted to hear. The only time she readily concurred with him was when she was devising a plan.

"Under no circumstance are you to ask Huntly to seduce Vinnie," Trent announced.

Amazed, Emma stared at him. "Why on earth would I do such an outrageous thing?"

She looked so innocent sitting there, her bright blue eyes blinking in surprise, as if she'd never done a hoydenish thing in her entire life. "Because that's what you asked me to do."

"Well, of course. You're a hardened libertine," she explained reasonably. "I have heard no such talk about the marquess. *Is* he a hardened libertine?"

He was nearly undone by the hopefulness in her voice,

but he kept a straight face and demanded she abandon whatever scheme she was devising.

"What scheme?" she asked.

"Emma," the duke said warningly.

"No, really, your grace, I have no scheme. I swear it," she said, raising a hand as if taking a pledge.

His grace was not fooled. "You mean you don't have a scheme yet."

Ever a straight shooter, she conceded this point. "I became aware of Vinnie's remarkable dislike not twenty minutes ago. I assure you, Alex, even I am not so ramshackle as to come up with a scheme that quickly. If it's to work, it must be well thought out and carefully planned."

That his wife was a thorough planner Trent knew very well from personal experience. Before breaking into the residence of her sister's despised fiancé, an excursion on which he had been invited to go, she gathered blueprints of the house from a footman and safecracking tips from the greatest lockpick in London.

Recalling the expedition, the duke felt a fissure of alarm, but he couldn't say for whom—his wife, himself or the Marquess of Huntly.

"And when you do have a scheme?" he asked, leadingly.

"I will consult with you, of course," she said with gratifying speed. "I would never implement a plan without your robust approval, for you are my most trusted ally."

It was a pretty speech, but the duke knew better than to believe a word of it. "Hogwash," he said, although he was fully aware of the futility of belaboring the point, for his wife would do just as she pleased. If marriage had done anything to change her behavior it had merely altered the first person to whom she was obliged to explain her actions. Previously, it had been her sister-in-law and chaperone, Sarah.

"Your faith in me is humbling," she said with an unholy glimmer the duke found impossible to resist, and while Tupper straightened the sideboard for the dowager's inevitable arrival in a few minutes, Trent kissed his wife with a hunger that continued to surprise him and lamented that poor Mr. Colson would have to wait on his pleasure after all.

CHAPTER FOUR

As soon as Lavinia glanced up from her newspaper and saw
the Marquess of Huntly browsing a bookshelf at Hatchard's
(Italian poetry), she realized her impulsive outing had been a
mistake and, quickly reviewing her options, settled on a fur-
tive exit as the only reasonable solution to her unfortunate
situation. The front door was a disagreeably far distance
from her location, but if she walked along the far wall and if
he remained near the fireplace and if all the other patrons
stayed exactly where they were, she should be able to squeak
by without discovery.

The plan was not without its risks, of course, but it was
better than sitting in the middle of the room like a winged
grouse in an open field.

Very carefully, Vinnie tucked the newspaper under her
arm and stood up slowly, determined to make no abrupt
movements that might call attention to her person. Then,
walking at what she considered to be an ideal pace—only
slightly faster than the rate at which one crossed the floor at
Almack's during the height of the season—she safely arrived
at the far wall. Once there, she kept her eyes trained on the
shelves to her right (Elizabethan verse, Restoration comedy,
Greek classics) so that Huntly, should he look over, would

be presented with the back of her head, which he could not be expected to recognize on such a short acquaintance.

She was a mere six or seven steps from successful execution when a clerk, no doubt intending to be helpful, called out, "Miss Harlow, please let me relieve you of that newspaper."

His tone, to be fair, was appropriately calibrated to the subdued environment of the bookstore, but to Vinnie's ears it sounded like a great, echoing roar from the depths of a cave and had the inadvertent effect of making her clutch the newspaper tightly in her grasp. Mr. Knoll, committed to his officiousness, tried to free the broadsheet from her grip, which Vinnie resisted from surprise and confusion, and a brief tug-of-war ensued.

"May I suggest, my good fellow, that Miss Harlow isn't ready to surrender her reading material just yet?" Lord Huntly said smoothly.

His appearance at the site of battle was so unexpected that the muscles in Vinnie's fingers went slack, and poor Mr. Knoll, suddenly unopposed, tripped backward and fell. Vinnie watched in horror as Huntly helped the kindly clerk to his feet while also rescuing from the floor the offending newspaper that had caused so much fuss.

Her face swathed in a blush, Vinnie immediately stepped forward to beg Mr. Knoll's pardon and to assure herself that he'd suffered no lasting effects from her ill treatment of him. He of course insisted on taking all of the blame—"Miss Harlow is circumspect about returning all materials, this I know and should have permitted!"—and swore that the red mark on his wrist had been there prior to the mishap. Vinnie was inclined to argue over both matters but forestalled herself with the idea that prolonging the incident could only make it worse.

She apologized again for the accident, commended him on his dedication to service and promised to return the periodical as soon as she was finished with it. This speech, delivered with the utmost sincerity, embarrassed Mr. Knoll so much that it was all he could do to mutter thank you in return before retaking his position behind the desk. She watched as he bent his wrist in various directions to test its effectiveness and worried that she'd done him permanent harm.

"That will teach him to do his job," Huntly said.

Vinnie, who had all but forgotten the Marquess of Huntly's presence in her distress, felt a new flush overtake her as she acknowledged the validity of his criticism. Determined to not cower, she threw back her shoulders and faced him with as much dignity as she could muster. She told herself to look on the bright side—all the participants in the drama were dry, at least at present.

"I must thank you, my lord, for calling me to my senses," Vinnie said, her voice as calm and composed as she could want. "I can't quite say what led to my unusual behavior, but my conduct was certainly wanting and I will be more conscious of it in the future."

The marquess nodded. "A worthy plan, I'm sure, but I hope you won't become too conscious of it."

Vinnie could see the teasing glint in his eyes and even heard it in his voice, but the comment felt like a rebuke and she stiffened her shoulders, determined to bring the interview to an end. "I appreciate your service," she said abruptly and held her hand out for the newspaper.

Huntly drew in his brows, unsure of what she could be indicating with the gesture, then realized belatedly that he still held the broadsheet. "Oh, yes, of course," he said, looking at the periodical, which was crumpled from abuse. "Please, let me lay it out on this table to remove the wrinkles."

He no sooner announced his intentions than placed the newspaper on the mahogany surface to perform the service. Vinnie's fingers twitched with the desire to pull the paper away from him but given how poorly her last attempt at such a maneuver had gone she knew better than to try. Consequently, she had to stand there silently as red suffused her face for the third time in as many minutes while Huntly read the headline on the edition of *The Times*.

She saw the look of surprise and then of pleasure

dance across his face. Of course he was pleased, Lavinia thought peevishly. It was a gratifying compliment indeed that she'd sought out his article.

"Miss Harlow, I'm flattered—"

"The dowager asked me to retrieve it," Vinnie said before he could finish the thought, for she couldn't bear the notion of him thinking so highly of himself at her expense. "She wanted to refamiliarize herself with the facts of the *Acacia anomala* so that she could speak intelligibly on the subject with you the next time you meet."

Huntly's lips might have twitched, but his expression remained somber. "Her grace asked you?" he asked.

Vinnie knew her explanation was flimsy at best and entirely unbelievable at worst, for nobody was less likely to request such a service as the unscholarly Dowager Duchess of Trent, but she had no choice but to brazen it out. "Yes, she sends me on errands such as these all the time. Just last week, I went to Hookham's to investigate"—she foundered for a topic and out of the corner of her eye saw poor Mr. Knoll rubbing his shoulder—"medicinal draughts of the Hellenesian peoples."

In fact, Vinnie was standing across from a shelf that said Hellenistic, but in her rush to come up with a believable culture she read it too quickly for accuracy.

"The Hellenesian peoples?" he asked with mild curiosity.

She scrambled for a locale. "Yes, from Hellenesia."

"Ah, yes, of course, near Polynesia?"

Vinnie couldn't tell if he was making fun of her or not, but she kept her face straight and stuck to her story. "Yes, you head there and make a right. You can't miss it."

Huntly nodded with the same sobriety with which he had conducted the entire conversation, but there was an unholy glint in his unsettling green-blue eyes. "Well, please tell the dowager that I can't remember when I have ever before been so complimented by someone's interest."

"Oh, I'm sure the dowager didn't mean it as a compliment, my lord," she said crushingly. "In refreshing her memory of your article she was merely showing the diligence which she considers your due."

Far from being deflated by this communication, the marquess seemed more amused than ever. "Whatever the dowager's intentions, I choose to take it as a compliment. I won't tell her that, of course, for to do so would only embarrass her, and will instead act surprised when she proves herself to be so conversant on the topic. She will have no idea I discovered you here in the process of fulfilling her request."

Vinnie knew it was all a hum—the naturalist was far too clever not to realize the truth—but she appreciated his allowing her the dignity of the lie. "I won't tell her either."

"Good, now tell me, what did you think of the article?" he asked, pulling out a chair. "Do please sit down. I've kept you standing in the middle of Hatchard's far longer than it is polite. Blame the nearly two years at sea for my appalling manners."

But of course his manners were everything that were correct and proper, which made Vinnie, whose own behavior had actually been appalling, feel even more uncomfortable. The last thing she wanted to do was extend their interaction any longer than necessary, but she could think of no way to pawn off her own desire to leave on the dowager, so she complied graciously.

Huntly sat adjacent to her at the large table, which was stacked with leather-bound volumes at the other end. As soon as they took their seats, an associate of Mr. Knoll's cleared the table so that they could spread out their things in comfort. Vinnie assured him that she wouldn't be staying long enough to get comfortable just as Huntly thanked him for his thoughtfulness.

As the marquess laid out the paper, Vinnie considered how to respond to his query. In truth, she thought the article contained a lot of useful information and his description of the slender, rushlike shrub, with its small yellow flowers arranged in cyndrical spikes, was so perfectly descriptive she had a clear picture of it in her head. Indeed, if she was going to be entirely honest, she would admit privately that she had realized her impulsive outing was a mistake long before she'd glanced up and seen the marquess browsing the Italian poetry shelf; she had realized it when she discovered his beautiful writing made it impossible for her to despise him entirely.

Vinnie knew, however, that it would never do for her to admit to such sentimentality to this man who was so used to compliments, he took them where they weren't even offered. No doubt, he was offered plenty by women of all ages and lineages, as he had every advantage of modern manhood: He was handsome, he was wealthy, he had a fascinating occupation, he was sophisticated, he was well traveled, he had breeding, he had poise. He was insufferably rude in his perfection, which was clearly what led him to treat her so shabbily yesterday.

Her late fiancé, Sir Waldo Windbourne, had been far from perfect. Not only was he a traitorous spy who tried to kill both her and her sister—a characteristic that had never counted to his advantage before now—he was also an intolerable windbag who could hold forth for hours on any topic he found of consuming interest. By the end of their engagement, she could little remember what she had found charming about him during their courtship, but she recalled now the hesitant little pauses he would sometimes take in the middle of his seemingly endless monologues, as if not sure of his next thought or its reception. As someone who frequently questioned herself, she'd found this trait endearing.

It had been months since Vinnie had thought of her former fiancé with anything other than seething hatred, and that she did so now because of Huntly was another point against the marquess. It was to her merely one more example of his thoughtless rudeness.

When Huntly was satisfied with the newspaper's arrangement, he said, "I would appreciate your thoughts. Alex tells me you're an accomplished botanist yourself."

As when anyone gave her a compliment, Vinnie's instinct was to demur and insist she was merely a devoted hobbyist. But her modesty depended to some extent on her audience not believing her and she feared in this case, Huntly would entirely agree with her assessment, so she said, "I recently published a pamphlet providing introductory information on drainage systems."

It was impossible to entirely suppress the pride in her voice, and when Huntly smiled, she felt for sure he was mocking her pretensions. How could a man who had traveled thousands of miles to examine the world's most exotic species be impressed with a dowdy spinster who wrote manuals on how to irrigate a garden?

"Well, then, I'm doubly interested in your opinion," he said.

Vinnie nodded consideringly. "I think it's a very fine effort, my lord. You should be pleased with yourself. The descriptions in particular are pleasingly workmanlike."

The marquess furrowed his brow, as if not sure what to make of this praise, which, as Vinnie intended, seemed faint at best. "Pleasingly workmanlike?"

"Rather than rigorously scientific, of course. That was your purpose, was it not, to make your description of the plant so bland and simple that anyone reading your article would instantly be able to imagine a familiar English plant she had in her garden, such as *Delphinium elatum*?" she asked disingenuously, for *D. elatum,* with its elegant spikes of bright blue and purple flowers, could not be any more different from *Acacia anomala.* Indeed, comparing one with the other was like saying a strawberry looked like a banana.

"*Delphinium elatum,* did you say?" he asked, confounded. "My description of the South Seas plant put you in mind of larkspur?"

"Exactly as you had intended," she said admiringly. "I thought it was very clever of you to leave out truly useful information such as measurements of the stamen and moisture level of the soil, for to do so would have confused readers, who only want to be assured that you are discovering new things. They do not require that you make those things known to them in a useful way. Truly, I think it's the veriest piece of populist botanicalesque journalism I've ever read."

The marquess was silent for a few moments, then he said, "Pardon me, but I'm not familiar with the term *botanicalesque*."

Vinnie trilled happily, as if charmed by his ignorance, though in truth he could not know what the word meant, for she had made it up on the spot. "It's a way of describing something that is close in nature to proper botanical study but not quite there. You see it used all the time in the journal of the British Horticultural Society, though there it is frequently used as a criticism and here I intend it as a compliment."

"I see," said the Marquess of Huntly stiffly.

She smothered a smile and nodded soberly. "Yes, I think you do."

An awkward silence followed this exchange, and Vinnie waited for the marquess to make the next move, which he did by announcing his departure.

Vinnie turned her lips down in regret. "That is a shame, my lord, for Mr. Knoll was just about to retrieve one of your other dispatches for me to read, as I understand there are several. It's so disappointing that you won't be here so I can compliment you in person on your unexceptional text."

"You are too kind, Miss Harlow," he said, managing a smile that seemed both grateful and sincere. "But I'm sure you've complimented me enough."

It was to his credit that his mask of good humor stayed firmly in place—Vinnie could readily acknowledge that—but it annoyed her nonetheless that he didn't show even the merest slip of temper. It demonstrated again, she felt, how highly he regarded himself and how little he regarded her.

"I know!" she said, as if struck by the best of good ideas. "I shall record my thoughts in an epistle and forward them to you at your residence. That way, you can read them at your leisure."

Huntly tried to demur by insisting he could not put her out to such an extent, but she assured him it was no effort at all—"Indeed, a mere trifle really, like the articles them-selves"—and in the end he agreed to read them at the earli-est opportunity.

Vinnie did not doubt that the opportunity, early or late, would never arrive, and she could hardly blame him, for her faint praise had been harsh indeed. With this happy thought in mind, she bid him good day and watched him leave the shop without purchasing a book or a newspaper. Whatever he had come to purchase during his visit had clearly been forgotten in his pique over their exchange.

In keeping with her word, Vinnie remained at Hatchard's for another hour, fulfilling her promise to pro-vide him with admiring notes. These compliments were in the same vein as the others, though in truth she was much impressed with his writing style, which was elegant, concise and evocative. As she read, she found herself envying not only the remarkable experiences he'd had but the freedom that let him have them. The unexpected longing for free-dom was a new sensation for Vinnie, who had never chafed at the confines of her life. Her sister chafed. Emma fre-quently railed against the firm strictures that dictated what a woman could or couldn't do, and some of her worst scrapes were merely attempts to free herself from what seemed to her an unfair set of rules.

But Vinnie didn't mind rules and indeed saw those same firm strictures as boundaries no more interesting and no less banal than, say, the walls of a room. One did not complain that the walls of the drawing room were too straight or too tall. Rather, one was grateful that they held up the room with such success that one's head stayed dry and one's bedroom above had a floor.

In this, as in all things, Vinnie was practical.

Or so she had thought before reading about Huntly's discovery of a small purple-and-yellow orchid with a fluted labellum and furled ribbonlike petals that was attached to the underside of a west-facing branch of a towering tree on an uninhabited island. In awe of its beauty, Huntly had dubbed the flower *Venustas sublimis*—sublime beauty—and just like that, a blossom never before seen by British eyes and rarely seen by human ones had a name.

This act of nomenclature seemed to her at once extraordinarily mundane and astonishingly fantastical, for what was more human than giving an unknown entity a name and what was more godlike than bestowing an identity upon a thing of creation. The boldness of it took her breath away.

As she was recording her thoughts on the marquess's article on *Lonicera serrata* ("Wonderfully vague description generously gives the reader an opportunity to create her own flower"), Mr. Knoll came over to the table to see if she required anything else, and it was only his presence that recalled to her the time. She had been there for more than two hours, and her poor maid Lucy was no doubt quite tired of the hard bench outside by now.

With a grateful smile, Vinnie told him she had everything she needed and would in fact be taking her leave of him as soon as she reassured herself that his wrist was not damaged from their earlier encounter. Mr. Knoll displayed several angles of movement without flinching and, convinced of his continued good health, Vinnie collected her things.

She was satisfied with that morning's work. No, it had not gone exactly as she'd intended and, yes, it contained more than one embarrassing episode, but she did not regret the impulse that had brought her there. She'd come because she was curious about the marquess's travels, and now that her curiosity had been appeased she would not think of the man any longer. He was a dear friend of her brother-in-law and she would no doubt stumble upon him a time or two in the conservatory or at the dining table, but she would pay him little heed, perhaps deigning only to inquire after his health to demonstrate that she, too, could behave with the utmost propriety.

She would be courteous and correct and comply with all the requirements of polite society, but she would not think about the Marquess of Huntly one single moment more. She simply would not.

CHAPTER FIVE

Although there were several dozen issues requiring the Marquess of Huntly's immediate attention, including some items that had been waiting for two years, he directed his curricle to the British Horticultural Society. His plan for the day had been simple: Following a brief visit to Hatchard's to purchase a replacement copy of Dante's *Inferno*, the original of which was destroyed in a typhoon (perhaps reading about hell was not the best way to handle a violent and unwieldy storm), return home to Berkeley Square to meet with the land agent. After his appointment with Mr. Branch, he had engagements with his banker and auditor and intended to review the accounts for the London house as well as those for the family seat in Devon and his various other properties.

Administering to the vast Dryden estates, a worthy and time-consuming effort, to be sure, comprised only half of his list of things to be done, for he had spent the whole of his journey taking copious notes and now required a well-ordered individual with a knowledge of botany to help him organize his material for publication. Once all the information was arranged in a logical and efficient system, he would hire artists to create watercolors from his drawings and engravers to make copperplate line engravings. The book he was to write, a vast compendium of all the strange and wonderful flora he had seen, would no doubt take him years to complete. Like a traveler who discovers forgotten mementos at the bottom of his luggage, he could no longer recall all of the items he had collected and was eager to refresh his memory.

As impatient as he was to begin, he could not forestall a visit to the horticultural society. Even as he swore he would not go, he turned his horses into Jermyn Street.

Mr. Berry, the energetic man of mild affability who neatly handled the organization's affairs so its members would not have to, greeted the marquess warmly and with great surprise, for he hardly expected the famous naturalist to call so soon after his return. "It is a great honor, my lord, a truly great honor. Please, do sit down and join me for a spot of tea. I've just made a fresh pot. Only if you have time, of course. Do not fear that I will pester you with hundreds of questions about your trip. I do have a list, of course, based on our correspondence, but I will wait for the lecture you are sure to give our worthy members."

The marquess hadn't factored in tea when deciding to stop at the society, and he resented the time it would take from his overly stuffed schedule. In the interest of fairness, however, he had to concede that he hadn't factored in anything at all in the decision, for the visit had been a whim he'd found impossible to resist, and a lengthy diversion was just what he deserved for acting so rashly.

"I'd be delighted," he said, removing his hat. The horticultural society's quarters were comfortable and airy, with bright patches of color supplied by pink bougainvillea and purple clementis and red roses, and as he sat down in the tall wingback chair to the left of Berry's desk, he felt surprisingly calm and unhurried. As a longtime member of the society, he'd spent many hours in the large room and in a lot of ways, it felt like home.

"To what do we owe the pleasure of this visit?" Mr. Berry asked as he handed the marquess a teacup with the society's thistle insignia. "Were you interested in something in particular or simply unable to stay away?"

"A little bit of both," the marquess said truthfully, though he was reluctant to divulge the entire reason, for he knew Miss Lavinia Harlow was making a joke at his expense. During the two years he was away, the word *botanicalesque* had not become common parlance in the society's bimonthly publication. Indeed, he rather doubted the word existed at all. Miss Harlow had already shown an alarming tendency to either tell outright lies or to garble the truth so completely that nothing made sense, as she had done with the staff at Trent's town house. As far as he could tell, all the familiar faces remained and none of the new ones had the name mentioned by Miss Harlow. He did not know what motivated the woman, nor did he want to know, and yet he couldn't simply let the matter rest. For some reason, he was compelled to confirm it by examining recent issues and seeing for himself.

The plan was untenable, of course, for he had far too many people waiting on him to spend several hours poring over two years' worth of journals for a word he knew wasn't in them. He'd come on a fool's errand, and feeling like a fool, he looked the editor of *The Journal of the British Horticulture Society* in the eye and asked him outright if he was familiar with the term *botanicalesque*.

Mr. Berry rubbed his chin thoughtfully and pursed his lips as if in deep consideration. "I don't think so, though to be completely candid I'm not as familiar with all the new terms as I should be. Perhaps it's of recent coinage. May I ask why you enquire, my lord? Is this a term we should incorporate in our discussions? Is the Society for the Advancement of Horticultural Knowledge using it?" he asked, unable to suppress his horror at the thought of the members of the rival society knowing something his did not. It was not part of Mr. Berry's responsibilities to nurse old wounds or to foster new enmity, and he did both of these entirely on his own as a voluntarily contribution.

Although more than twenty years had passed since the Society for the Advancement of Horticultural Knowledge was formed by discontents fleeing the British Horticultural Society, many current members of the BHS still saw it as a mutinous faction. Tensions between two different schools of botanical thought—knowledge for knowledge's sake on one side and knowledge for the advancement of human society on the other—had been growing for years, and the split finally came when Sir Walter Campbell advocated for a plaster made of cow dung, lime, wood ashes and sand to be applied to wounded trees as a restorative measure. A report commissioned by parliament concluded that the unpleasant concoction had no effect on the trees at all, neither good nor ill, but Campbell remained passionately committed to his invention regardless of its usefulness, and unable to save the majestic oaks in the royal forest, he decided to save himself by forming his own organization.

"You may remain calm, Mr. Berry," Huntly said with all due sobriety, though, in fact, he found the rivalry between the two societies to be endlessly amusing. "As far as I know, the Society for the Advancement of Horticultural Knowledge does not have an lexiconical advantage over us."

Mr. Berry exhaled loudly in relief. "Thank goodness for that, my lord. From whence, then, does this word come? And what does it mean exactly?"

If Huntly had considered the sort of conversation engendered by his question, he would no doubt have preferred taking the time to do the painstaking research himself. But he hadn't thought that far ahead, and reluctant now to dignify Miss Lavinia Harlow's absurdity with any more of his attention, he asked the clerk what advancements the other society had made in his absence.

As expected, this question successfully diverted Mr. Berry, and for several minutes straight he assured the marquess that the Society for the Advancement of Horticultural Knowledge had so far from advanced anything that it had actually—gasp of horror!—*regressed.* "They are recommending that one no longer rotate one's crops, for fear of letting valuable farmland grow fallow, if you can believe it, sir, and there's no reason you should not!"

While Mr. Berry railed against the folly of sunken gardens (not since the Middle Ages!), Huntly contemplated how to extricate himself from the situation he'd created. But no, he thought, this circumstance was not of his doing; 'twas Miss Harlow who was to blame, with her sugarcoated insults and her backhanded compliments. He had been unable to tell during the entire conversation if she was giving her truthful opinion about his work or offering intentional slights. Her manner had been everything that was honest and sincere as she blinked at him with wide-eyed innocence, her admiring tone at once genuine and abashed.

He knew now, of course, what her true purpose had been in offering these so-called compliments and calling his work botanicalesque—she was being deliberately insulting—and the Marquess of Huntly, whose person had never before been the target of deliberate insults, couldn't imagine what he had done to offend her. His behavior from the moment she had doused him with her ridiculous exploding hose had been nothing but circumspect: He greeted her politely when introduced by the duke, he made no mention of the incident, he smiled when she introduced a comment into the conversation, and he tipped his hat to her upon taking his leave. He had behaved exactly in the way a man of his breeding, station and taste was supposed to, and she, intemperate female that she was, had behaved like a veritable cracked pot.

And now, because of her, he was stuck listening to Mr. Berry air old grievances rather than attending to his estate, which required his attention far more than the garrulous clerk, and he resented the fact that he resented the fact that he was there.

It was an absolute muddle from top to bottom, and knowing that he was ultimately responsible for it made him even more angry with Miss Harlow.

"Understand, of course, that I'm not advocating for additional members," Mr. Berry continued, "for I know very well that it's quality that matters rather than quantity, but I cannot ignore the fact that the rebel society now has more members than we do."

At this information, Huntly's head tipped up sharply and a light entered his eyes as an idea occurred to him—a perfectly horrible, wonderful, wretched idea. It was not the sort of idea that befitted a man of his breeding, station or taste, but acting in accordance of all three had wound him up there and he was annoyed enough not to care. He would deal with Miss Harlow in exactly the same way she had dealt with him: by offering an insult wrapped in the fine paper of a compliment.

"You are right, Mr. Berry, we must be judicious in whom we stand as members," Huntly said agreeably, "for we have a proud lineage and cannot corrupt it by stuffing the ballot box, as they say. But new blood is always good for the stock."

"Very good," said Mr. Berry, happy that his idea had found favor with the marquess. "I shall put the matter on the agenda for the society's next meeting. The imbalance is not huge and horticulture, of course, is not a matter of numbers but of feeling. Still, I can't help but feel a few new members would serve us well."

"As I said, I agree entirely and would like to propose a new member myself," Huntly said.

Mr. Berry picked up a quill and took a fresh white sheet of parchment out of his desk. "I would be honored to record it. Please proceed."

"Miss Lavinia Harlow," Huntly said firmly.

The clerk nodded and scrawled *miss* with confidence as well as the first three letters of *Harlow* before the words he was writing penetrated his consciousness. Then he paused and looked up at Huntly with a furrowed brow, as if incapable of trusting his own ears. "Miss Lavinia Harlow, you say?"

"Yes, Harlow with a *W*, not to be confused with Harlo

without a *W,* which has a slightly forlorn look about it," he said helpfully.

As much as Mr. Berry appreciated the marquess's attempt to clear up his confusion, he didn't find the effort particularly helpful, as the problem was not the spelling of the name, of which he was already quite familiar. "She—being a *she*—is female," he said.

"Astutely observed, my good man," Huntly said with all seriousness, although his lips twitched with the desire to break out into a broad smile.

"We do not have any provisions for females," Mr. Berry said.

Huntly knew that by the word *provisions,* the clerk intended to say that the society was not set up to accommodate female members, which was entirely true. The British Horticultural Society was a fair-minded institution that allowed ladies to participate in activities appropriate to their sex such as entering flowers in its annual show, but it in no way considered women worthy of membership to its exclusive club. The society was far too rigorous and serious for such a distinction, for it had been created to provide men of a certain botanical bent with an opportunity to share thoughts and ideas through discussions, lectures and published articles.

The marquess knew what Mr. Berry meant, but he found it expedient to his purpose to deliberately misunderstand. "As always, you are correct. There are no provisions in the bylaws that bar the application and acceptance of females into the society."

At this statement, the efficient little man's face turned white, then bright red, for he had committed the charter to memory during his first month of employment and knew that the marquess spoke the truth: There was nothing in the document that specifically addressed the issue of women. Far from being an oversight, this omission was an intentional acknowledgement that the notion of admitting females into the organization was so absurd as not to need addressing.

Unsure of the marquess's purpose in making such an extraordinary suggestion, Mr. Berry did not let his mortification show and instead took a practical approach to the problem. "Yes, indeed. There is the matter of the application. According to the bylaws, in order for a candidate to be eligible for consideration, he—or, um, *she*—must publish a paper on an appropriate topic and present it to the society."

"I have it from the candidate herself that she recently published a pamphlet on drainage systems," Huntly said.

For a moment, Mr. Berry looked quite taken aback by this information, then his expression turned disgruntled. "She did indeed, my lord. It was actually published by the society," he admitted, his tone suddenly faint as he recalled the pamphlet that he himself had commissioned at the behest of the Duke of Trent.

The Marquess of Huntly was not a cruel man and he found it unseemly to take one's enjoyment at the expense of others, but he couldn't help being amused at the predicament this confession created for Mr. Berry. The gentleman seemed at once affronted and aggrieved, as if he had blindly fallen into a trap not visible to the unaided eye.

"I have it right here," Mr. Berry admitted with great reluctance as he retrieved the offending pamphlet from the stack of papers on his desk. It was so easily accessible because he had been perusing it earlier, for it contained information that pertained directly to a problem he was having with his own garden on Upper Seymour Street. The clerk knew it wouldn't do to admit such a thing, but he felt compelled to say, either out of sense of fair play or respect for the lady, who had impressed him with her rationality and clear thinking, that he thought the pamphlet had a few useful ideas. He paused, seemingly done with the thought, then added as if by compulsion, "It is written very well."

Huntly accepted the pamphlet, which was called "A Horticulturalist's Rudimentary Guide to the Implementation of Drainage Systems" and ran an even fifty pages. "Good. Then there can be no objection to her application."

"Oh, there is," insisted the clerk, his efficient mind quickly sifting through all the information he had to arrive at yet another concern. He did not devote himself to the task so fully because he was an ardent horticulturalist. Rather, Mr. Reginald Berry was a zealous British Horticultural Society-ist and he knew—could not *bear*—the may game the Society for the Advancement of Horticultural Knowledge would surely make of them when the truth became known. "She is in mourning, my lord, and as such could not attend the social event that her presentation would be."

At once, the marquess straightened his shoulders and leaned forward in his chair, for this was information that was entirely unknown to him and for some reason, it didn't sit right. Miss Harlow was an unbalanced creature, to be sure, but she did not seem unbalanced by grief. Her sense of humor was far too well intact for a widow wearing the weeds. "For whom is she in mourning?" he asked.

"Her fiancé, Sir Waldo Windbourne, a baronet from Derbyshire with political aspirations," Mr. Berry said. "He died six months ago in a wardrobe-related mishap, and Miss Harlow has been in black gloves ever since."

In the whole of his entire adult life—and that summation included two years at sea with several dozen fascinating men—Huntly had never heard any description as intriguing as *wardrobe-related mishap*. He could tell that his companion was eager to elaborate, and rather than appear unduly interested in the private matters of people not intimately known to him, he simply waited the necessary few seconds for Mr. Berry to burst with impatience.

"It was his stays, my lord. He pulled them so tight he suffocated himself," he said, striving for what he hoped was a tone that implied only academic interest. Despite his efforts, however, an unseemly, high-pitched giggle escaped him. Quickly he added, so as to cover up the undignified sound, "It was ruled death by misadventure, although there was some talk of charging his valet with murder. I believe the Duke of Trent interceded on the young man's behalf."

The story was incredible, and indeed the marquess could not believe it. He had heard of women fainting from corsets that were too snug but never an instance in which a life was lost, and he very much doubted it could happen. He assumed the true story was considerably more mundane—the baronet had choked on a haddock—and had grown increasingly fantastical with each retelling until the fish bone was a whalebone and the victim done in by grotesque vanity. The next time he saw Trent, he would get the truth.

"You are right to raise the concern," Huntly said, "and I understand why you do so, but I happen to know that the young woman will be at her sister's wedding ball in a week's time. If she can attend that after the first sixth months of mourning have passed, then I'm sure she can attend one of our little presentations, which could hardly be raised to the felicitous level of social function, let alone event."

If Mr. Berry wanted to press his point further, he certainly would not do so while the marquess was present. He would wait until he left before giving voice to a variety of very reasonable and well-articulated arguments. "Right you are, my lord. I shall add her name to the list, then, shall I?" He phrased the statement as a question in one last hope that the marquess would see the folly of his ways and recant.

"You are completely obliging, Mr. Berry, and I appreciate it. I trust you will send the invitation immediately?" Huntly asked.

The little clerk blanched but kept his horror firmly in check with a subdued nod. "There is, of course, paperwork to be done first, a file to be started and various other sundry protocols to be followed, but as soon as all that is complete, I will send the invitation immediately," he explained, grateful to have an excuse to delay the inevitable. Thankfully, the process for acquiring new members was an involved one, regardless of gender.

Satisfied with this answer, Huntly said, "Good. Now on to my other business."

"Other business?" he squeaked, unable to imagine what

else there could be to discuss. They had already covered the marquess's travels and the possible destruction of their beloved institution. Was that not enough for one afternoon?

"I need to hire an assistant to help me put the notes from my travels in order," the marquess explained. "I have hundreds of drawings and almost a dozen journals that need to be catalogued and organized for the compendium I mean to write. Do you know anyone with the proper knowledge who might be in want of a position?"

Much relieved to be on familiar territory once again, Mr. Berry brightened and said he knew just the person for the job. "Actually, several persons who are very well educated and should be suited to the task. I will gather the names and recommendations and forward them on to your secretary."

"I have yet to engage a secretary, so you can address the information to me," Huntly said, standing.

Mr. Berry hopped to his feet as well. "Very good, my lord. If I may be so presumptuous, I will also included a few persons who I believe would serve well as factotums."

"You're a regular mop fair, Mr. Berry."

Pleased with the compliment, the clerk looked down at his fingers and assured the marquess that he was happy to do what he could.

Retrieving his hat, Huntly again expressed his appreciation, for he didn't doubt that the efficient clerk would send along several excellent applicants and that the task of organizing his book would soon be under way. As much as he'd resented the minutes lost to the unplanned visit (47 and counting), he had to concede now that it was time well spent. Not only had he engaged Mr. Berry's help in arranging sundry business affairs, but he'd come up with a way to tweak Miss Harlow's ego in a similar way that she'd tweaked his. He didn't mean her any harm in standing her for membership, and he couldn't imagine anything ill coming of it. In all likelihood, she would get the invitation to join, realize he was having a bit of fun at her expense and send a polite but strongly worded letter declining the honor.

He found, to his surprise, that was he looking forward to receiving the letter, which would no doubt be strewn with the same sugarcoated insults as her praise. He couldn't say why such a prospect appealed to him, except that from the remove of a few hours—and the keen satisfaction of a cleverly executed revenge plot—he could appreciate the skill with which she had taunted him. He still thought she was a nonsensical woman given to odd starts and mad fits, but now he could now see there was a method to her madness.

The Marquess of Huntly took his leave of Mr. Berry and climbed into his curricle, determined to salvage something of the day. It was still plenty early—only a little after one—and when he arrived at home, he would request a light meal to be served to him in the study, so that he could eat while discussing the estates with Mr. Hardwicke. He knew there was much to get through, but he felt confident that he and the steward could dispense with many of the more pressing issues before Mr. Graney from the bank arrived at four. It was merely a matter of devoting all his attention to the issue at hand—putting his nose to the grindstone, as he had charmingly heard it put more than once on the ship—and not letting minor things distract them. It was easy enough to accomplish.

And yet twenty minutes later, his curricle was still parked in front of the British Horticultural Society as he read just one more page—and then just one more page—of Miss Lavinia Harlow's oddly fascinating text on how to implement a drainage system.

CHAPTER SIX

If anyone were to lay odds in the betting book at Brooks's which Harlow sister would appear in the betting book at Brooks's, the clever money—indeed, all the money—would have been on Miss Emma Harlow. That she had managed to avoid such a distinction in all of her twenty-four-plus hoydenish years surprised everyone who knew her, from her aggrieved mother to the scullery maid at Crescent House, who regularly found the impertinent young miss with her fingers in the larder at three in the morning.

The Dowager Duchess of Trent was not only astonished by this accomplishment but grateful for it because it meant one fewer direction in which she had to extend her credit—although, to be fair, she didn't doubt for a moment that her consequence could easily bring such a scandal to heel.

On the night of her ball to celebrate her son's wedding, the betting book at Brooks's—or even White's or Boodles—was the farthest thing from her grace's mind. During the last frantic week of planning, she'd thought about the menu and the decorations and the musicians and the placement of the ice sculpture of two intricately carved swans. She'd debated the merits of rosettes *and* swags for her blue silk gown (perhaps a little too youthful) and the wisdom of doubling the layers in the freestanding trifle (a marvel to behold but architecturally compromised). She had worked tirelessly to pull off the grandest event London had seen in a decade with the sole intent of intimidating the *ton* with excess—to, in effect, cower Emma's critics with caviar—and putting to rest once and for all any discussion of her new daughter-in-law's scandalous past.

Now that the evening had arrived—the wine was flowing, the guests were dancing, Prinny was offering compliments on her son's choice of brides—she thought it very likely she had succeeded beyond her own considerable expectations. She knew better, of course, than to count her chickens before they hatched, but she felt the deep fissures in the eggshells indicated a certain inevitability on which, if one couldn't exactly count, one could take comfort.

Then, not ten minutes after Prinny had taken his leave, Lady Dalyell punctured her grace's sanguinity when she was overheard informing Mr. Crispin Joseph of a "delicious *on dit*" involving a wager, one hundred guineas, Lord Hastings and "that Harlow chit." The exact nature of the business the dowager could not discern, for at that moment, the famously indiscrete Lady Dalyell chose to cultivate discretion and lowered her voice several notches. Her grace tilted her head to the left to ascertain more information but was thwarted by the unprecedented dulcet tones of her ladyship.

Unable to decide if she was more angry or irritated at being exposed to a new scandal at an affair calculated to squelch an old one—a development that further angered or irritated her—the dowager sought out her daughter-in-law to collect all the facts before settling on a suitable course of action. (Forcefully removing Lady Dalyell from the party, though a very satisfying response, was not a viable option.) She found Emma near the ice sculpture talking to her sister-in-law Sarah, a sensible woman with little patience for the Harlow Hoyden's high jinx and even less aptitude to rein them in.

Emma, dazzling in a red silk gown trimmed with pearls

and lace, her hair gathered in a classic chignon, her eyes glinting with irrepressible humor, greeted her grace with a delighted smile. "You'll be relieved to hear, ma'am, that Sarah was just rhapsodizing over the champagne and saying that this is quite the loveliest ball she's ever been to. She has no idea she's being lulled into a state of complacency about my many sins. One more glass and she will congratulate you on your excellent good luck in acquiring me as your daughter-in-law."

The dowager, whose chief method for handling Emma's nonsense was to ignore it, took this statement in stride, but Sarah immediately turned pink and began to stutter an apology for her former charge's rudeness. Unconcerned, the duchess waved off the other woman's distress with a flick of the wrist and turned to Emma, who stared back at her with a look of appealing curiosity. Impertinent baggage!

"You wretched girl, what have you done now?" she demanded curtly, her face a mask of polite good humor, which revealed not a hint of her aggravation to any interested guests who might happen to glance their way.

Emma's smile did not waver at this accusation. Indeed, the dimples in her cheeks deepened as she launched into a list of recent peccadillos. "An hour ago, I stepped on the Earl of Montagu's toes, which was his fault, for he inserted his foot under my shoe in a rush to get away from Miss Crossdon. As I was sympathetic to his plight, I did not hold his complicity against him and apologized so prettily that even Sarah would have been pleased. Then, about fifteen minutes ago, I dropped an olive into Lady Keppel's ratafia. It was an accident, of course, but I didn't think she would believe the ridiculous series of events that culminated in an olive in her wine, so I promptly hid behind Mr. Ashley-Cooper, who is as good as a column for providing cover. Despite my cowardly retreat, I was sensible of my responsibility and kept an eye on the good woman to make sure the olive did her no lasting harm, which, I'm happy to report, it did not. I believe that's it. No, wait, I also told Lady Jersey that she didn't strike me as quite the chatterbox her nick-name implied." At Sarah's gasp of horror, she rushed to explain. "I only said it because *she* had observed that *I* didn't strike *her* as the hoyden my reputation suggested and I want-ed to assure her that the label was well earned. Of course, as soon as the words were out of my mouth, I realized they didn't sound quite like the compliment I had intended and I rushed to apologize. It was touch and go for a moment, and I thought for sure I would be barred entry to Almack's for the rest of my life, but then she smiled and said we must have a coze later. And that, ma'am, is a complete catalog of what have I done now."

The dowager listened to Emma's absurd speech, un-certain if her new daughter-in-law was jesting with her, for now, as always, her cornflower blue eyes blinked with inno-cent frankness. "I'm referring to the wager Lord Hastings laid that involves you," she explained calmly. "What outra-geous claim have you recently made? That you can beat your own record to Newmarket?"

"I have said on several occasions that I could improve upon my racing time from London to Newmarket," Emma said mildly, "but I wouldn't call that an outrageous claim, as it's entirely true."

Her grace's smile grew brittle, and Sarah said her sister-in-law's name in the same warning tone she used with her children. The Harlow Hoyden, who had never failed to own her sins regardless of how disgraceful they were, rushed to assure the dowager of her innocence. "I swear to you, ma'am, I have done nothing to warrant a wager to be placed. Truly. I know how important this evening is to you and would never do anything to undermine its success."

The sincerity in Emma's voice was undeniable, and the dowager had no choice but to believe her, for though her new daughter might be a minx and a scapegrace, she was a brutally honest one. Indeed, it was her stubborn re-fusal to comply with the superficial dictates of polite socie-ty that most frequently got her into trouble. The Duchess of Trent could respect it, even if she couldn't understand or admire it.

"Perhaps the cause of the bet isn't entirely Emma's fault," Sarah offered.

Emma, who was used to this sort of abuse from her sister-in-law, laughed. "I'm humbled by your faith in me and not the least bit put out by your cautious use of the word *entirely*. No doubt we shall discover that I'm responsible to some extent, no matter how blameless I actually turn out to be. Shall we investigate? We will cover more ground if we split up. Your grace, you take the south portion of the room. Sarah, you go north. I'll start along the east wall and work my way west."

Although the dowager could not imagine what an investigation by the Harlow Hoyden would entail, she knew for certain she didn't want one in her ballroom. Before she could utter a single word of protest, however, her nephew Philip, a lively young man from Yorkshire who had yet to cultivate town bronze despite nine months in the metropolis, came over to express his disappointment at Emma's poor spiritedness. "Such a bang-up lark, bearding those stiff-necked gardeners in their hallowed den! Worthy of the Harlow Hoyden. But I suppose now that you're married to Trent, you will have to settle down and adopt the matronly airs of a proper duchess," he conceded with surprising graciousness. "Trent's a right 'un and deserves a bit of peace, even if he did just call me a nodcock."

"I believe the term I used was *clodpole*," the duke said as he appeared at his wife's side, his handsome countenance enhanced by a broad smile. "And it's a fitting description of anyone who puts his elbow into Lady Villier's wine."

Much offended by the unjust accusation, Philip straightened his shoulders, lifted his head and declared with all due dignity that the glass had been empty. Then he presented two pristine elbows as proof. "Not such a clodpole I'd start rumors about my own cousin," he muttered.

"All right, cawker, you have my apologies," the duke

said without a trace of sincerity. "In future retellings I will distinguish between a full glass and an empty one. Now, if you will excuse us, I've come to claim my wife for the waltz."

His mother, who had visibly tensed upon hearing Philip use that deplorable nickname for Emma, gasped in horror at this announcement. That Trent had accompanied the statement with a fond look at his wife only made the transgression more appalling, and the dowager was properly dismayed that any son of hers would so blatantly flaunt his happiness in front of the *ton*.

"You cannot dance with your wife at your own wedding party," her grace said scandalized. "It's beyond all things ramshackle."

"Actually," Sarah interjected with a hint of a smile, "it might be the most respectable thing Emma has ever done."

"Don't mean to contradict you, Mrs. Harlow," said Philip, whose admiration for the Harlow Hoyden was still fervent despite recent indications that she might be losing her gumption, "but I should think saving England from a French invasion was the most respectable thing she's ever done."

Emma smothered a smile while the dowager, frustrated by her family's lack of respect for her efforts, glanced around to make sure nobody heard Philip's outrageous claim. It might be true that Emma's interference saved the lives of several dozen British spies and perhaps some of the guests there tonight, but it would never do for everybody to know that. Even her considerable consequence could not overcome the notoriety of having a heroine in the family.

"I appreciate the tribute, Philip, but would rather hear more about the stiff-necked gardeners you mentioned," Emma said, "for I suspect that's the missing piece of information her grace was looking for."

The dowager did not instantly grasp the implication, but Sarah did and she stared at Emma in shock. "*Vinnie?*" she asked, unable to conceive of her sensible and reserved sister-in-law doing anything that would cause the gentlemen at Brooks's to utter her name, let alone record it in the betting book.

Philip nodded proudly. "She put herself up for member-ship to the British Horticultural Society like a regular Trojan. First female to try. Lord Hastings bet Mr. Irby one hundred guineas to ten that she'll get in. I think she will, too. Don't you, Trent? You'll vote for her, won't you?"

Before Trent could answer in the affirmative or the negative—it was unclear from his expression which he in-tended—Emma said, "Of course he will," just as the dowa-ger said, "Absolutely not."

Both women were equally annoyed, and as they glared at each other with narrowed eyes, the dowager so forgot herself that she let out an irritated huff. It was an inelegant sound, quite unlike anything that had ever emanated from her refined person before, and Sarah glanced around to make sure the unusual noise hadn't excited interest. To her dismay, she noticed several attentive bystanders looking their way—and no wonder, with the duke, his mother and the infamous Harlow Hoyden gathered so closely together. Anyone, even the least curious among them, would want to discover the topic under discussion.

Trent realized the same thing and sought to defuse the situation by suggesting it was all a hum. "For I'm certain Vinnie would not do something like that without consulting me. Philip must have misunderstood. Wet elbows or not, he's hardly the most reliable source of information."

"I say, cuz, cut line!" he demanded, his face pink with in-dignation. "I got it from Morgan Pearson, who, I'm sure you'll agree, has never dipped his arm into Lady Villier's glass."

As the state of Pearson's clumsiness wasn't the matter up for debate, nobody responded to this absurdity. Instead, the duke announced he would clear up the confusion with his friend immediately, Emma stated she would get the true story from Vinnie, and the dowager insisted that everyone remain exactly where they were so as not to arouse further suspicion in the group of onlookers now gathered around them.

"This is how we will proceed," she said, quickly devising a plan that would halt both gossip and the progress of any newly hatched chickens that tried to escape. "Trent, dear, in the tone of voice you use to scold your nephew and niece—that is, loud enough to be heard by those immediately surrounding us but not so booming as to disrupt our guests by the refreshment table—will tell the story about the time Brummell used your cravat to shine his Hessians. When he is finished, we will all trill delicately with amusement, including you, Philip. Then I will say, 'How droll, dear,' and suggest that Lord Darby, who is standing three feet to our left, would delight in that anecdote as well. A moment later, Emma will politely excuse herself to greet her friend Kate Kennington, an estimable young lady no doubt trapped in conversation with the overly solicitous Lady Fellingham to our right. Sarah will remain here with Philip and ask about his recent fishing expedition on the Thames. Philip will then relate an engrossing tale about hooking a large perch. I, of course, will continue to lull our guests into a state of complacency with fine champagne, as my lovely daughter-in-law so charmingly put it. We will all carry out our various tasks with broad smiles on our faces and without the slightest hint of self-consciousness. We will be natural and unaffected."

The dowager paused for a moment and silently lamented the fact that she had to enlist their help at all, for she knew the likelihood of success decreased as the number of participants increased. But there was nothing she could do about it, so she gave each one an admonishing look and asked if she'd made herself clear. Three heads bobbed up and down—Emma's, the duke's and Sarah's—while Philip started to protest his assignment on the grounds that he had never caught a perch in the Thames, large or otherwise.

"I once caught a trout in the Serpentine River in Surrey, but I would hardly describe it as large. It was more mediumish like a...." He trailed off as he met his aunt's impatient glare. "Yes, ma'am."

"Good," she said firmly. "Now let's implement the plan. Alex, you may start talking now and remember to inflect properly. A story is only as good as its telling."

Duly chastised, the Duke of Trent launched into the Brummell tale, the details of which were hazy to him several years later. Rather than risk his mother's ire by appearing less than confident, he made up the specifics as he spoke and avoided his wife's determined gaze, for he knew if he looked at her now, he would break into uncontrollable laughter and that unusual sight would invite more speculation than the dowager could withstand.

Miss Lavinia Harlow had never been the most popular girl at the ball—her looks, though pretty and blond, were too anemic to hold interest, her countenance too withdrawn and pale—but she had never been a pariah like her sister. During the course of a typical evening, she would gossip with other young ladies, converse with inquisitive matrons and stand up with eligible *partis*. That she participated in these activities less frequently than her peers was understandable, as the majority of the young ladies and inquisitive matrons and eligible *partis* wanted to talk about the most recent exploits of the Harlow Hoyden, a topic naturally unappealing to Vinnie.

Attending her first function as a woman in mourning, however, made her look on her previous unpopularity in a fresh light, for compared with her new social status, she had once been the belle of the ball.

Her conduct, of course, was circumspect and complied with the dictates imposed by grief. She was properly attired in widow's weeds: bombazine silk, subdued lilac, wide hem—all appropriately dull to lower a young woman's spirits if the death of her beloved hadn't sufficiently accomplished the task. She was correctly seated among the chaperones and wallflowers, who chose to partake of the festivities by not partaking. Her expression was suitably bland, her hands were decorously clasped in her lap, her toes were befittingly still. She hadn't done a single thing that wouldn't be found on a list of approved behaviors for young widows, and yet she could feel the disapproval all around her.

The problem was the timing of the ball, which fell just three days after the end of her official six-month mourning period. The dowager had insisted the seventy-two hours provided a sufficient cushion for any stickler who might nip-cheese the dates, an argument to which Vinnie had reluctantly submitted because she didn't want to miss the happy event. Instead of appeasing the zealously critical members of the *ton,* however, the three days incited their scorn by implying a cool-minded calculation that many guests found off-putting. To them, it signified an overeagerness to get out of mourning, which in turn indicated a disinclination to enter into it. Their gracious hostess was, of course, exonerated of all culpability because she had merely offered the invitation; the fault was her guest's for accepting.

Vinnie, who had overheard enough snippets to know what people thought of her (as they had intended, of course), found the situation excruciating. To be in mourning for a man whom one did not mourn—indeed, for whom one actually shot dead—was onerous enough, but to then be accused of not wanting to mourn for him when, in fact, one had not, was unbearable. She realized all they wanted was some outward display of grief, such as a forlorn tear down her cheek or a wince at the sight of happy couples, but she refused to pander to their vanity by trying to convince them that her insincere mourning, which, for the record, had faithfully followed Countess de Boufflers's *Maxims and Rules for the Conduct of Women,* was in actuality sincere. They would simply have to accept her stiff upper lip as proof of her anguish or dismiss her entirely.

Her pride, however, was only part of the difficulty. More to the point was her complete inability to dissemble. Yes, she was more schooled in the ways of polite society than her sister, who could never bestir herself to feign interest in a dull conversation, but in the whole of her life, Vinnie had never pretended to be anything other than what she was. In this, she and Emma were in perfect accord.

It was little wonder, then, that people were talking about her. Vinnie told herself she didn't mind, which wasn't completely true. Naturally, she minded being the subject of ugly rumors, for who save her sister *wouldn't* mind, but it was better that they supposed her to be ruthlessly on the prowl for a new husband than suspect the truth. She would gladly suffer any amount of gossip to avoid being branded a murderess.

These thoughts kept Vinnie happily occupied for some time. Well, she conceded silently, *happily* might be overstating the case, but she appreciated having something to think about while she waited for dinner to be announced. Dancing was off-limits, as was smiling, laughing or any display of merriment, but eating made the list of approved activities. Indeed, it was encouraged, for one must keep up one's strength during these difficult times.

Vinnie was calculating just how many minutes remained before the dinner announcement when the Marquess of Huntly appeared suddenly before her.

"Miss Harlow, we must speak," he said firmly.

Although she knew it was absurd, Vinnie swore she could hear the room around her hush as several dozen interested heads turned her way. Inside, she withered from the attention, but she kept her face impassive as she stood up to greet Lord Huntly with polite indifference. She was not feeling entirely indifferent, of course. Ever since their exchange at Hatchard's, she had been anticipating their next meeting with unusual eagerness. It wasn't because she liked him any better than when she'd first met him but because she was interested to see if he would respond to her critique of his writing. As almost a week had passed, he'd surely gotten her note with her comments on his other articles. No doubt he'd figured out that her tepid compliments had been pointed insults and wanted some small revenge.

Vinnie stood up to greet him and spoke loudly and clearly for the edification of her audience, for to speak any lower would be to excite more interest. "Good evening, my lord. It's a pleasure to see you. I trust you are enjoying yourself."

"Splendid affair," he said, his tone as clipped as his nod. Then, mindful of the crowd around them, he added softly. "There is a matter I would like to discuss."

Mindful as well, Vinnie paid no heed to his request for a tête-à-tête. She might not know how to mourn to the *ton*'s satisfaction, but she certainly knew how to conduct a respectable conversation. "It is indeed splendid. Why, even Prinny has given his stamp of approval."

Huntly leaned closer to Vinnie and said directly into her ear. "We must talk."

The inexplicable urgency in Huntly's voice intrigued Vinnie, but she refused to indulge it and took an extra-large step back to double the distance between them. The movement was exaggerated, like a performer in a pantomime, and she feared that it made her look ridiculous.

Perhaps this indelicate attempt at a private conversation was Lord Huntly's revenge.

"I believe Prinny's gone now, but he stayed for a good number of minutes and even offered his compliments to my sister," she said, wondering what inane topic she could prattle on about once she had exhausted the subject of the regent's visit. "I'm sure the dowager was quite pleased."

Huntly's frustration was apparent in the way he pressed his lips together, but before he could issue his request for an astonishing fourth time, the orchestra played the opening notes of a waltz. His expression immediately lightened, and, relieved, Vinnie assumed he would excuse himself to claim the lady to whom he was promised for the dance.

Instead, he seized her elbow and said, "Our dance, Miss Harlow," with authority and conviction. Surprise propelled her forward a few steps, and by the time her senses returned, she realized it was too late. She was well on her way to the dance floor, with dozens of censorious eyes watching her, and to stop now and tug her arm from his grasp would not only raise eyebrows even higher but make her look absurd as well. Dancing the waltz just three days out of mourning was scandalous, but being dragged by a marquess across a ballroom was scandalous *and* mortifying, which was just a little more than Vinnie could bear.

Furious at the situation and powerless to alter it, Vinnie placed her hand on Huntly's shoulder and resolved to get through the experience without further humiliation. She would dance gracefully and silently until the music ended, then return to her chair amid the wallflowers and sit down with a woeful grimace. If she could manage it, she would squeeze out a tear or two to suggest that dancing with a man who wasn't her dearly departed was too painful to be contained. Perhaps she could even convince her bottom lip to quiver.

"I realize my behavior was unorthodox, but it's imperative that we speak," Huntly explained masterfully.

Vinnie, who refused to dignify his shabby treatment of her with a response, kept her attention firmly focused on her feet. She had danced the waltz several times before—once unmemorably with Sir Windbourne—and knew the steps, but the careful study gave her a reason to avoid his eyes.

Huntly, his shoulders tense despite the graceful way he twirled her around the floor, said, "I must explain before this goes any farther."

Unable to withstand the provocation, Vinnie lifted her angry eyes to his. "I don't think there is any danger of that, my lord. I'm fairly certain you have taken my ruination as far as it can go," she announced.

The marquess winced. "I am sincerely sorry for the harm I have done you. In my defense, however, I would like to point out that I could not have foreseen the scandal it would create."

"You could not have foreseen the scandal?" she repeated scathingly, the scorn in her tone contrasting strongly with her graceful movements. She would not admit it to anyone, of course, but the marquess made an elegant and agile dance partner. "The customs involving mourning in our society are well established and known to all so I fail to understand how you could not have *foreseen* the scandal your making me dance the waltz when I'm not a full week out of black gloves would create."

"It was a private conversation between Mr. Berry and myself, and I did not—" He broke off suddenly as he digested her words and looked at her with a puzzled expression. "What are you talking about?"

Lavinia was equally confused by the mention of a Mr. Berry, the only one of whom she knew was employed by the horticultural society. "What are *you* talking about?"

"The one-hundred-guinea bet Lord Hastings placed that you would be accepted into the British Horticultural Society as a member," Huntly explained, his brows drawn.

The idea of her acceptance into the society was so unexpected and extraordinary that Vinnie broke out into peals of delighted laughter. The organization, which graciously deigned to let women participate in its annual exhibition at Temple Gardens, would never countenance a female member, a fact so well established she could not conceive of how the wager originated. It had to be a hoax by a bored nobleman who could not think of an outcome more outrageous than a woman gaining admittance to those sacred halls.

Vinnie knew she should be offended that she was singled out, for clearly the reason was her excessive unsuitability. There was no more improbable candidate than the somewhat reserved and retiring older sister of the notorious Harlow Hoyden. There were plenty of other ladies who regularly exhibited at the show who could have been selected for the prank—none high fliers, of course, though a few were fashionable leaders of the ton.

But in truth, Vinnie wasn't the tiniest bit offended. Rather, she was so amused by the absurdity, she could not contain her delight. It was, she decided, a fine thing—a truly, genuinely, very fine thing—for her to be the scandalous Miss Harlow at her sister's wedding party. Emma would be shown to advantage, which would no doubt please the dowager.

"You must stop laughing," Huntly commanded softly. "People are looking."

He was right, of course, but Vinnie found she couldn't rouse herself to care. People were always looking, or, as in this case, glaring with disapproval. From the moment she had arrived at the ball in the company of her brother and sister-in-law, her eyes turned down, her pale skin pallid against the lilac silk of her dress, she had been the target of censure and reproach, and now she was giggling as one of London's most ardently hunted quarry—an eligible bachelor with no prior attachments—twirled her around the dance floor. There was nothing for it but for her to admit the truth: She was a failure as a widow.

The thought of her supposed mourning brought her back to her senses, and she had enough wits about her to stop laughing. She didn't halt it entirely in a moment, for to do so would be to imply that her laughter was something to be ashamed of. It was inappropriate, yes, but had she actually been mourning the death of a loved one, she knew she would have found relief in the outburst.

When she had herself sufficiently under control, she said, "I must thank Lord Hastings for his faith in me."

Huntly, whose fingers on her shoulder had tightened during her laughing fit, said, "Hastings was not displaying faith in you but rather tweaking Mr. Irby, who, as a member of the British Horticultural Society, naturally finds the idea of a woman among our ranks repellent. Hastings belongs to the Society for the Advancement of Horticultural Knowledge, a rival organization, and would love to see our esteemed institution brought low by the inclusion of a female." Sensing her rising anger at his frank speech, he hastened to add, "I seek only to clarify your understanding of the matter, Miss Harlow. I would loath for you to overestimate your importance in the matter."

Although this attempt at clarification—or, rather, conciliation—only made the situation worse, Vinnie regarded him calmly, as if not in the least put out by the insults he'd dealt her. "Of course, my lord, I would never presume to consider myself anything but a pawn in the machinations of important men. I trust it's all right if I thank Lord Hastings for choosing to use me in his maneuver rather than one of another dozen or so insignificant females? Or am I not allowed to be flattered by that either?" she asked mildly, fluttering her eyelashes in what she hoped was a fawning manner.

"You are cross with me for being so honest," Huntly observed. "Perhaps I should have not used the word *repellent,* as your sensibility is too delicate for such a harsh word. I apologize for my immoderate speech and promise to conduct myself more appropriately in the future."

Without question, Vinnie took exception to the word *repellent* in the context in which he'd used it—and she had something improper to say about *brought low,* as well—but she would never admit that to him. The overly solicitous nature of his response reminded her of their exchange at Hatchard's, and she wondered if he was using her own tactic against her. It certainly felt as though she was being mocked.

Nevertheless, she smiled sweetly at him, determined to appear unruffled. "You are correct. Descriptions such as *repugnant* and *revolting* are much more suited to my sensibilities. I would add *nauseating* as well, but I'm afraid something about the word makes me squeamish. Then, of course, there's the adjective *disgusting,* which has always struck me as so singularly unappealing as to be, well, disgusting. When one thinks of it, there are so many words you could have used to describe my possible admittance to the British Horticultural Society. I will, of course, be sure to thank Lord Hastings for opening me up to all of them with his thoughtful wager."

To her surprise, he blanched, and rather than make the rallying response she anticipated, he said with sudden stiffness, "Miss Harlow, I must confess that it was not Lord Hastings who opened you up to various comments that one could interpret as insulting but rather myself."

Vinnie, who found this revelation to be as extraordinary as the previous one, stared in amazement. "You, my lord?" she asked blankly, as if unable to digest the information. When her name had been chosen by a stranger seeking to maximize the effect of his childish prank, she had felt no injury, for her person had merely suited his aim. But discovering that the source was someone already known to her changed the complexion entirely, turning a random occurrence into an intentional slight. She knew their short acquaintance did not reflect well on her, and that was hardly surprising given its inauspicious beginning. If she lived to be one hundred years old, she would never fully live down the humiliation of soaking him with her exploding hose, but it was probably unfair of her to take out her discomfort on him with those comments at Hatchard's, which, though pointed, had been made mostly in jest. She didn't mean to do him any genuine harm, for, in truth, what harm could she possibly do him? He was an adventurer, a world explorer who had seen more amazing things in a single day than she would in her entire life, and she was an unmarried lady on the verge of becoming an old maid. She never imagined she could puncture his vanity.

But she must have punctured it quite badly for him to have retaliated like that. If so, she had done him yet another bad turn.

Mortified anew but determined to behave in the correct manner regardless of how uncomfortable it was, she said with quiet dignity, "I am sorry, my lord, for the wrongs I have done you. What I said about your articles at Hatchard's was meant only to tease you, not to provoke a response that—"

"I must insist that you stop apologizing, Miss Harlow," Huntly interrupted with surprising vigor, "for either by design or by chance, you are making me feel more wretched. As much as I would like to disavow all responsibility for this contretemps, it's entirely my fault. Your comments at Hatchard's certainly provoked me—and please let me express my admiration for your skill with the sugarcoated insult—but they in no way warranted such a large and public retribution. That was never my intention. I hope you believe that."

He spoke so simply and with such sincerity, she had no choice but to nod. She was too disconcerted by the intensity in his strange aquamarine eyes to speak, so she waited for him to explain further. Out of the corner of her eye, she glimpsed the dowager duchess. She was chatting with Lady Bolingbroke by the edge of the dance floor. Her smile was as serene and composed as ever, and if she had heard about the scandalous wager, nothing in her manner revealed it. Vinnie, who was easily intimidated by Trent's imposing mother, hoped with all her heart that the story hadn't reached the woman's august ears before she had a chance to explain. It was futile, of course, for even if she didn't know about the appalling bet, she was fully cognizant of the shameful waltz, which would surely eclipse all else on the tips of wagging tongues.

I am sunk, she thought.

As if reading her thoughts, Huntly said, "All is not lost. I acted rashly, yes, and failed to properly consider the consequences, which was lamentably irresponsible of me. When I put your name up for membership, it never occurred to me that members of a rivalrous society would seek to humiliate us by—"

"Famously rivalrous," she said.

"Excuse me?"

"I was observing that the rivalry between the two organizations is rather well known," she explained, "and one needed but only a little imagination to conceive of the Society for the Advancement of Horticultural Knowledge members delighting in the prospect of the British Horticultural Society being—how did you so concisely describe it?— *brought low* by the admittance of a female."

Huntly stiffened at her words, which were an indictment despite the fact they were said with a mildness that could be described as indifference. "You are right, of course, and if you would like to continue to complain about my behavior, I cannot protest. Recriminations, however, will get us nowhere."

Vinnie smiled wryly. "Won't get *you* anywhere, to be sure. Recriminations would allow *me* to vent my spleen, which would get me a good distance from frustrated and angry. But I will refrain because I'm curious to hear your plan for salvaging the situation."

"We shall say that I proposed your application at the behest of Sir Windbourne," he said.

At these words, Vinnie faltered. She had conducted the entire conversation, remarkable in so many respects, while twirling effortlessly around the ballroom, yet at the utterance of her dead fiancé's name, she stumbled. Nobody would think it amiss—indeed, Huntly certainly did not as he steadied her with a sure hand—but she was appalled by the implied frailty. Even though she knew a display of weakness was to her benefit, she hated for anyone to think her grief was so deep, she could barely remain upright at the mention of her beloved.

Before Huntly could apologize or treat her with the marked concern one typically reserved for the elderly or the infirm, she said matter-of-factly, "You never met Sir Windbourne."

Taking his cue from her, he said with equal pragmatism, "A minor detail that nobody will question, for what cause would they have to doubt my word? In actuality, however, I do believe I met him once at an embassy party. We did not have a private exchange, but we were introduced by our hostess, Lady Smithington. He seemed like a decent fellow. Lady Smithington said he was very good at whist."

As Sir Windbourne was in reality atrocious at whist and at any other game in which one could possibly lose money, Vinnie assumed this was polite chatter on the part of either Lady Smithington or Lord Huntly. "He could not have made his behest to you because you were at sea for the entire length of our relationship," she pointed out reasonably in hopes of dissuading him from his plan. Her dislike of Sir Windbourne was such that she couldn't bear the thought of accepting help from him, however posthumously or unknowingly it was offered.

Huntly easily dismissed this concern with more invention. "After Lady Smithington so graciously made the introduction, we kept up a dedicated correspondence. Naturally, he wrote to me when he become engaged to the lovely Miss Lavinia Harlow, and being a devoted swain and in full admiration of your horticulture skills, asked if I could possibly help arrange membership for you. He realized it was unlikely, given the fraternal nature of the organization, but he could not refrain from asking when he knew how much it would mean to you."

The gentleman he described, who bore no resemblance to her deceased fiancé, was exactly the sort of man she wished to wed. It would be beyond everything wonderful to marry a man who had so much faith in her talents and so much concern for her happiness that he would make such an outlandish request. Of course such a paragon did not exist, and awareness of that disappointing truth choked her throat and brought unexpected tears to her eyes.

Blasted, she thought.

Seeing her distress, Huntly was instantly contrite. "I'm a beast for forcing such an upsetting topic on you. As you have reminded me, you are only three days out of black gloves, and the wound must be quite fresh indeed. Please know that I would not intentionally hurt you for the world."

All Vinnie could manage was a nod as she struggled to swallow back tears. She knew she was being completely absurd—only a ninnyhammer cried for something that could never be—but that knowledge merely made it worse.

"As unpleasant as the subject is," Huntly continued, determined, it seemed, to plow through it all at once, "I am honor-bound to devise a scheme to save your reputation, since it is I who put it at risk. Therefore, we shall proceed with my plan. I will put it about that Sir Windbourne's last request was that I propose your candidacy. The timing is not ideal, as you are only just out of deep mourning, but nobody save a complete stickler could quibble about my motives. I'm sure we will quickly win over the more sentimental ladies of our acquaintance and the rest will obligingly follow."

While he spoke, Vinnie marveled at the marquess's ability to always say the right thing—as in the conservatory when he stood there soaking wet, water dripping into his eyes, and assured her it was his fault for coming upon her unannounced. In this way, he was the perfect gentleman, calling forth the proper words for every occasion, even the most unlikely one. But, she realized now, that didn't mean his behavior was equally circumspect, for how else to account for the two egregious disservices he had done her in rapid succession: putting her name up for membership and dragging her onto the dance floor. These injuries, she decided, were greater than her own, which happened in the privacy of the duke's town house and not in the middle of a lavish event for anyone with eyes to gawk over. At this thought, she felt her mortification, which only a few minutes before she'd resigned herself to carrying to the grave, leave her.

Taking her silence as assent, Huntly said, "Once the story is widely accepted, you will inform your intimates that although you are flattered by the invitation, you can't possibly accept."

He spoke with such authoritarian confidence that Vinnie felt possessed of the same mischievous fiend as when she was at Hatchard's, and rather than accept what she, too, knew to be the truth, she decided to compel him to provide a list of excuses. She expected it to be a long catalog as he enumerated reason after reason why a female was unsuitable for membership, and she prepared to memorize it so she could mock each one with Emma later. "Why, my lord?"

"Well, I don't think it would be quite the thing for you to broach the subject with Lady Jersey," he explained reasonably, "though we could all agree that would be the most efficient way to broadcast the information. It's much more appropriate if you share your decision with your sister and sister-in-law and let them spread the word."

Vinnie, who noted again how flawlessly he knew the proper customs of society and how poorly he himself followed them, shook her head. "No, I meant why can't I possibly accept the invitation?"

He looked down at her with surprise. "I should think it's obvious."

She blinked back, all innocence and ignorance. "Not to me."

"Well, we can't have a woman in the British Horticultural Society. It's simply not done," he said.

Vinnie waited for him to elaborate—to mention, for example, how a woman's presence would mar the congenial nature of the gatherings or how a woman's interest in gardening was not as serious as a man's—but he said nothing more. As far as the marquess was concerned, his brief answer was sufficient. The fact that she wasn't worth the effort of summoning a tedious list of excuses made Vinnie annoyed all over again, and she felt herself seized by a contrarian devil. "Perhaps the only reason it's not done is because it hasn't been done," she suggested.

"I beg your pardon?" he asked, his brow furrowed as if she had spoken in a foreign language or, at the very least, too quickly for coherence.

"I apologize for speaking obliquely, my lord. Let me be more clear," Vinnie said with a wide grin. She could only imagine what the gawkers would make of that unrepentant expression. "I'm flattered by the invitation and delighted to accept."

Huntly's shock was almost visible. His gait remained smooth, but Vinnie thought for sure he'd almost stumbled. "You can't mean it," he said, his tone vaguely horrified.

"I can't?" she asked with an eyebrow raised tauntingly.

The truth was, no, she didn't mean it. Or, rather, she had not. But now that the words were out of her mouth, she realized she meant it with everything that she was. Six months of fake mourning, seven days of mortification, two hours of targeted gossip and one humiliating waltz stiffened her spine in a way she could not have imagined. As always, she had followed the rules. The practical Miss Lavinia Harlow, having had the misfortune to shoot her despised fiancé, had submitted to her fate without a single complaint. She had done everything society and the Countess de Boufflers prescribed to avoid even a hint of impropriety in Sir Windbourne's death. And where had it gotten her? The subject of gossip and idle speculation. She knew everyone in the ballroom was talking about her. They'd been talking about her from the moment she had arrived, and as far as she was concerned, they could continue, for they would with or without her permission. If she was to be the topic of the day, she might as well get some enjoyment out of it.

That she would enjoy being a member of the British Horticultural Society wasn't in doubt. She could think of few things more satisfying than being a part of a congenial group of similarly disposed individuals discussing a shared passion.

After several moments of startled silence, the marquess said, "You must see it's impossible."

"The way I see it," she said calmly, "is either the invitation is legitimate, in which case the society, as an ethical institution, owes me the courtesy of allowing me to accept or decline, or the invitation is false, in which case I've been shockingly abused by an institution that's as heartless as it is immoral. Which is it, my lord?"

"The invitation is genuine," he said stiffly, seemingly offended by the implication that the society might not have been square in all of its dealings. "It was delivered this morning, which is how word of it got out. The courier who was given the invitation thought it was highly amusing that it was going to a lady and mentioned it to several of his associates, one of whom is employed by the Society for the Advancement of Horticultural Knowledge."

"In that case, I think I have no choice but to accept," she said, her smile revealing deep dimples in both her cheeks. Her heart felt lighter than it had it months, which, she thought, proved just what a perverse creature she was. And for all these years, they'd assumed Emma was the only Harlow girl who didn't know how to behave. "As it was my beloved's last wish for me, how could I deny it? I owe it to him and his memory to try to fulfill his ambitions for me. To do anything less would be disrespectful."

"Miss Harlow," he said firmly, "I fear you don't—"

"You must not worry," she said, rudely interrupting

him but doing so in a soothing tone, as if genuinely trying to relieve his concerns. "I will not make any public statements to that effect. I have a strong sense of propriety and will speak of it only to intimates. But I will be sure to repeat it several times to ensure that my sister and sister-in-law know exactly what to tell Lady Jersey."

Huntly shook his head and took a deep breath, as if gathering his thoughts for another attack. Vinnie, who had found the lively discussion invigorating, hoped he would put genuine effort into making his case, for, she realized as she waited, all she really wanted was to be considered a worthy opponent. She did not want to be dismissed or overlooked or ignored as she had been that first day in Emma's study.

Before the marquess could open his mouth, the music stopped and the waltz, which had seemed like it would go on forever or at least until they concluded their business, suddenly ended. Neither Huntly nor Vinnie appeared to entirely grasp that fact, for they stood silently in the middle of the dance floor while other couples cleared the way for the next set.

How long they would have remained there unmoving was impossible to say, for not one moment after the orchestra's last note faded away, the dowager was at Vinnie's side with a quelling look at Huntly. He promptly bowed—appropriate as always!—thanked Miss Harlow for the dance and promised to continue their discussion at a later date.

Not nearly as bold despite indications to the contrary, Vinnie immediately tilted her head down upon spying the intimidating dowager and examined her gloves with undue fascination. She knew she was owed a stern talking-to, if not a severe lecture, from both Trent's mother and Sarah, and the evening, which had already felt interminably long, just got a little longer. Yet, as the dowager led her through the crowd to the abandoned chair that would be her home for the rest of the ball, she couldn't resist looking back, catching Huntly's eyes and mouthing the words *thank you*.

Whether it was for the dance, the argument or the invitation, she couldn't quite say.

CHAPTER SEVEN

When Fleming announced the Duke of Trent at ten-thirty the next morning, the only thing that surprised Huntly was that his friend had managed to rouse himself so early from his slumber. The ball, despite a few hiccups, including but not limited to the scandalous behavior of Miss Lavinia Harlow, had been a resounding success. More than a few guests lingered when the marquess finally said his good-byes a little after three, and he imagined that Trent had scarcely taken to his bed before leaving it again to make this call.

That the call would be made at some point during the day had been an inevitability established even before Huntly had dragged the duke's poor, grieving sister-in-law onto the dance floor, a gaffe so egregious he still couldn't say what had come over him. Yes, he had been away from polite society for nearly two years, but he had been instructed in the rules of civility from the cradle and the proper way to treat a lady was simply not something one forgot after a few months at sea. Even if basic courtesy had not been in-grained in him by thoughtful nannies and tutors, he was still the Marquess of Huntly, a gentleman known for his urbane address. He was not a famous flirt in the style of, for example,

Lord Deverill or even the duke himself, but he certainly knew how to endear himself to a lady.

Lord Huntly could think of no reasonable explanation for his behavior other than an undue anxiety to confess his sin. As a well-regarded gentleman—by the *ton* as well as himself—he rarely made a misstep, and, upon finding himself on the rare occasion of being in the wrong, he had felt an urgent need to set it right. His impatience stemmed not just from knowing he had made a gross miscalculation but from realizing that only a bufflehead run-a-muck would *not* have comprehended immediately exactly how gross the miscalculation was. As the injured party herself had pointed out, the rivalry between the two organizations was famous, and none but the greenest greenhorn would have failed to foresee the outcome. Of course Lord Hastings had laid a wager upon discovering the identity of the British Horticultural Society's newest recruit. Even if Huntly himself would not have done the same thing—because, ironical as it may seem, he'd never bandy about a lady's name—he knew the vast majority of his associates would not hesitate. Even the dignified Mr. Berry would have gleefully used the information to taunt his counterpart at the competing institution.

The marquess, who was not accustomed to feeling like a naïve addle-wit, found the sensation unpleasant, and that discomfort only added to his impatience to straighten out the matter with Miss Harlow. He didn't want merely to demonstrate that he could resolve the difficult situation but that he could do so easily and with a modicum of fuss. His solution, which seemed to him both elegant and effective, accomplished all that he required, but it failed to account for the emotional sensibility of a young woman in mourning. Sir Windbourne had been only a name to him, a thing that he could wave in the air like a magic wand to make the problem disappear. He did not consider that the name was attached to a real, live human being—well, a former real, live human being—and that the mere mention of it might bring pain to the woman who had loved him.

That misstep bothered him more than any of his other recent blunders, for he hated the thought of inflicting pain on any creature, let alone a gentlewoman whose heart was so obviously broken. He could read it plainly in the stricken look on her face and the way she had stumbled in his arms.

Given her fragile emotional state, Huntly was little surprised that she insisted on accepting the society's invitation to membership. Grief often made women irrational, and no doubt in Miss Harlow's anguished mind, the phony behest had created a link with her departed beloved that she was now reluctant to let go.

The explanation made perfect sense to Huntly.

Yet there was that delighted smile she'd flashed at him as the dowager was leading her away—how did one account for that? And the words she had mouthed: *thank you.* At that moment, her cheeks had dimpled and her eyes sparkled and her whole face seemed lit with satisfaction, if not outright happiness.

Huntly had no idea what to make of it, except to wonder if she was laughing at him again. It did not seem possible, considering how she had cried only a few minutes earlier, but then, the marquess admitted, Miss Harlow was by far the most unusual female he had ever met. Green misses and Cyprians alike had always been easy for him to decipher, for their wants and needs were written plainly on their faces. Whenever he was in Miss Harlow's presence, however, he genuinely had no idea where he—or she—stood.

While he tried to make sense of the bewildering Miss Lavinia Harlow, he retreated to his study to review the papers left by his secretary and to wait for the duke's call. He assumed he was settling in for a long, tedious morning of estate business, but no sooner had he reviewed the list of improvements for the tenants' cottages at Langston (all of which seemed reasonable) than Fleming made his announcement.

Rising to greet his guest, Huntly asked Fleming to bring a fresh pot of tea. "May I get you something to eat?" he asked. "Considering the hour, I can't imagine you had time for anything but a roll on your way out the door. Perhaps some eggs?"

The duke smiled and assured Fleming that tea would be sufficient. As soon as the butler closed the study door, he turned to his friend and said, "How much?"

Huntly, who had planned to defer the inevitable reprimand with polite conversation until after the tea arrived, stopped short at this question. "Excuse me?"

"How much to get you to leave town on another expedition?" Trent asked, striding over to his friend. "The cost of a ship, of course, and a crew, plus wood, livestock and various sundry supplies. Provide me with a figure—a rough estimate is sufficient—and I will have my secretary give you a check by the end of the day."

The marquess grinned at his old friend. "Things a bit uncomfortable at home, are they?"

Trent smiled back and sat down in the large leather armchair next to the fireplace, as his host did the same. "You could not have created more pandemonium if you'd hired a circus troupe to set up its tent in the drawing room. Vinnie, who is determined to go through with her application, is working on her presentation to the society, while my mother alternatively tries to cajole and dishearten her into changing her mind by insisting at once that she's much too good for the organization and not good enough. Emma is delighted by her sister's trailblazing spirit and is resolved to assist her in the most helpful way possible, which she has identified, rightly so, if I may say it, as altering my mother's opinion about the situation, and, failing that, halting her ceaseless chatter on the topic. When I left, Sarah had just arrived to offer her support, which, oddly, has nothing to do with the membership and everything to do with the thoroughly inappropriate waltz you imposed on poor Vinnie. Sarah seems to think there might be some mental distress involved. So I ask you again, my friend, how much?"

Although it was impossible not to smile at the absurd picture Trent painted—pandemonium indeed!—he smothered a grin and tried to look contrite. "Leaving town won't undo the damage. The die, as they say, is cast."

"No, but it would save me from the obligation of calling you out," Trent explained amiably. "Good god, Felix, what were you thinking?"

Just then, Fleming entered with the tray and placed it on the low table in front of the fireplace. Huntly graciously accepted the cup of tea, but as soon as the butler left, he put it down and walked over to the side cabinet. "I think I need something a little stronger," he said, picking up a bottle of port and pouring two glasses. He handed one to Trent and sat down with a sigh. "May we put it down to brain fog that comes from too much travel or a tropical ailment from the bite of a pernicious bug?"

The duke took a deep sip of the port and waited.

"To be honest, Alex, I have truly no idea what I was thinking," he confessed. "An inexplicable fugue state makes as much sense as any other. I took leave of my senses and embroiled your family in a fresh scandal without ever intending to. I'm deeply sorry for it. I am particularly sorry for the pain I've caused Miss Harlow. Although I knew she was in mourning, it did not occur to me that it might be not only inappropriate for her to dance but painful as well. Your sister-in-law makes me…. I find that she is—" He broke off as he considered his words. He wanted to make a clean breast of it to his friend, but he couldn't figure out how to tell some of the tale without telling all of it, and telling all of it would make him look like a petty fool. He didn't mind the first and would easily admit to having unintentionally caused the pandemonious ordeal in a fit of pique. But the fool part gave him pause. He didn't understand why Miss Harlow had driven him to unprecedented heights of pettiness, and until he could explain it to himself, he didn't want to explain it to anyone else. So instead he said, "I hope you won't be offended when I say your wife's sister is a very difficult person."

The duke's expression did not alter, but he leaned forward in his chair, resting his elbows on his knees as he looked at the marquess. "You think Vinnie is difficult?" he asked mildly.

Huntly nodded, relieved to see only interest in his friend's face. "Yes, I find she's one of the most difficult women I've ever met. She's capricious and unpredictable. You think she's joking but maybe she's sincere, and then you think she's sincere but perhaps she's joking. It's thoroughly unsettling never to know where precisely you stand with a person. But I don't have to tell you. You know what she's like. Lucky for you, you married the sensible sister."

Trent's lips twitched, and he sought to hide his amusement in the wineglass. He did not succeed, and Huntly, seeing his enjoyment, said, "I'm sure you find my predicament vastly amusing, but I assure you, it's devilishly uncomfortable, and I will gladly accept your offer of funding if it means I will be spared another run-in with Miss Lavinia Harlow. I do believe you said I would have the check by nightfall. If you'll just wait while I run through a series of quick calculations, we can have the matter settled before nuncheon."

"The offer is off the table," the duke announced.

Huntly looked at him balefully over the rim of his glass. "You dirty-dealing thatch-gallows. A man's promise is as good as his vowels."

Unmoved, Trent said, "Nevertheless, it is rescinded."

"It's because I called your sister-in-law difficult and capricious, isn't it?"

"Yes," Trent agreed at once, "but not for the reason you think."

As Huntly never had any intention of leaving town—just as the duke never had any intention of providing the conveyance—he did not try to make sense of his friend's ambiguous remark. Instead, he refilled his glass, drank deeply and said, "She's working on her presentation?"

"Drainage systems, of course," said Vinnie's brother-in-law. He paused until the marquess's eyes met his and then asked in all seriousness, "What do you plan to do?"

Huntly smiled wryly. "I have no idea. What do you plan to do?"

"Offer my support," he said simply, "to both of you."

"So she has your vote?" Huntly asked.

"She is a skilled horticulturalist who would, I believe, add as much to the organization as she would take from it," he explained. "But even if she were merely an enthusiastic hobbyist, I would support her application because she is a very dear friend and I want her to be happy."

The marquess should not have been surprised to hear Trent speak so ardently in support of a friend, for he himself had been the grateful beneficiary of his assistance far too many times to count, but the fact that a woman had earned his loyalty astonished him. The duke had always been a plain dealer in his transactions with all females, respectable or otherwise, but—and perhaps this was because they were indeed transactions—he treated even the best of them with a cynical detachment. Now he had not only given his allegiance to a wife but to her sister as well.

It was one more thing about Miss Harlow for him to puzzle over.

"Your mother can be very persuasive," Huntly observed hopefully.

"She can indeed," Trent agreed with a grin. "I'm not sure she's equal to the task this time, but she's certainly persistent. Why else do you think I'm here at ten-thirty in the morning?"

"Ah, so the indomitable Duke of Trent is hiding in my study," he said, smirking with satisfaction. "Alert the dailies!"

"Not hiding," Trent corrected as he poured himself another glass of port, "lingering."

Although the distinction was too slight to exist, Huntly didn't raise an objection and instead pointed to a black crate that rested against the wall to the left of the sideboard. "If you care to linger for the rest of the morning, you can make yourself useful and help me unpack that trunk. It contains samples from my trip, many of which I'm sure you'll find, if not fascinating, then highly interesting. I have another dozen crates in the cellars waiting to be sifted through as well. With one thing or another, I haven't had a chance to hire an assistant," he explained, "so if you know of anyone suitable, please don't hesitate to send them to my secretary."

The duke looked at the trunk with a predatory gleam in his eye. "You know perfectly well that I've been itching to get my hands on your New Hebrides orchid for months now, as I mentioned it in several letters, and do not require the pretext of pandemonium in my home to offer my help. In fact, if you hadn't asked me within the week, you would have come down one morning and found me elbow-deep in your trunk."

Huntly laughed, for despite the duke's considerable consequence, he could easily imagine him being caught in such an undignified pose. "Then I suppose it's a good thing I've brought your sister-in-law to the brink of ruin. Come, let's get started. I shall take notes and let you do the honor of unpacking the flora. I believe the *Dactylorhiza fuchsii* and *Bulbophyllum auratum* are near the bottom on the left. First, however, let me ring for Fleming and arrange a light collation. Shall we say twelve-thirty?"

With an absent nod, Trent strode over to the trunk, unlatched the clasp and lifted the lid to reveal several layers of carefully preserved specimens. Indifferent to his valet's thoughtful administrations, he knelt down on the floor to examine the contents and waved off Huntly's offer to move the crate to a table. "Entirely unnecessary," he said.

After ringing the bell, Huntly gathered supplies from his desk—pen, ink, leather-bound book—and joined his friend on the floor. When Fleming entered the room a few minutes later, he found both lords on their knees digging through the trunk with rapt expressions, like two children in the garden searching for worms.

When the duke arrived home in the late afternoon, he found Emma locked in her study, which wasn't in itself peculiar, for she often secured the door against intrusions from his mother and sister. What was unusual, however, was the fact that the knob turned but the door did not open. It seemed to be in some way jammed shut.

"Emma," he said, knocking on the door. "Are you in there?"

"Who is it?" she asked cautiously.

"You know who it is."

Although she did indeed know, she asked him to prove it.

He blinked at the absurd request. "What?"

"Prove you are Trent."

"Emma," he said with a hint of impatience.

As she was very familiar with that warning tone, she agreed to open the door, and he heard a strange scuffing sound before one beautiful cornflower blue eye peeked out of the crack to make sure he was alone. Once she was satisfied, she opened the door wider, gestured for him to enter quickly and immediately shut the door behind him. Then she slid the white chair from the side table under the doorknob.

He watched her ministrations with mild curiosity. "What are you doing?"

"Fortifying the citadel," she explained. Then she held out a tray, "Scone?"

He declined the pastry and examined his wife, who was still in her morning gown despite the lateness of the hour. That she was engaged in some great enterprise was clear from the dozens of folders on her desk and the several stacks of carefully organized papers.

"My mother?" he asked, unable to imagine anyone else against whom his bride would have to fortify herself.

"She has switched tactics," Emma explained, sitting down on the settee to eat the scone herself. It was the last one she had, and she offered it to her husband only out of a sense of obligation. "Having made no headway in her attempts to sway Vinnie, she has decided I am the more tractable twin and is now devoting all her argumentative powers to convincing me to convince Vinnie not to apply for membership.

Honestly, if I weren't so exhausted from fending off her attacks, I'd be offended at being thought of as tractable."

Trent nodded at this seemingly reasonable explanation but looked again at the chair. "But why—"

"Shhh," she ordered, raising her finger to her lips and vigorously shaking her head. Just in case the duke was disinclined to follow instructions, she stuffed the remaining scone into his mouth.

A moment later, there was a knock on the door and Tupper inquired after her health.

"I'm fine," she said, her shoulder pressed against the door.

"I have Dobbins with me, your grace, from the stables," the footman announced. "He has a metal bar and is going to try to pry open the door.

"Hello, Dobbins," she said. "Thank you for trying to get me out. I don't know why the door is stuck, but nothing seems to budge it."

"Me pleasure, yer grace," Dobbins said. "Now move yerself several steps and let me know when ye are a safe distance."

Emma sat down in the chair, then counted to three before calling out that it was all right to proceed. With an enthusiasm he usually reserved for the horses he trained, the groom slid the metal bar into the crack between the door and the frame and applied all his strength to levering the door open. He made several attempts, though none that could dislodge Emma and the chair, and succeeded in only scratching the frame and the door further, for which he was very apologetic.

Assuring him that the damage was entirely her fault— "for being such a pea goose as to get trapped in my study"—Emma thanked him for his efforts and sent him to the kitchen to get some of Mrs. Chater's walnut scones, which were most likely still warm from the oven.

"Never fear, your grace, we'll get that door open by hook or by crook," Tupper said, afraid that the duchess must be on the edge of despair, for it had been several hours now.

"Don't worry about me, Tupper," Emma said. "At the risk of sounding overly cheerful, I'm quite comfortable, I've got plenty to occupy my time, and I won't be hungry for a few hours yet."

"If I may say so, your grace, your bravery is an inspiration," the footman confessed before leaving to explore the next solution.

As soon as the servant's footsteps had died away, the duke said, "A few hours yet? How long do you intend for this siege to last?"

Emma confirmed that the chair was firmly lodged under the doorknob and then leaned against her desk, wishing she hadn't used her last scone as a muzzle. Despite her bold claim, she was actually a little peckish. "I think we are in the final stages. Within ninety minutes, Tupper will have the door off its hinges."

Although the duke couldn't contemplate the total destruction of one of his doors without at least a little bit of concern, he instead concentrated on the neatly stacked piles on her desk. Curious, he picked up one of the folders. "Dare I ask what has driven you to such extreme measures? The lock wasn't sufficient?"

Laughing with delight, she leaned over and gave him a kiss on his cheek. "Oh, you delightful, naïve man. You are adorable," she said, shaking her head in wonder. "Mrs. Crenshaw has the keys, and your mother did not hesitate to apply for her assistance in gaining entry. It required some quick thinking on my part to keep her out, if I do say so myself. Your mother suspects something havey-cavey but can't prove it and has had poor Tupper try everything short of a battering ram."

Trent, who knew himself to be the far more sophisticated partner in their relationship, marveled at the extremes to which she would go to avoid a conversation with his mother. "So much for the fearless Miss Harlow," he said wryly.

Emma refused to rise to the bait. "We both know I can hold my own against your mother. But I had more important things to do than to spend the day quarreling with the dowager, and you know as well as I do that she could go on for hours. She is, as the saying goes, like a dog with a bone when she gets something between her teeth, though, don't misunderstand me, a dog who throws a wonderful party."

Rather than enter into a debate about his mother's debating skills, which were, he allowed, inexhaustible, he looked at the file in his hand. Written on the label was the name Stanley Chetwynd, Seventh Earl of Talbot. He opened the folder and read the top page, which listed the basic facts of the man's life: birth, schooling, property, family tree.

Startled, the duke looked at his wife. "What is this?"

"My dossier on"—she leaned over to read the label—"Talbot. Do be careful. I have them all arranged in alphabetical order by family name."

Trent stepped back and looked more closely at the files piled neatly on his wife's desk. With a growing suspicion, he scanned the labels quickly, noting the familiar names: Abingdon, Capell, Irby, Morton, Rothes. Yes, he confirmed, all twenty-six members of the British Horticultural Society were present and accounted for, including himself.

"You have a file on me?" he asked, not sure if he was amused or aghast at his wife's thoroughness. Then he flipped through the folder, found a page detailing the names and dates of several of his former mistresses and decided he was aghast.

"I did not commission that one," Emma rushed to assure him. "As you can imagine, my ability to communicate has been somewhat hampered by the siege and I didn't have a chance to clarify that a dossier on my husband was unnecessary. I can gather information on you quite well on my own. And you needn't worry," she said with a grin, dimples showing as she correctly read his expression, "there's nothing in that file that I didn't already know."

The duke wasn't convinced that was true but knew better than to enter into an argument for which winning would have no benefit. "I cannot conceive of a reason why you would compile dossiers on any of the members of the British Horticultural Society, let alone the entire organization."

"Votes," she explained simply. "In order to determine how to best procure the votes of your fellow society members—cajole, blackmail, bribe, reason, et cetera—I need information. I can't do that without a thorough investigation into their backgrounds and current situations."

Trent, who had thought his unlikely courtship of Emma had revealed all the little Machiavellian corners of her mind, stared at her in astonishment. He had known his wife was an inveterate schemer, a dyed-in-the-wool plotter who could not leave a situation alone until it complied utterly with all her demands, but until that moment, he had not fully comprehended the depths of her depravity. To even contemplate blackmailing or bribing the honorable members of the horticultural society was beyond the bounds of anything good or decent. It spoke of a truly corrupt mind.

Yet as appalled as the duke was at her capacity to conspire, he couldn't help but admire not only the way she set goals but also the skill with which she achieved them. Even barricaded in what used to be the front parlor, with his mother demanding her attention and Tupper intermittently pounding at the door, she had gathered intelligence information on her quarry with the efficiency of the commander-in-chief of the British Army. Wellington himself could not have done a better job.

To his horror, he found he respected the pragmatism of her approach even more—it was coldhearted, yes, but practical.

Despite these revelations, what stunned him the most and had him staring silently at his wife for more than a minute, was the fact that he had failed to anticipate her response. When he had left this house this morning, he had truly believed she would devote herself entirely to changing the dowager's mind, as if his mother's opinion had any bearing on the outcome at all. It didn't, of course, and Emma would never waste a moment on something that had no bearing, or only a very little, on a devoutly wished-for outcome. Like all efficient commanders, she cut straight to the heart of a matter, for there was no time for trivialities on the battlefield.

"I didn't say seduce," Emma announced.

Dumbfounded, Trent stared at her. "Excuse me?"

"In the list of tactics I plan to employ to get Vinnie the votes she needs for membership, I did not say seduce," she explained. "I recall from our recent conversation on how to bring off a match between Vinnie and Huntly, you had specifically requested that I not ask anyone to seduce anyone else. I mentioned this as a way of proving that I do listen to you, despite your frequent assertions to the contrary. You are my most trusted ally, and as such your input is invaluable to me."

Although he had been called her "most trusted ally" enough to realize it was merely an honorary title, the duke was touched that she included him in her scheming at all. He knew that she thought she could pull off even the most outlandish scheme entirely on her own.

He also knew her well enough to recognize when she was being deliberately provocative and chose not to be sidetracked by a distraction. "If I had realized bribery and blackmail came as easily to you, I would have included them in the injunction."

Emma, who had been genuinely pleased by the opportunity to demonstrate how reasonable she could be, found these additional constraints vexing. If Trent had his way, all she would be able to do was beg for votes, which would be humiliating—for Vinnie, of course, not for her. She herself was immune to embarrassment of any kind. But if Vinnie was going to be a full and equal member of the British Horticultural Society (and to be completely honest, Emma had been surprised to discover that she wasn't already), then she needed to begin her tenure from a position of strength. Blackmail and bribery demonstrated strength; begging demonstrated its opposite.

Before Emma could explain this to her husband, whose

sense of honor somehow excluded ill treating other gentle-men but included barring half the human race from public life, she heard a gentle rapping sound on one of the windows.

"If you'll excuse me," she said, "I have a meeting with one of my associates."

"*One* of your associates?" Trent asked, following her to the window along the east wall. Unlike the bow window, which overlooked the square, it faced a battery of trees and a less-frequented side street. The shrubbery offered some protection from prying eyes, but the window was hardly a private conference chamber. "How many do you have?"

"Six or seven, depending on whether you consider Mr. Adams an associate or an apprentice," she explained, as she opened the sash and leaned over the pane to address her visitor.

Looking over her shoulder, Trent was unsurprised to see a petite figure in a well-worn brown topcoat and a green beaver. "Good afternoon, Mr. Squibbs," he said, greeting the best lockpick in all of London.

The little man doffed his hat in return. "The duchess isn't at the docks, your grace," he said cheerfully and with a fair amount of satisfaction, as if that happy circumstance was of his contrivance. The duke did not doubt that it was. "When I arrived this morning for our first meeting, she was in the process of climbing out the window, but I suggested that she would be more useful staying here and setting up a central command post."

Trent flinched at the image of Emma hanging out of the window in her morning dress. "I am in your debt yet again," he said sincerely, for he owed the lockpick several times over for helping Emma—once when she was accost-ed on a solo visit to the docks and again when she had pur-sued her traitorous future brother-in-law to Dover without telling a soul. Mr. Squibbs had defended her against drunken ruffians in the former and provided the duke with valuable information in the latter.

"Nothing to it, your grace," he said. "I'm happy to help."

101

Emma sighed loudly and looked first at her husband, then at her associate. "If you gentlemen are done with your chitchat, I would like to get down to business," she said impatiently.

Mr. Squibbs laughed. "Yes, your grace."

The duke looked on as Emma conducted her meeting through the open window, reviewing documents, asking questions and providing avenues to be explored next. She was not only satisfied with the information her network of spies had gathered but much impressed with their speed and cunning. Mr. Adams, in particular, had uncovered a fact concerning Lord Bilberry so salient as to firmly establish the young apprentice among the ranks of associates.

"Excellent work, Mr. Squibbs," Emma said approvingly. "Truly excellent work. We will take up the matter of compensation for you and your associates tomorrow, when I will be more free to move about. In the meantime, I trust you will have no difficulty tracking down those final few details."

"None at all, your grace," the lockpick said confidently. "By the time we're done, we'll have enough dirt to ensure your sister is president of the society. It's only what she deserves."

Emma smiled with pleasure. "Thank you. I will tell Vinnie you said that. She will be delighted."

"I'll be off, then," Mr. Squibbs said, doffing his green beaver again.

"Until tomorrow," Emma said, with an informal wave that would have appalled the dowager if an entire conversation held through the opening of a window had not already done so. Then she took her stack of new papers and brought them to the desk for proper perusal and filing.

Trent leaned against the window and caught the eye of the little man before he turned to leave. "Thank you," he said simply.

"My pleasure," he said, understanding the depth of the duke's gratitude. "May I offer congratulations on your wedding, your grace? I was pleased to hear it, as you and she are well matched."

Knowing in what high esteem the lockpick held his wife, Trent recognized it for the lavish praise it was. "You may indeed, and I very much appreciate it. Good day, Mr. Squibbs," he said and slid the window closed. Then he turned to his wife. "Have you been holding meetings at the window all day for anyone on the street to witness?"

Emma, who was filing the new information about Lord Bilberry in the proper folder, did not look up as she said, "I believe the foliage provides sufficient coverage, but if it does not, you have only yourself to blame. Do recall that I specifically requested a room downstairs and in the back of the house for my study."

She kept her head studiously tilted down, but Trent could see the smug little smile tugging on her lips and it was all he could do not to seduce her right there and then. The only thing that stopped him was the thought of Tupper charging into the room with a battering ram.

Instead he said, "Although you have failed to ask after my day—married six months and already you've lost interest—I do have a tidbit that you will find fascinating."

Emma was skeptical that her interest would rise to the level of fascination but decided to give him the benefit of the doubt. He was her husband, after all. "I'm sorry, your grace. How was your day?" she asked with a brash grin.

The impertinent look was more than he could withstand and before she could grumble about keeping her well-arranged papers in order, he lifted her onto the desk and captured her lips with his own. He intended it to be a brief kiss, as a way of saying hello at the end of an unusually busy day, but once his lips touched hers, once he felt her enthusiastic response and the ever-familiar tug of desire, it turned into something far more. He pulled away a few minutes later, despite her groan of protest, and rested his forehead against hers.

"My day was good," he said softly, "and getting better."

"Mine, too," she said, wrapping her legs around his waist and shimmying closer. "Given that the average interval between offensives has been seventy-three minutes and that Tupper had to send Logan to fetch a screwdriver from the blacksmith, I would say we have twenty-one minutes before anyone disturbs us. Shall we get on with it, Alex?"

Trent did not doubt the accuracy of her calculations, and as he looked down at her, the picture of innocence in her white lawn morning dress, her face naturally flushed, her eyes gleaming with desire, he was tempted, so very, very tempted, to get on with it. And it was not the threat of Tupper and his battering ram or even Logan and his screwdriver that had him taking two cautious steps back. Rather, it was the memory of the last time she had him in a similar situation—in a locked room, on the verge of impropriety. On that occasion, it had been her brother's drawing room, where they, as an engaged couple, had been allowed to say good night privately following one final harrowing episode with Sir Windbourne. Her brother, Roger, had knocked on the door at a particularly inconvenient moment, which Emma had found remarkably funny, and the duke was forced to put a nightgown back on his giggling beloved while her protective brother called out questions from the other side of the door.

No, he was not going through that again.

Emma looked at him through her lashes and called him poor-spirited. "I thought you had more gumption, your grace."

Familiar with his wife's tactics, Trent knew what she was trying to do and he refused to be provoked into another compromising position. Instead, he said, "You will stop pouting when I tell you Felix called Vinnie capricious."

As predicted, Emma bolted upright and stared in wonder. "Our Vinnie?"

"Felix said she was the most difficult woman he has ever met. He said it is impossible to figure out where one stands with her. He said that *I*"— here Trent's voice took on a tone remarkably akin to glee—"had married the sensible sister."

"The Vinnie who has been around my whole life?" she asked, trying to make sense of such an inexplicable claim. "The one who is nine minutes older than me? Thinks watching a plant grow is thrilling? *That* Vinnie?"

"Yes, imp, that Vinnie," he said fondly.

Emma jumped off the desk and squealed with delight. "I told you there was something between them," she said, clapping her hands. "I told you. I knew there had to be something, for Vinnie has never reacted so strongly to another human being in her entire life. She's so even-keeled and placid, she likes everyone, even the boorish Lord Windbag before he revealed his murderous nature, but from the very moment she met Huntly, she has found him intolerable. It's above all things wonderful."

Thinking of his sister-in-law, whom he held in the highest esteem, the duke had to concur, and with Vinnie's happiness in mind, he sat down with Emma on the settee to concoct a plan that would bring Huntly and she together. They both agreed the application for membership was a great opportunity to throw the pair together, but Emma thought it was merely a solid foundation upon which to build a more elaborate scheme. With a pensive nod, the duke mentioned that his friend was looking for an assistant to help him catalog specimens from his travels, and Emma, immediately grasping the implication, was so impressed by her husband's devious mind, she felt compelled to kiss him. Trent, whose resistance had been worn down by his earlier refusal, succumbed wholly to his wife's enthusiastic appreciation, and when Tupper succeeded in removing the door from its hinges ten minutes later, his eyes took in the shocking display of the duke passionately embracing his duchess. Appalled, the footman stammered an apology, turned on his heels and fled down the hallway. The Dowager Duchess of Trent, entering the room only a moment later, was equally shocked to see her son in his wife's arms, though not because of the activity in which they had so obviously been engaged—for that was only to be expected of a newly married couple in a locked room—but because Trent, unlike her, had managed to gain entry into the supposedly impenetrable citadel. Next time, she would go through the window, damn her dignity.

CHAPTER EIGHT

Vinnie was in the middle of the fifth draft of her letter to the British Horticultural Society when the dowager duchess burst into the room to insist that she decline the invitation immediately. Although she had been resolute in her intention to apply in her conversation with Huntly the night before, sleep—all two hours of it—had brought counsel, and in the clear light of dawn, she realized she couldn't possibly go through with it. Her sister could do it. Emma would not only *not* flinch at the challenge, she would relish it in all its difficulties. But Miss Lavinia Harlow was not the sort to inflict her presence upon a group of gentlemen who did not want it. Recognizing this, she rose from her bed, ordered a pot of tea and sat down to compose a polite thank-you-but-no-thank-you note.

She had run into trouble almost at once, for she couldn't figure out why she should thank anyone for making her the object of ridicule. She should instead be taking Huntly...Mr. Berry...the whole society...to task for treating her with such cavalier disdain. One did not issue invitations that one did not sincerely mean. That was a basic tenet of etiquette that even the smallest child in the schoolroom knew.

Her first draft was a paradigm of moderation and appreciation, full of praise for the society's good work and respect for its time-honored traditions—which was why she tore it up. She wanted to be moderate and appreciative, yes, but with an undercurrent of immoderation and unappreciation. She wanted her letter to express the correct thoughts and feelings, while at the same time making it clear to its readers that she was expressing the correct thoughts and feelings only out of a sense of social obligation. She begrudged every word, and she wanted them to feel her begrudgement.

It was a difficult tone to achieve, and by the time the dowager entered her bedroom issuing orders—without even knocking—Vinnie's temper was considerably frayed from the effort. The two hours' sleep, squashed between postparty anxiety and predawn worry, did not help the situation.

Intimidated by the duchess's stern demeanor, Vinnie listened quietly as her host enumerated all the reasons why she must not apply for membership, reasons that she herself had arrived at only a few hours before. When the dowager pointed out how uncomfortable it would be for her to attend meetings knowing none of the other members wanted her there, she nodded with vigor and even tried to explain that she agreed wholeheartedly. But her grace, who could brook no interruptions when she was in the middle of a reprimand, silenced her with a hand. Suitably chastened, Vinnie bowed her head and waited for her turn.

And then the duchess made a fatal mistake. While elaborating reason number four—it was not appropriate for a grieving woman to have any interests outside the home—she described the bloom in Vinnie's cheeks as "unbecomingly healthy."

"I would never presume to tell another woman how to mourn the death of a loved one, as such advice is coarse and insensitive, but I must say that for myself and others it's entirely disagreeable and unsettling to observe such a bright look on a widow's face," she explained. "If you won't think of yourself, think of Sir Windbourne. What would he say to see that rosy glow so soon after his death?"

At the mention of Sir Windbourne, Vinnie's entire demeanor underwent a radical transformation. In an instant, her back straightened, her lips tightened, her eyes hardened and her shoulders stiffened. She was heartily sick to death of people using Sir Windbourne's memory to direct her behavior to suit their own ends. Huntly had employed the same tactic last night. If she were genuinely in mourning, she would in all likelihood find these constant reminders of what she had lost excessively painful. Fortunately for her, she was not in mourning, and as such she found them only excessively irritating. Indeed, the duchess's attempt to dissuade her from a course from which she had already been dissuaded reignited Vinnie's contrarian spirit.

But it was not merely a desire to thwart the will of censorious busybodies that had her resolving yet again to follow through with the application. It was also the unexpected thrill she felt upon hearing the words *rosy glow* and *bright look* applied to her, as nobody had ever described her as such. Emma was the unbecomingly healthy twin, her cheeks always abloom, her eyes always aglow, her countenance always a lively mix of excitement and eagerness. Pallid from long hours bent over rootstocks and drain pipes, Vinnie was quite literally a pale imitation. That she compared unfavorably with her twin in respect to appearance did not bother her, for it seemed only fair to her that Emma, who was constantly being taken to task for her ill-bred vivacity, have some advantage. Of the two siblings, Vinnie, with her calm disposition and sensible outlook, was the infinitely preferred one, a fact that had angered her from the moment she'd realized it, for even as a little girl she had loved and admired her sister's daring. Fault her as you would, but Miss Emma Harlow never feared public rebuke or private reproach, and hearing the dowager criticize her own unbecomingly healthy bloom made Vinnie feel as if she didn't either.

Damn the consequences, she thought, the rosy-cheeked, bright-eyed Harlow girls do what they want.

As fearless as she felt, Vinnie was not brave enough to

interrupt the dowager for a second time and let her continue with her enumeration, of which she was now up to reason six (gardening was an inappropriately propagative subject for an unmarried female). While her host rambled, she sipped tea and mentally reviewed the list of requirements for admission: a treatise on the value of a society dedicated to horticultural pursuits, a presentation and an interview. Of the three, she was the least worried about the presentation, for she knew she could speak quite knowledgeably and effectively on the topic of proper drainage. True, she had never spoken on it in a lecture hall in front of two dozen equally knowledgeable men, many of whom would be waiting for her to make a mistake, but she refused to be cowered by the daunting prospect.

Vinnie refreshed her tea and wondered if she should offer the dowager a cup, for the long lecture—fifteen minutes and counting—was surely causing her throat to feel dry. Despite the protracted speech, the duchess showed no signs of flagging and enthusiastically launched into a lecture on the joys of a more suitable hobby, which might have been called How Embroidery Will Save the Empire and Find One a Husband.

Amused, aghast and exhausted, Vinnie sighed, swallowed a yawn and twisted her back in an attempt to stretch her shoulders without appearing to fidget from boredom. As she tilted her head to the side, she caught a glimpse of her sister peeking in the doorway. Although the Harlow Hoyden had a reputation for impetuousness, Vinnie knew she was in fact the opposite: Emma was very good at observing a situation and gathering information before settling on the best course of action. If her thoughtful process had any deficiencies, it was in her understanding of what the word *best* meant.

For now, Emma stood silently on the threshold and watched her sister for an indication of how to proceed. Meeting her curious gaze, Vinnie shrugged her shoulders as if to ask what could one do other than wait for the duchess to finish her diatribe. It was a rhetorical question, of course, but her sister had no patience for situations without clear resolutions and strode into the room to take charge of the matter. The dowager, having established her presence in the bed chamber a full twenty minutes prior to Emma's arrival, considered the matter already in her charge (thank you!) and insisted that her new daughter-in-law, who had behaved very prettily at last night's affair (thank you again!), entrust her to resolve the difficulty in a manner satisfying to all parties involved. Emma immediately countered that as the "difficulty," a designation to which she strenuously objected, involved one party and one party only—that is, Miss Lavinia Harlow—they should entrust *her* to resolve it to *her* satisfaction. Needless to say, this sort of willful self-determination did not sit well with the Dowager Duchess of Trent, and she instantly began to browbeat Vinnie into accepting her wise counsel, though *she* strenuously objected to the designation of her robust encouragement as "browbeat."

At first appalled by the scene unfolding in her bedroom, Vinnie quickly saw the absurdity of it and had to bite back an almost uncontrollable desire to giggle. It was not only the argument itself that was ridiculous but the method with which it was being conducted as well, with tranquil smiles and soothing voices, as if no difference of opinion actually existed between the two women. To her credit, the dowager retained her excellent manners and tried to include Vinnie in the conversation by addressing her comments—sometimes scathing, sometimes complimentary—directly to her, but Emma, an ill-bred hoyden to the last, did not give her sister an opportunity to answer for herself. The discussion was overlong and overheated, with Sarah showing up at some point to offer her sympathy and support, and just when Vinnie worried that her twin might actually be on the verge of screaming in frustration, Emma caught her eye and winked.

Wonderful impertinent girl!

Seeing that her sister had everything well in hand, Vinnie

decided it was safe to sneak out to work on her presentation. Since Sarah was at the duke's town house, she knew her brother's drawing room would be quiet, calm and empty and requested the coach take her there before anyone else realized she was gone. Roger, who had always been a doting if distracted sibling, welcomed her with a delighted smile, urged her to partake of breakfast as there was far too much for him to eat, apologized for his wife's absence and returned to his newspaper.

Vinnie remained in the Mount Street residence for the rest of the day, staying to enjoy an informal meal with her sister-in-law, and when she returned after dinner, she found the house as quiet as a church. Upon inquiring, she discovered that the dowager had decamped to Lady Courtland's for a card party and that Emma and Alex had already turned in for the evening. As relieved as she was exhausted, she retired to her room, changed into her nightclothes and climbed into bed. There, on the nightstand, was a note from Emma. "Don't fret," it said in her sister's florid script. "Solution in the works. Everything well in hand. More to come." Too tired to decipher the ambiguous message, she promptly closed her eyes and fell asleep.

In the morning, she expected another round of vigorous discussion, but when she came down for breakfast, she again found the house quiet. Unwilling to question her good fortune, she helped herself to a generous serving of eggs and plum cake before retreating to the drawing room to tackle the intimidating treatise. She had just finished the first draft when Caruthers announced the Marquess of Huntly to see her.

"Me?" she squeaked.

If Caruthers noticed her inordinately shrill tone, he gave no indication. "Yes, miss. Shall I show him?"

Although her first impulse was to say absolutely not, she repressed it and nodded sedately to the butler. "Yes, thank you. And please ask Mrs. Crenshaw for tea."

Caruthers bowed his head in assent, and as soon as he turned to leave, Vinnie began to fidget with her appearance, straightening her pale-blue walking dress and smoothing her curls. She had no idea how she looked, though the dark circles under her eyes, caused by the ball's late night and yesterday's early morning, were thankfully gone and her hair felt neat and presentable.

She realized it didn't matter—the Marquess of Huntly wasn't there to admire her appearance but to talk her out of her decision—but she couldn't smother the twinge of vanity or the jolt of excitement she felt. Part of her, that contrary part she had only just discovered, had hoped he would call so they could continue their lively discussion of her membership. She knew she had exasperated him with her stubborn refusal to go along with his plan, for she could read it plainly on his face, and something about his response made her feel oddly giddy. As sensible as ever, she tried to consign the emotion to mere novelty, as she had never exasperated anyone before, but she was too smart to fool herself. The truth—the absolutely awful, wretched truth—was that she enjoyed arguing with him and unsettling those unsettling blue-green eyes. She was, she acknowledged now, as perverse a creature as her sister, poking a sleeping tiger for the sheer joy of hearing him roar. Perhaps hoydenism ran in her family like eye color.

When Caruthers admitted Huntly, she stood up, resisting the urge to tidy her curls yet again, and walked around the settee to greet him warmly. "Good morning, my lord," she said with a bright smile. "Your timing is impeccable, for I have just now finished the first draft of my treatise. I hope you will read it and, as a member of the society, advise me on how I may improve it."

Although she meant this to be provoking, Huntly nodded amiably and sidestepped the topic entirely with a compliment on her appearance. "You are looking decidedly well," he observed. "I trust you are completely recovered from the ball. As I had said to the dowager in a note yesterday, the festivities were a rousing success and I believe there will be no more chatter about her son's unconventional choice in a partner."

Polite discourse was the last thing she expect from the

marquess, but she was gracious enough of a hostess to converse congenially in return. "Please sit down. Caruthers is bringing in— And there he is," she said when the butler entered with a tray. He placed it on the gold-inlaid table, inquired if there was anything else and quietly left. Vinnie filled two cups and handed one to Huntly. "I agree the ball was a triumph. Her grace was well satisfied and could speak of nothing else yesterday."

"Really?" Huntly asked softly, a slight curve to his lips. "She could speak of *nothing* else?"

Amusement shown in his strange-colored eyes, not exasperation, and Vinnie discovered that she was the one who was unsettled. She knew how to respond to his anger—it was merely a matter of parry and thrust—but his mild good humor made her self-conscious and awkward, as if she had doused him again with her exploding hose.

"Well, she *might* have devoted one or two words to the society membership on offer," she admitted, hoping to get a rise out of him. "She is not pleased with my decision to accept it."

"I thought the turtle soup was particularly excellent," he said calmly as he raised the cup of tea to his lips. "Her grace's French chef quite outdid himself. I must be sure to congratulate him, for I know how challenging it is to coordinate an elaborate spread such as the one he provided."

Disconcerted by both his refusal to be drawn out and his knowledge of kitchen matters, she said, "Ah, yes, Monsieur Charpentier did a superior job. Everyone was well satisfied. I imagine the society has its own chef who provides meals for the members upon request. Do we ever host banquets?" she asked, confident that the inclusive *we* would elicit a response.

Again, she was to be disappointed.

"The flowers were also stunning," Huntly said. "I'm sure I detected a few of Trent's own specimens in the arrangements. I know he is partial to orchids, but he has done wonders with some of the rose species he has cultivated."

With this statement, which was, to be fair, as accurate as it was benign, Vinnie sighed loudly and put down her teacup with a sharp rattle. She could continue to make leading comments for the rest of the afternoon—it was easy enough to come up with obliquely related topics—but she didn't have the patience. Having anticipated this meeting for two days, she knew exactly what she wanted to say to him. Her arguments were nicely arranged in numerical order, just like the dowager's, and the more he put her off with polite nonsense, the more disordered her thoughts grew.

"I don't understand why you are here if not to try to talk me out of applying for membership," she said forthrightly.

If the marquess was surprised by her frankness, he didn't show it. "To make amends," he said.

Now she was even more confused. "Excuse me?"

"I treated you abominably at the ball, and I'm appalled by my own behavior," he explained, placing his teacup gently on the table. "You are in mourning, a fact of which I'm entirely sensible, and I should have been more considerate of your feelings. I know from personal experience how devastating it is to lose someone you love, for my parents died in a carriage accident when I was eleven years old, and I imagine it's even worse when you lose the person with whom you intend to spend the rest of your life. Opening you up to public ridicule and vulgar gossip when you are also dealing with the devastating loss of your fiancé was inexcusable of me. I cannot undo the damage I have done, but I can attempt to make amends if you would let me."

Vinnie, who had thought she'd experienced every unpleasant sensation to be derived from falsely grieving during the six months she'd pretended to mourn, discovered a whole new level of misery as she listened to him speak. It was one thing for people to pat her on the hand with compassion or to cluck their tongues with pity, for these gestures were obligatory, even compulsory, and she accepted them with the insincerity with which they were offered. But Huntly's speech resonated with earnestness, as if he were

THE OTHER HARLOW GIRL

showing her a secret part of himself, and that honesty, when she had none to give in return, was agonizing. Until this moment, her false grief had felt like a superficial detail, an insignificant fact of who she was that had no bearing on anything, such as, for example, saying one didn't like peas to avoid eating a particularly mushy mound of them at a dinner party. Now she knew it was a fundamental misrepresentation of who she was, and while she kept up the lie, she could never get to know anybody, including Huntly.

For reasons she couldn't begin to articulate, this revelation made her feel like crying. Knowing that would only make it worse, she took several deep breaths and nodded yes. Even without the tears, her mute response coupled with her bowed head had the unfortunate effect of making her false grief seem deeper.

There was nothing to do, she realized, but to embrace the present as it existed. Wishing things were different would not make them so.

With this in mind, she raised her head, looked directly into the Marquess of Huntly's beautiful blue-green eyes and said with admirable calm, "I would like that, my lord. What do you propose?"

His lordship smiled. "I would like to leave it as a surprise. If you will come with me?" he asked. "I assure you, it's not a long drive and it won't occupy your entire day."

Although Vinnie was suspicious of surprises, for usually they meant Emma was trying to hide something, she fell in with this plan and asked Huntly to wait while she fetched her pelisse and her maid. Once in the carriage, she tried to guess where they were going by observing the route, but she quickly found herself in an unfamiliar part of London, for the stately white houses and pretty green squares gave way to large factories. When they stopped in front of a tall gray building with dark windows, she thought for sure they were in the wrong place. What surprise could be waiting for her here? But Huntly smiled at her, his eyes bright with anticipation, and opened the door before his groom even got down from his seat.

"After you, my dear," he said.

Warily, she climbed out of the coach, noting an acrid smell in the air, and looked up at the imposing edifice before her, still not convinced they were in the right place— or, if they were in the right place, not convinced this wasn't another terrible prank on Huntly's part.

Then she read the name on the building and turned to him agog. She opened her mouth to speak, but no words formed. She was, for the first time in her life, simply too surprised to speak, for she was, to her utter amazement, standing in front of the Brill & Company shoe factory. It was here, in this very building, where Samuel Brill invented a method by which cloth could become waterproof, a method she had been trying without success to tailor to improve the elastication of the common watering hose for the garden.

Vinnie's shock at being there was twofold. Obviously, the first cause was the importance of the place itself and the knowledge she could acquire by simply being there. The thought of talking to Mr. Brill himself or consulting one of his assistants literally made her knees weak. Indeed, she had to hold on to the coach handle to retain her balance. But the second reason was equally destabilizing, for it humbled and astonished her that the Marquess of Huntly not only recalled her experiments and the trouble she was having but also thought enough of them to arrange this visit. She would not have believed him—or any man—to be that thoughtful.

"Well?" he asked with an air of amused expectation.

Striving for a little dignity, which of course meant not letting her jaw hang open, she said with a mildness she did not feel, "This is a very nice surprise, my lord, thank you."

Huntly smiled again, clearly gratified by her wide-eyed wonder. "Shall we go in?" he asked, offering his arm. "Mr. Brill is expecting us."

Her heart hitched at this announcement, and she gratefully accepted his escort to the building door, which was answered so promptly by the clerk it was clear the young man had been keeping an eye out for them. Mr. Peale was as excited by the visit as Vinnie, for, as he explained as he led them through the factory floor—past workstations and bolts of fabrics and hydraulic lifts—they had never welcomed a gentlewoman-inventor before. Naturally, Vinnie blushed to hear herself described so, and she rushed to explain that she was merely a horticulturalist who wanted to find a better way to water her plants. Huntly, disagreeing with this assessment, assured Mr. Peale that anyone who makes turpentine solutions was not a mere anything. Rather than demur further, Vinnie meekly accepted the description, and when Mr. Brill, a kindly man with a ferocious mane of white hair, made the same observation as his clerk, she graciously thanked him for sharing his time and expertise.

"My pleasure, my pleasure," Mr. Brill assured her. "Now, I'd arranged for us to have a spot of tea before we got down to the business of chemistry, but I can see from the way you are gazing all around you that that will never do. Let's delay the tea until after we address your issue. You are attempting to use my method to increase the flexibility of the hose."

She nodded briskly. "Yes, sir. Inspired by your innovative use of India-rubber, I've been trying to make the watering hose more elasticated. I've tried several formulations—seven, in fact—and they have all ended in disaster."

"Some being more disastrous than others," the marquess observed with a twitch of his lips, and Vinnie, noting the mild good-natured tone with which he made the observation, was again struck by the kindness of the gesture. He could not wish to be there, at a shoe factory in the middle of Acton Vale discussing turpentine. Surely, he had more important things to do. And yet he seemed almost as delighted as she. It was, she acknowledged, another point in his favor.

"Good, good," Mr. Brill said approvingly. "There is no progress without setbacks. If you had several hours, I could tell you about all my disasters."

Vinnie, of course, was about to assure the kindly gentleman that she did indeed have several hours—and more than that besides—but fortunately she realized that it wasn't just her time being expended but Lord Huntly's as well. He did not deserve to have his generosity repaid with such a cruel turn. No doubt when he envisioned this outing, he assumed it would last an hour or two.

Mindful of this, Vinnie readily agreed when Mr. Brill proposed they visit first the distillation laboratory, a long narrow room with bare walls and windows, and she wasted no time in raising pertinent questions. Although she had never imagined this meeting, she knew exactly what she wanted to ask. Hours devoted to tinkering with his method, making incremental changes to her formulations in hopes of finding the perfect solution, had left her with a concise understanding of what she didn't understand. The information she had obtained about his process, cobbled together from patent forms and a report for investors, was limited, and the ability to get answers directly from the source was thrilling.

Mr. Brill, who was surely as busy as Huntly, with his factory of more than three hundred workers to run, answered her questions in remarkable detail, pausing on more than one occasion to marvel at her astuteness.

In his admiring presence, Vinnie didn't just bloom; she blossomed. Her eyes glittered, her cheeks glowed, and her entire countenance seemed to shine with the bright light of understanding. It was not her own understanding—and this was the important thing to comprehend—but Mr. Brill's, for her joy was the kind that came from being in the company of another human being who was in perfect sympathy with one. She had experienced it before, with Emma, of course, since they were very small children and, more recently, with Trent, who treated her as an equal in every respect, but she had never felt so fully appreciated for her knowledge and so certain of acquiring more.

It was a heady feeling.

While she and Mr. Brill discussed the intricacies of working with India-rubber, a challenging ingredient, to be sure, Huntly stood quietly to the side, determined, it seemed to Vinnie, to remain removed from the discussion, which could hold no interest for him. But out of either consideration for his host or genuine interest in the topic, he sauntered to the table to observe Mr. Brill's calculations. He even asked questions, some of which were quite perceptive for a novice.

By all accounts, the Brill Improved Method for Waterproofing was simple: One merely dissolved India-rubber in spirits of turpentine and then spread the mixture by manner of a brush onto the cloth or other material. Amending the process to increase the elasticity of the product was the complicated part, and Vinnie knew the challenge lay in mastering the details: how much turpentine, how much India-rubber, how long to let the mixture stand, how to identify the ideal texture of the mixture. That Huntly quickly grasped these particulars impressed her immensely. His interest was such that he asked Mr. Brill about the impetus for his invention, which Vinnie, who was consumed by the science, never even wondered about.

All in all, the visit to the distillation lab was a stunning success, and when Mr. Brill suggested they return to his office for tea, Vinnie happily agreed. She did not know if she would be able to attain the dearly wished for results when she got home, but failure would no longer be for want of information.

A lovely sitting area had been arranged in Mr. Brill's office, which was not often the site of such frivolity, and Vinnie gratefully partook of the congenial serving of cheeses and bread, for now that she had sat down, she realized she was quite frightfully hungry.

Although Mr. Brill had intended to enjoy the light repast with them, he was quickly called away to attend to what his clerk described as an unexpected shoemaking incident.

"Oh, dear, oh, dear," he said, setting his teacup down on the table with a clang. "An incident. That's our internal description of a code red, which is very serious indeed. Please excuse me. I shall say my good-byes now, for I don't expect you to linger long. It has been an absolute pleasure, Miss Harlow, and I regret that I have to be the one to end our little meeting of the minds."

Touched again by his kindness, Vinnie thanked him wholeheartedly for opening his factory doors to her and assured him that she quite understood his need to rush off—though, in fact, both *code red* and *unexpected shoemaking incident* escaped her understanding entirely and she itched to discover their true meaning. Huntly was intrigued, too, for as soon as Mr. Brill closed the door behind him, he began to speculate as to what they could indicate.

"I know nothing of the finer points of manufacturing shoes, but given the size and complexity of some of the machines we saw, I can easily imagine an operator losing an arm or a leg," he observed mildly. "In which case, blood could be the red in *code red*. Or maybe the event is considerably less intricate and decidedly more common, for example, two laborers coming to fisticuffs. That begs the question, of course, over what would shoemaking laborers come to blows? Could it be the shine on the shoes? Is that something that can move the pugilist spirit? Having never shined a shoe, I can't say, but I must admit that seeing mud caked on my Hessians has been known to put me in a belligerent mood. Either way, I must admit, I'm fascinated."

Vinnie, caught somewhere between a giggle and a laugh, emitted an amused sound that could only be described as a gurgle. It was not so much the marquess's words that set her off but his tone of academic conjecture, as if trying to decipher how the Great Pyramids of Egypt were constructed.

If the gurgle sounded strange to him, he did not indicate with a look or comment, but it certainly drew his attention, for he quickly added, "I must also admit that I entered into this outing with the spine of a Spartan, determined to get through it without a single complaint but not actually expecting to derive any joy from the experience. I have not only failed to *not* enjoy it, I've found it a true pleasure. Thank you."

Although Vinnie knew that it was she who should be offering her thanks again and again (and again), she could do nothing in the face of such sincere graciousness than to say, "You're welcome."

Her first impression of the Marquess of Huntly had been of a peer whose sense of propriety outweighed his sense of humanity. His good manners seemed to extend from a desire not so much as to impress other people as to impress himself. This attitude was not surprising, as she had encountered it many times since her come out and understood the value of it. But although she supported noblesse oblige in theory, in practice, when it was directed at her, she found it insulting and demoralizing. She would rather be treated rudely as an equal than kindly as a subordinate.

But there, in the confines of Mr. Brill's mahogany office in a shoemaking factory in Acton Vale, she formed an entirely different opinion. This Marquess of Huntly wasn't merely personable but likeable as well. His questions to Mr. Brill revealed a lively and interested mind, and his actions demonstrated an unprecedented level of thoughtfulness. He was funny, sincere, patient and kind—an entirely human human being.

As if to prove how thoroughly inaccurate Vinnie's original impression had been, Huntly added, "My experience with chemicals is limited to the blending of snuff, at which, I will admit, I am merely proficient, unlike Trent, who has the devil's own nose, but if you require assistance with your next formulation, I would be happy to lend mine."

The proposal was so implausible, Vinnie assumed she hadn't heard him correctly. "You would like to help me make my next mixture?" she asked, a wrinkle of confusion between her brows.

Huntly nodded as he took a sip of tea. "Having heard all about the process, I would like to see it firsthand. As a naturalist, I do have a scientific bent, you know, and, as such, recognize and accept all the risks involved. If the hose explodes on me again, I will accept full responsibility."

Vinnie could hardly believe the offer was in earnest— imagine, the Marquess of Huntly in his waistcoat measuring out turpentine—and immediately dismissed it as unworthy of comment. Even if he had meant it, she could not accept. As a sensible young woman with a steady head, Miss Lavinia Harlow was not given to fits of nerves or waves of anxiety, and yet she feared having Huntly working alongside her would discompose her entirely. It was not merely that she was accustomed to toiling alone, although that circumstance was, of course, a contributing factor, but also that she suddenly found Huntly to be uncomfortably appealing. Sitting next to him now, she discovered her heart beat a little faster and her breath came a little swifter.

Despite the fact that she'd been engaged for more than a month and had, upon occasion, entered into intimate embraces with her fiancé, Vinnie had never experienced anything like a racing heart or shallow breaths. Her relationship with Sir Windbourne had been predicated on a different set of criteria—most significantly, his interest in her. Other men had shown her attention, but he was the first one to persist, pursuing her with zeal as if she were irresistible, which, in turn, made her feel as if she was. Of course, he had other traits that appealed to her. His confidence, for one, was inspiring, and she liked being around someone who knew his own mind so well, he didn't hesitate to speak it freely—so freely, in fact, that it relieved her of the obligation of speech.

Her sister, recognizing his tendency to pontificate as the boorish behavior it was, immediately dubbed him Sir Windbag, and it was upon this foundation that her dislike of him was based. Although Emma's aversion turned out to be prescient, even she could not have imagined him for the traitor, spy and murderer he revealed himself to be.

As much as Vinnie hated to recall her dead fiancé, she expected such unpleasant thoughts would have a beneficial effect on her present state by calming her unsettled nerves. But Lord Huntly contrasted so sharply with Sir Windbourne all his memory did was underscore the marquess's positive attributes, making her even more keenly aware of his appeal.

Absurd, she thought, unsettled by an emotion she couldn't describe. You are absolutely absurd.

Determined to rise above these sudden and irrational feelings, she searched for something innocuous to say, and recalling his last comment about shouldering all the blame should the hose fail again, observed that he had accepted full responsibility last time.

Recalling how he had indeed stood in the conservatory with water dripping off his nose and insisted the dousing was his fault made Huntly laugh. "I did, didn't I?" he said thoughtfully. "What to do when one is doused by an exploding hose was not a topic covered by my nanny or tutors, and it seemed to me the safest route was simply to take the blame. I find as a general rule in society that the best way to handle a disconcerting event is to claim responsibility and apologize."

At the bright, crisp sound of his laughter, Vinnie's heart hitched, and she stared at him, arrested by the pure delight in his eyes. It was that look, she decided later, that pushed her over the edge—first the visit, then the offer, then the laughter and finally the unholy amusement in his gorgeous aquamarine eyes. How could she resist it? How could anyone?

Acting on instinct, her mind lulled by the impossible beauty of his eyes, she leaned forward and pressed her lips against his. It was a soft brushing, more like a gentle caress than an actual kiss, and as soon as she felt the wonderful warmth of his lips, her heart rolled over. Dazed and oddly content, she pulled back and stared at him. She waited for the horror to come, a mortification a hundred times worse than anything she'd experienced before, but as she gazed into his eyes, all she felt was an inexplicable peacefulness.

Huntly's mood was harder to decipher, though he did not seem entirely repulsed by her act, and she was thoroughly puzzled by his seriousness when he said softly, "I'm sorry."

Vinnie smiled because she recalled his inclination to accept blame regardless of culpability, and finding she couldn't let him take responsibility for a deed that was utterly her own, said, "That was my fault."

Now Huntly smiled. "Not for that," he said, lowering his head. "For this."

His lips captured hers in a searing kiss, and that was all Vinnie could think—that she had somehow been taken captive. Huntly moaned softly in his throat as he gently held her head in his two strong hands, running his tongue smoothly over her lips until she opened them. Deepening the kiss, he pressed her back against the cushion, his movements wild but assured.

Vinnie, her arms climbing up Huntly's arm...around his shoulders...into his hair, felt her heart slam into her chest as Huntly's lips moved slowly from her cheek to her jaw to the cleft of her neck. The sensations he created with his tongue and his hands, which were now causing tingles up her arms, was beyond anything she'd imagined existed. She didn't know she could feel like this. Indeed, she honestly didn't know what *this* felt like. It was so blissful and heavenly, she didn't quite believe it was real, although there was an element of discomfort, just a slight yet growing sense that she could never have enough. She and Huntly could sit on this settee engaged in the same activity for eons to come and she would never be satisfied.

Although her mind was lulled, there was just enough of sensible Vinnie still working to find the notion of an unquenchable hunger to be disturbing. Her need for Huntly felt like a deep, dark hole from which she might never return.

At this thought, her mind began to clear, though not enough to end the embrace, for the sensations were far too pleasurable. It was only when she felt Huntly's hand touch her breast, which sent a marvelous new shot of need coursing through her body, that she had the strength to pull back.

Wild-eyed and trembling, Vinnie stared in shock at the damage she had wrought with her single kiss. The Marquess of Huntly was breathing heavily, his hair was tousled and a look of horror had replaced the amusement from only a few minutes before.

With a calm she was far from feeling, she swallowed

her mortification—ah, yes, there it was—and resolved to apologize with all the dignity she could summon. She did not relish the further humiliation, but Miss Lavinia Harlow did not shirk her responsibilities and this debacle was entirely of her own making. Poor Lord Huntly had simply been sitting on a settee drinking tea and making polite conversation when she'd accosted him. She didn't know much about men, but it seemed likely that even the best of them would have little resistance to the wiles of an unprincipled woman.

"Now I must apologize, my lord," she began, grateful that her voice wasn't weak or reedy, "It will sound like a feeble excuse to you, I'm sure, but I got swept up in the moment. I was so happy to be in this wonderful place and so grateful to you for arranging it that I behaved in an indecent and wholly unacceptable way. I hope you will accept my apology, which is heartfelt and sincere, but I will not hold it against you if you cannot."

Midway through her speech, Huntly began to shake his head and as soon as she finished, he said, "Miss Harlow, I cannot let you—"

"No," Vinnie said, her tone firm as she stood up, forcing the marquess to rise as well. "You must not feel compelled to do the so-called proper thing. I know you have beautiful manners and you think it's your obligation to take responsibility for all disconcerting events. But this is my disconcerting event, and I beg you will please allow me the dignity of taking responsibility for it."

Although the marquess looked like he very much wanted to argue further, he sighed and said, "Very well, Miss Harlow, I will abide by your request and will, if the offer still stands, accept your apology in the spirit with which it was offered."

Relieved, Vinnie nodded and felt some of the anxiety leave her. Her heart was still beating wildly, but presumably even that would return to normal in a minute or two. "I'm grateful, my lord, and I genuinely hope that the…ah"—how to describe it?—"unpleasantness hasn't marred your enjoyment of the visit. I assure you, it hasn't ruined mine. It's still one of the nicest days I've ever had and I remain indebted to you for making it possible."

Huntly examined her for a long while before answering, and Vinnie began to worry about her appearance. Neither one of them was as kempt or as tidy as when they'd arrived, but she had straightened her dress and smoothed down her hair. At least she'd thought she had. Perhaps an unruly curl was sticking out of the side?

Finally, he spoke, "Nothing can ruin my enjoyment of this day, and if I may just add that I am humbled by your gallantry."

Although gallantry was not something to which Vinnie aspired, she recognized when she had been paid the highest compliment possible. "Thank you, my lord. Now, shall we be on our way? You are far too courteous to let your impatience show, but I'm sure you have plenty of other things to accomplish today."

The marquess opened the door and followed her out. "I'm happy to escort you home now, but to be completely honest, I'd much rather skulk around the factory to discover the meaning of a code red incident. I find the description so evocative of an emergency that I'm inclined to use it with my staff. Code red, Petrie, my Hessians have a scratch. Or code red, Mrs. Dundee, the tea is cold."

Vinnie laughed at this nonsense, as the marquess had intended, and felt confident they were once again on solid footing. Whatever had sparked the...ah—well, she couldn't really call it unpleasantness because that description was far from accurate—disconcerting event remained behind in Mr. Brill's comfortable office. It did not follow them out the door, through the factory and onto the street—of that, Vinnie was certain. As she had said, her behavior was the product of a remarkable confluence of forces that would never occur again. For this reason, she felt perfectly composed as she climbed into Huntly's conveyance and she was able to make polite conversation with him the whole way home.

They talked about Mr. Brill and his associate Mr. Peale and code reds and turpentine and even exploding hoses.

The conversation was easy, with one topic leading naturally to the next, and Vinnie felt so entirely comfortable in his presence that she almost forgot the incident in Brill's office. She could not erase completely the memory of his touch or his kiss or the desperate look in his aquamarine eyes from her thoughts, but she was able to push it to a corner of her mind, where it could do the least amount of damage. What she did forget about entirely was the invitation to apply to the British Horticultural Society, which was why, when Huntly brought it up, she was momentarily stunned.

If he noticed her surprised expression, he did not let it dissuade him from his course. "As you know, we must discuss it, for it looms large over both of us."

Although the invitation certainly did hang over Vinnie in a particularly looming manner, she felt his choice of words rather overstated the case. "I wouldn't say *large,* my lord. It looms small to middling."

Huntly conceded this point with an absent nod and continued, "Although I cannot fathom your interest in joining an organization that is ill-suited to your person, I respect the fact that the choice is yours to make."

"Thank you, my lord," she said wryly.

He was too intent on his purpose to observe the sarcasm. "Knowing you have a multitude of interests, I proposed today's expedition in the hopes that it would provide you with an occupation sufficiently engrossing as to override your interest in the society," he explained.

Vinnie felt her face grow hot and her heart thump, and she could have sworn the entire world turned red for a moment, so intense was her anger. She curled her fingers into fists but otherwise kept an outward calm. "Excuse me?" she asked coldly. She had heard him clearly the first time but felt a perverse desire to make him say it again.

"It's my hope that our visit to Mr. Brill's factory provided you with so much useful information that you won't have time left over to apply for membership in the society," he repeated helpfully and then added a smile to imply that he was thinking only of her welfare.

A smile!

Remarkably, nothing in her life had ever made her as furious as that smile—and, given that she had shot her murderous fiancé just as he was about to gut her with a fish knife, that was saying an awful lot.

The entire day had been a ruse to get her to withdraw her application. Every single thing Huntly had said and done had been carefully planned to draw a particular response from her. He had acted with chilling premeditation.

"Please bear with me as I struggle to understand exactly what you're saying," Vinnie requested, her soft tone a clear indication of her anger. "Far from being the restitution you described when proposing the trip—I believe the actual words you used were *make amends*—the expedition to the factory was in fact an exchange. You give me Mr. Brill and his improved method for waterproofing, and I give you my agreement not to apply. Is that correct?"

"No…well, not exactly," he said, faltering a little as the carriage stopped in front of her house. "You make it sound rather calculated, and I assure you, my intentions were—" But Vinnie didn't want to hear about his intentions and cut him off. "Was it not a quid pro quo, my lord?"

"Again, I must protest your characterization as a—"

"It is a simple yes-or-no question," she pointed out stonily. "Was this expedition a tit for tat?"

He leaned against the back of the seat, his shoulders stiff, and said, "I suppose by some measure, yes."

Vinnie felt no satisfaction at the concession, and yet she persisted. "So it was not a sincere attempt to make amends for sins committed against me, as you originally stated?"

Now the marquess's smile was wry. "Can it not be both?"

Although her expression did not change, Vinnie felt something inside her crumble and die. The day—the wonderful, bizarre, remarkable, happy, unexpected day—had been a lie. What she thought was their first honest exchange, their first conversation without an agenda on either of their parts, had been simply another move around the chess board for him. He had been playing a game, while she had been in earnest.

And the kiss.

Ah, yes, the kiss.

Well, she had gotten exactly what she deserved for being so bold a hussy as to kiss a gentleman on the lips. She had known there was something unreal about it—the inexplicable passion, the even more puzzling confluence of forces that created it—and had already accepted that it didn't exist outside Mr. Brill's office. Naturally, she had assumed the unreality was the kiss itself and the wild tumult of emotion it created. She never once imagined that it was the man who was not real, but the Marquess of Huntly whom she'd felt compelled beyond all reason to kiss was merely a creature of her own making. He was a phantom.

Gutted by this realization—yes, fish knives could do a lot of internal damage but emotions certainly created their own brand of sharp, stinging pain—she acknowledged for the first time how much the experience had meant to her. It was not the kiss itself that was rife with meaning but the compulsion that produced it, for Miss Lavinia Harlow had never been compelled to kiss anyone before, least of all her fiancé.

What did it say about her that the one man she felt driven to kiss was a figment of her own imagination?

Unwilling to think about it further, Vinnie pulled her pelisse tight around her shoulders and thanked the marquess for his honesty. She wanted to add a snide comment about it being better late than never, but she refused to give him the satisfaction of a response, any response. It was better to be calm and indifferent, to simply leave the carriage on a high-minded dignified note, than to descend into petty insults.

But it cost her. Oh, did it cost her something fierce not to call Huntly a bounder and a villain and the worst human being she'd ever had the displeasure to meet.

Vinnie unlatched the carriage door and found Huntly's coachman waiting patiently to help her down. She turned back to the marquess and gave him what she hoped was a cool, apathetic look. "Good day, sir," she said.

She expected him to make another attempt to justify his actions, perhaps to explain how the expedition could have been both a means to an end *and* a way to make amends, but he simply responded in kind. "Good day, Miss Harlow."

This, too, struck her as an insult, for surely after spending almost an entire day with her, he should thank her for the lovely company. It would be an empty gesture, of course, but their entire world was composed of polite nothings and she would have liked to be considered worth the effort.

One insult more or less didn't make a difference, for she had already settled on a course of action. She wasn't a schemer by nature and she certainly didn't look at life as if it were a chess board full of pawns, but she knew one person who did and she did it better than anyone in the known world, and as soon as she handed her pelisse to Caruthers, she ran up the stairs to plot strategy with Emma.

CHAPTER NINE

The first Huntly heard of the dossiers was from Mr. Luther Townshend, who insisted upon seeing the marquess immediately, despite being told several times that he was interviewing candidates for the position of cataloging assistant—"to help him organize and classify flora from his voyage, sir"—and was not to be disturbed.

"Very well," snapped Mr. Townshend, whose patience had been worn thin by the first five refusals, "I should like to put myself up for the position."

Fleming, resentful of any attempt to circumvent his authority, kindly requested a résumé, an act that had the unfortunate affect of turning Townshend's face purple.

"Devil take it, man, I'm the deputy director of Kew Gardens," he all but screamed. "Now, tell the marquess I must see him at once."

The butler was saved the trouble of interrupting Huntly's interview, for as soon as Townshend had finishing making his demand, the study door opened and Huntly's head stuck out. "What seems to be the trouble, Fleming?"

Townshend opened his mouth to reply, but the trusted retainer spoke more quickly and at a greater volume. "This gentleman—a Mr. Luther Townshend—would like to see you when you have a moment, my lord. He understands you are already engaged and is happy to wait in the drawing room with a pot of tea."

Huntly, who knew Fleming well enough to realize that wasn't quite true, nodded his head abruptly. "Very good. I'm almost done here, so I shall be in there directly."

Realizing he had been outflanked, Townshend meekly followed Fleming to the drawing room, where he was of-fered not only a cup of perfectly brewed tea but a plate of warm scones as well. Given the oddness of the hour—after morning calls, not yet afternoon visits—he was impressed with the freshness of the pastry and comfortably finished the entire serving before the marquess came in to apologize.

"I would like to blame Fleming, for he does tend to get territorial, but in this case he was simply following my or-ders," Huntly explained as he drew the doors closed behind him. "I've been home three weeks now and have yet to en-gage an assistant, which is unfortunate for everyone in-volved, as my study is practically consumed by trunks from my journey. Today was specifically set aside for interviews."

Townshend, who had stood as soon as the marquess entered the room, nodded agreeably, his frayed temper con-siderably smoothed by the interval with the scones. "Of course, my lord. I apologize for my bellicosity. I am usually more temperate in my responses."

Huntly nodded as if he knew this to be true, but in fact Townshend was the single most argumentative member of the British Horticultural Society. As the deputy director of the gardens, he was accustomed to ordering people around and had little patience when others did not bow to do his authority, even the equals who made up the membership of the society. He wasn't unreasonable, of course, and inevita-bly apologized for his inappropriate outbursts only mo-ments after he'd made them. For this reason, it was hardly remarkable to hear him shouting at poor Fleming in the hallway. No, the remarkable thing was his presence in the hallway. In all the years of their being in the society together,

Townshend had never before visited Huntly at his home.

"No need to apologize," the marquess said, taking a seat and indicating that his visitor should do the same. "I'm sure whatever has driven you to that extremity is as dire as you perceive. Please tell me how I may be of assistance."

Although Townshend spent several hours a day prowling the fields at Kew, his taste for sweets and his advanced age of sixty-six gave him a rather inflated middle, which he now rested his hands on. "It's that woman you proposed for membership," he said with distaste.

Of all the things the marquess expected him to say, this was absolutely the last and he bolted upright in his seat. "Miss Harlow?" he said.

"Yes, Miss Harlow," he spat. "Her dossier on me is pure libel and certainly more denigrating than her dossier on Sir Barton."

At the mention of Miss Harlow, the marquess felt his heart jump and in an instant he saw her as he always saw her—in Mr. Brill's office, her breasts heaving, her eyes half shuttered, her lips swollen from his kisses. It was a potent image, and he repressed it now as he had done every day for the last week.

Instead, he called up the picture of Sir Charles Barton's nose. There were few things less lascivious than the hairy mole on the end of that good gentleman's hawklike beak.

It did the trick and gave Huntly the opportunity to respond to Townshend's statement. "I'm sure you—" he began, fully intending to assure him that the situation could not be as dire as he thought. But then the words themselves penetrated. "I'm sorry, did you say Miss Harlow has a dossier on you?"

"On me, on Barton, on everyone," he said, his voice rising again. "That wretched woman has compiled dossiers on the entire society and is using the information to coerce members into supporting her candidacy. I assure you, it's the most damnable thing."

Although Huntly heard him clearly, he still could not

properly understand what he was saying. "Miss Lavinia Harlow has compiled dossiers on every member of the society?"

Townshend sighed heavily and snapped, "For God's sake, man, keep up. This is very basic information. I'm surprised you don't know it already. I can imagine the dossier on you is the most extensive by far, as you are the one who set her up for this humiliation."

The deputy director went on for some time, complaining about not only Vinnie but also about women, parliament and the appalling ignorance of the average visitor to Kew Gardens. A great number of subjects had earned his ire in six decades of life, and he seemed content to voice all of them in the Marquess of Huntly's drawing room.

While Townshend ranted, Huntly tried to make sense of his revelations, for it seemed inconceivable that the Lavinia Harlow he knew would try to coerce anyone, let alone an elderly gentleman. Recalling their exchange at Hatchard's, he conceded that she had a piquant sense of humor and would not hesitate to tweak an ego if she felt it needed deflating. He also knew she was stubborn, and he felt that some, if not all, of her desire to become a member of the society was spurred by his desire that she not become one. During their dance, he'd felt her back stiffen with contrary resolve with every reasonable suggestion he made.

These failings, however, were minor—and, indeed, he could not quite bring himself to even think of them as failings. He admired her pluck and liked her sense of humor, and when he remembered her in Mr. Brill's office, asking with the dignity of a queen to be allowed to take full responsibility for her actions, he was in awe of her bravery.

He could do nothing save grant her request, but listening to her take the blame for something she was hardly responsible for nearly broke his heart.

It was almost comical that she thought the scene in the office was her fault. True, she had initiated the event with her kiss, but that chaste peck had been as sweet as it was innocent. He understood human nature and the sometimes horrible inadequacy of words. It was just like she said: The kiss extended from an overwhelming combination of emotions—happiness, excitement, gratitude—that could not be expressed with mere speech. It required an action, and he, being a bounder and a cad, took unconscionable advantage of that. He had known what he was doing the entire time, pulling her deeper and deeper into the web of desire because he couldn't bear the alternative: that she didn't want him as much as he wanted her. All afternoon, while she was in the distillation lab with Mr. Brill, her face vibrating with excitement as he tinkered with his formula, Huntly had felt his desire growing. He had tried to stay aloof but could not resist being drawn in by her warmth.

He knew she was mourning the death of a beloved fiancé. He had seen the way she responded to mentions of Sir Windbourne and felt the connection to be deep and abiding. For that reason, she could not be held responsible for her actions. No doubt she missed the bond they'd shared as a couple and, when she felt that overwhelming gratitude toward him, mistook that closeness for intimacy. Realizing he was a poor substitute for her beloved, she had thrown off the heavy weight of passion and conversed easily with him in the carriage. Such a thing probably happened all the time with widows.

But it never happened to him before. Huntly could not remember a time when he desired a woman to the brink of madness and had to let her go.

He'd made a significant misstep in the carriage—he'd known it as soon as she spoke in that chilly voice—but surely he could be forgiven for not thinking clearly. How could he possibly keep his wits while confined in a small space with the woman whom he had nearly ravished a half hour before? The provocation was too great, and all he was thinking was that it had to end. She couldn't possibly join the society and torture him on a regular basis. No, the only way forward was to avoid her entirely, and convincing her not to apply was vital to that happening.

He knew how his proposal had sounded to her, and

she was right to be offended. His intentions, upon arriving at her town house that morning, had been pure. He had thought of nothing but making amends. It was only after, when he realized how untenable further contact would be, that he devised the other motive. But the sole reason he suggested it was he had genuinely thought she would rather work on her invention. A year of meetings of the British Horticultural Society could not possibly give her as much joy as a single afternoon at Brill & Company.

Although Huntly thought he knew women fairly well—with his unusual eyes and his even features, he'd been petted and adored by ladies from an indecently early age—he admitted he didn't know the first thing about Lavinia Harlow. She had been a mystery to him from the moment they'd met, when she rambled on nonsensically about the duke's staff. He still had no idea what made her invent a fictional housekeeper, but he didn't doubt she had her reasons.

Recalling that encounter and others, he decided Miss Harlow most likely did have a dossier on the members of the horticultural society, and he interrupted Townshend's diatribe against pigeons to ask what his file said.

The question, which seemed to Huntly to be the logical follow-up to the declaration that he had a file, disconcerted Townshend, either because he was so in thrall to his own ideas or because he hadn't planned on sharing the information. "Well, you see, it's really a minor…certainly nothing to, uh, kick up a fuss over," he explained. "Entirely false, I assure you, entirely false. No crime has been committed."

Unsure how to respond to this strange speech but seeking to put his friend's mind at ease, he said, "If that is the case, it seems you have nothing to worry about. I beg you to put it out of your head."

Townshend sighed loudly, closed his eyes and shook his head. "The charge of plagiarism is accurate," he announced boldly, then opened one eye to see how the marquess responded to this confession.

Huntly drew his brows in confusion and surprise, for

he had read Townshend's outstanding text several times and found it very useful in his own research of different species of flora. *Botanicus* was a concise and articulate resource for anyone who enjoyed the study and cultivation of flowers.

"I'm afraid I don't understand," Huntly said.

His friend seemed to shrink into the settee, though, with his substantial middle, he couldn't make himself disappear entirely. "Writing a volume as compendious and significant as *Botanicus* is a remarkable endeavor, and I am the deputy director of Kew Gardens, a responsibility that requires a large amount of my time. To compensate for these disadvantages, I relied on descriptions of flora from books previously published on the subject. As you know, it is standard procedure for authors to employ other authors' work in the production of their own. Shakespeare used passages from Plutarch's *Lives of the Noble Greeks and Romans* for his plays and has been lauded for it," he said defensively, his spine stiffening as he warmed to his subject. "I have done no differently, and yet Miss Harlow is trying to cast my innocent act as a crime. She seems to feel that I should have come up with all the words in my book entirely on my own and failing that, should have given credit to my source material. Have you ever heard anything as absurd?"

Although Huntly had indeed heard many things not only as absurd but also more absurd, he wisely kept his own counsel. Instead, he assured Townshend that he had his continued respect and would no doubt retain the respect of every member of the British Horticultural Society.

Taking little comfort from this statement, Townshend looked at him bleakly and said, "But the Society for the Advancement of Horticultural Knowledge would delight in humiliating me. They're a monstrous throng of heathens who have no understanding of scholarly procedure and will make hay over this information. Our entire organization is at risk if word of this got out. It is not myself I am thinking of but each and every one of us. It is simply imperative that you talk to Miss Harlow and bring an end to her machinations."

Now Huntly's spine stiffened. "I?" he asked, lifting an eyebrow.

"You have brought disgrace on the society with your cavalier invitation to Miss Harlow. Yes," he added forcefully, "I said *cavalier,* for although I do not know what prompted the invitation, I know it was not made in earnest. You were having a little joke, which is, of course, your prerogative, but it will not be at my expense. Now, sir, you are obligated as a gentleman to undo the damage you have caused and I suggest you do it at once."

As much as Huntly wanted to resist Townshend's directive, he knew the problem was entirely his fault and that, yes, the onus fell on him to fix it. Only a week before, he had resolved to avoid Miss Harlow as much as possible and now was in the damnable position of having to call on her. As Townshend had said, he had no choice.

He knew this development should trouble him, for just the thought of seeing Miss Harlow again brought the image of her in Mr. Brill's office searingly forth in his mind, but he was more sanguine. He had done the proper thing and made the virtuous resolution to avoid her, and now matters beyond his control were throwing them together again. He was powerless to resist fate.

"I will speak to her posthaste and resolve this matter," Huntly assured his visitor, "but I urge you to calm yourself. There's nothing to be accomplished by getting aggravated, for you are hardly at point non plus. As you say, the practice is common and no doubt members of the Society for the Advancement of Horticultural Knowledge have done it themselves."

At this statement, Townshend perked up. Indeed, he rose to his feet with considerably more dexterity than one would expect to find in a man of his age and size. "Of course! You are a genius, Huntly, a true genius, and I apologize if I let my concern rule my mind. I will do exactly as you suggest. Thank you."

Although the marquess was happy to accept the designation of genius, he preferred to know what for. "You're welcome, though I'm not sure what I suggested."

Townshend, who was marching toward the drawing room door, halted with his hand on the knob. "A preemptive strike against the enemy, of course! The members of the Society for the Advancement of Horticultural Knowledge *are* probably guilty…er, familiar with the practice as well. Therefore, all I need to do to ensure the society is not a threat is locate a book in which one of its members plagiarized…er, relied on an earlier work. I must begin at once. Thank you again, Huntly, for your wise counsel."

Huntly knew it would take days, if not weeks, for Townshend to trace a half dozen texts back to their original sources, assuming, of course, that they had original sources, but he thought his friend would be better off if his hours were consumed with research rather than worry. Realizing the monumental nature of the task, he wondered how Miss Harlow had uncovered the truth about *Botanicus* so quickly and made a mental note to ask her.

During the half hour he had been bracketed in with Townshend, three letters from other society members had arrived, begging an interview with him immediately.

Miss Harlow's work, he thought without heat. He knew he should be more appalled by her behavior and some part of him was properly horrified that any gently bred lady would stoop to such vulgar tactics, but mostly he admired her spine. It was he who had embroiled her in the membership dispute—she had not come knocking on their door, demanding entrance—and somehow insulted her with each new request that she back down. He liked to think his intentions were always good, but his behavior since he'd met Miss Harlow had been too erratic for him to properly understand his motives. She unnerved him in a way he'd assumed no woman could, interrupting his thoughts when he was engaged in important activities such as cataloging specimens from his voyage.

Following through on his promise to address the problem

right away, Huntly promptly informed Fleming he was going out and turned down the offer of a carriage, for it was quicker if he simply walked the few blocks to Grosvenor Square.

When he arrived at the duke's town house, he discovered that the duke was away from home, a development that didn't affect him in the least, and that the dowager was not, a development that required a minor detour from his purpose, for he could not deny a visit with the woman who had raised him as much as his own parents had.

As he had been only eleven when his parents died in a carriage accident, he could not recall them clearly, except as benign spirits who sometimes visited the nursery with sweet words and treats. Jane, Duchess of Trent, was not the doting type either, but she found the treatment of her orphaned neighbor, who had been sent home to live with servants when he proved too unruly for elderly relations, to be insupportable and arranged for the boy to attend Eton with her own son. During breaks and holidays, she insisted he stay with them rather than at his own estate, which marched along their north border.

For these considerations, Huntly was eternally grateful, for there was nothing more lonely and desolate than a family seat with no family.

Their comfortable tête-à-tête was disturbed after twenty minutes, when Caruthers announced the arrival of Lady Britten.

"She is planning the come out of her youngest daughter and asked for my guidance on a variety of important matters," the dowager confided. "Her taste in presentation gowns is a little gaudy, and I hope today to steer her toward something simpler and of course with fewer white feathers. Two or three plumes in one's hair are charming, but there's nothing elegant about wearing an entire ostrich."

As there were few things more pleasing to the dowager than overriding the poor sense of others, Huntly knew she was in for a delightful afternoon.

He made his good-byes quickly in an attempt to avoid

Lady Britten in the hallway, but the mother of four daughters sensed there was a bachelor underfoot and stalled in her removal of her pelisse in hopes of greeting him. For several minutes, he nodded politely as her ladyship detailed her daughters' love of flowers. Amazingly, all four of them were floraphiles, which, of course, revealed that they were indeed not, for the proper word was *anthophile*.

The dowager very kindly put him out of his misery by insisting Lady Britten join her for tea immediately, for she was parched and could not possibly partake while a guest was still standing.

As soon as the door was closed, he asked Caruthers where he could find Miss Harlow and was immediately directed to Emma's study. He didn't know what he expected to find upon opening the door but certainly not the Harlow twins bent over the mahogany desk plotting strategy like generals in a war. Fascinated by the uncensored glimpse into how their minds worked, he stood in the doorway without announcing his presence. Neither young lady seemed to notice.

"What is the status on Bolingbroke?" Emma asked as she picked up a chess pawn with the baron's name written on it.

"Defiant but wavering," Vinnie reported matter-of-factly. "He is not convinced that the influence of the Harlow Hoyden, however well married, will help his daughter. But Lady Bolingbroke feels the dowager's ball firmly established your position and is in transports over the prospect of the new duchess taking Lady Agatha Bolingbroke for a ride in Hyde Park in her curricle."

Emma nodded thoughtfully. "Maybe we should up our offer to two rides in Hyde Park *and* a coze at Mrs. Douglas-Home's rout on Monday."

Vinnie glanced at her quizzically. "I thought you were not attending Mrs. Douglas-Home's rout."

Her sister shrugged. "I wasn't. I find all routs to be dreadfully dull and none of my hosts seem capable of arranging proper ventilation, but it's a small sacrifice and I'm happy to make it."

"Well, I cannot accept it," Vinnie said with a firm shake of her head, "for you will no doubt do something outrageous to relieve your boredom and get into a whole new scrape, for which the dowager will hold me responsible. Let's abandon the rout idea and invite her to go to the theater with us in a few weeks. It's *Merchant of Venice,* which means you will be thoroughly occupied and won't cause a bubble bath."

"Although I take offense at your insultingly poor opinion of my ability to withstand boredom—was I not a pattern card of correct behavior at Lady Ilchester's card party last night?—I find your reasoning sound and agree. A theater box provides Lady Agatha with a greater opportunity to be seen with the Duchess of Trent. Her mother will be pleased and will sway her husband. Very well, then," she said, selecting another pawn, "onto Mr. Edward Lincoln."

From his perch in the doorway, Huntly was too amazed by their efficient calculations to decide if he was horrified or impressed. Their summation of the Bolingbrokes was entirely accurate, and he could easily imagine the discussion in which Lady Bolingbroke convinced Lord Bolingbroke that their plain-faced daughter's chances would be greatly improved by an association with the popular Duchess of Trent.

Watching Emma twirl the chess piece marked Lincoln, Huntly realized it didn't matter how he felt on the matter—what they were doing was wrong, for they held the lives of real people in their hands.

With four long strides, he was at the desk. "I apologize for the intrusion, but I really must protest."

Emma looked up and grinned hugely at the marquess. "Lord Huntly, your timing is impeccable," she announced, as if he were there by invitation or even command. "We were just discussing the estimable Mr. Lincoln and would welcome your opinion on how to proceed. Our research turned up two helpful facts. One: that he is horse mad but cannot find a stud worthy to mate with his beloved mare, Daisyfield. Two: that he is a devoted boxer but has been unable to attain private instruction from Gentleman Jackson. Which do you think bothers him more?"

At Huntly's stunned looked, Vinnie rushed to explain, "That is to say, for which problem should we offer him a solution? If it were I, I'd prefer the former, for I think one has a closer relationship with one's trusty steed than with one's boxing instructor. But that's why we are so glad to see you, for perhaps as females we are underestimating the importance of an athletic instructor. Please advise us."

Although the marquess knew they were teasing him, for there was no way they could possibly be sincere in asking him how best to manipulate a fellow society member, he was too fascinated to resist answering. "Ordinarily, I'd agree with you, Miss Harlow, and say that the horse is a better value, especially in the circumstance you are devising. However, Mr. Lincoln's older brother is a noted pugilist and I fear there is an element of rivalry with his sibling in his interest in boxing. For that reason, I would suggest you offer him the latter prize. May I ask how you will arrange it?"

While Emma made a notation in Lincoln's file, Vinnie explained that Alex had offered his assistance in any way possible and would kindly make the request on their behalf to Mr. Jackson. "As you know, he has been going to his saloon for years and is a particular favorite."

"Alex?" he asked in surprise. "He's agreed to aid and abet this madness?"

Emma laughed. "Yes, though he did lay some ground rules before agreeing. No bribery or blackmail."

"Or seduction," Vinnie added with a twinkle. "I believe he was very adamant about that."

At the word *seduction,* Huntly whipped his head around to stare at her and he noted how vibrant she looked in her pretty yellow walking dress. It seemed to him she always looked bright and alive, her eyes glinting at some private joke. It was an illusion, just a trick of light, because he knew how deeply in mourning she was.

He knew and he had to struggle to keep it in mind, for he must not accost her again. To that end, he looked away, first out the window to the left of her shoulder and then at the table covered with files.

The room was silent for almost a full minute, then Emma said, "You must want to see your own dossier. I have it in the other room. While I'm gone, Vinnie, ask him about the Earl of Moray."

Before the marquess could protest, she was out of the room and he was left alone with Vinnie. Keeping his eyes purposefully down, he read the labels on the files, looking for Quentin Wallop, Earl of Moray.

"She's just provoking you, my lord," Vinnie said softly. "You don't have to rise to the bait."

Huntly found Moray's file underneath Townshend's, opened it and flipped through it without reading a single word. He wasn't interested in what it said; he simply needed something to look at so he wouldn't stare at Vinnie. "I understand the appeal, you know, of what you're doing: strategizing, moving the puzzle pieces around until they all fit. And I understand why you're doing it."

"I appreciate your understanding," she said.

Now Huntly glanced up at her, searching for some hint of irony or sarcasm in her voice or face and finding none. "Would you stop if I asked?"

Vinnie folded her arms across her chest and smiled faintly. "I don't know, my lord. What will you offer me in exchange?"

Huntly should not have been surprised by the reference to the scene in the carriage, and yet it took him entirely unaware. He'd been so focused on resisting her, on keeping his mind in the moment and not in Mr. Brill's office, that he'd forgotten how their outing to the shoe factory had ended. "You are still angry," he stated flatly, unsure if he was relieved or disappointed. Logically, he knew he should be the former, for it put her even more firmly out of his grasp.

"No, I'm really not," Vinnie said with a thoughtful look. "At the time, of course, I was distressed to learn you had an ulterior motive for doing what was genuinely the nicest thing anyone had ever done for me. I'd had what I thought was the perfect day, and you betrayed that memory by informing me it was all a lie. But to be completely honest, I cannot blame you for what you did. You're in an untenable position and are entitled to try to extricate yourself by any means at your disposal. I should not have expected otherwise."

This gracious speech should have pleased Huntly, but instead he found her calm acceptance of his betrayal to have a disconcerting effect on him, for it created an ache somewhere near his heart. He didn't know how to account for it and could attribute it only to the madness of the situation, which had somehow gotten entirely out of hand.

To his dismay, he discovered the new sensation was even more disturbing than the memory of Miss Harlow in Mr. Brill's office (breasts heaving, eyes lidded, lips swollen), and he immediately looked down to study the Earl of Moray's file as if the information it contained was vastly engrossing. Scanning the first page, which comprised the rudimentary facts of the earl's life, he tried to find something to comment on in order to end the silence, which was far too potent for his peace of mind. When Vinnie didn't speak, he read the note scribbled at the top of the page, "Desires a French cook," and looked at her. "Is this really how you want to gain admittance?"

It was a fair question, Huntly thought, but Vinnie's long, hard stare made him feel as if he'd inquired about the state of her ankles. Finally, she said, "How else will I gain admittance? A strong essay, an informative presentation, an intelligent interview? You must admit, my lord, the deck is stacked against me. What are the odds down at Brooks's these days? I believe the original wager was given three to one odds that I wouldn't get in and now it's up to ten to one."

As Huntly preferred not to think of the wager placed in the betting book at Brooks's, he did not know where the odds stood, but he couldn't deny they were not in her favor. "I will admit it," he said readily. "But you must admit in turn that the only reason you want in is because I told you to stay out. You seek to thwart me."

"Not just you. The dowager, too. I can't decide whom I hope to thwart more," she said, her dimples peeking out as she smiled. "In some respects, you are right, my lord, but in others you do me a disservice, for I would truly value being a member of a society that feels passionately about the subjects I feel passionately about. I would relish that sense of community and common purpose, and I think I would contribute something of value. Having admitted that, however, I cannot deny that your and the dowager's insistence that I must not apply has strengthened my resolve. For most of my life, I've been an unassuming person with modest ambitions. Emma would call me docile, for I tend to stay where I'm put because it's more practical than engaging in a pointless argument. I've chosen not to want things because I've spent my whole life watching my sister struggle to have more and being punished for it. But then something happened, something worse than anything I ever thought could happen."

The ache in Huntly's heart grew as he realized to what she was referring. "You mean your fiancé's death," he said softly.

She seemed surprised by his astuteness, for she stared at him a long while before saying, "Yes, my fiancé's death. And it made me realize we all get punished regardless of what we do and that the truly pointless thing is to give up before we even try. So I am trying," she said earnestly before assuming a less personal, more businesslike tone, "which is why I would be very grateful if you'd weigh in on the matter of Lord Moray. We've established two possible courses of action."

"Yes, I see opportunity number one is a French cook. Short of giving him Alex's own chef, I can't divine how you will perform that trick. What's the second option?" Huntly asked, accommodating her need to change the subject and lighten the mood. He did so eagerly because he found he didn't like thinking about her fiancé, this departed paragon who held her heart. It bothered him more than he could say that he couldn't go toe-to-toe with the gentleman and take his measure.

"Get him back into Weston's good graces," she said, leaning over the desk to straighten the files, which were scattered everywhere. She seemed intent on arranging them in a single pile. "Moray had the very unfortunate luck to be caught altering one of the esteemed tailor's finest master-pieces: a slim-fitting double-breasted coat made of the high-est-quality wool facecloth. He was displeased with the heft of the silk velvet collar."

"Displeased with anything Weston does? Unfathomable!"

"Well, the earl doesn't have your low standards and asked Stulze to make a few adjustments, which he did, al-though he was not delighted to be reworking a coat rather than making one," she explained as she tidied the already neat stack of folders.

"Did Stulze cry rope on him?"

Seemingly satisfied with her ruthless organization of the files, Vinnie placed the ordered pile on the desk and stepped back. "No, but there appears to be some disagreement over how Weston showed up at Mr. Jennen's shop at the particular moment the button maker was crafting new gilt buttons to replace the ones that had been lost during the alterations."

"I trust Stulze retained ownership of Moray's silk vel-vet collars?"

"Yes, and although the change in tailors created no marked difference in the earl's impeccable style—his waistcoats remain the envy of all—the loss has haunted him ever since."

The marquess smiled faintly. "And you and Emma are going to put him out of his misery."

"Weston owes her a favor."

Huntly somehow resisted asking why the most sought-after tailor in London owed the Harlow Hoyden a favor—no doubt it was a long, involved, fascinating tale—and un-did all of Vinnie's fine work as he looked through the dossi-ers for another victim.

"Lord Peter Waldegrave," he announced. "What do you have in store for him?"

"Ah, old Nippy," she said with relish. "An excellent choice."

Vinnie launched into their plan for old Nippy, who, at twenty-three, was actually the youngest member of the society and the hardest to sway, for all he seemed to want was his father's approval and neither she nor Emma could figure out how to get that for him. (The marquess offered no solutions.) Nevertheless, they were working on an approach and thought perhaps the mentorship of an esteemed elder such as the famous naturalist Sir Joseph Banks might make a fine substitution for paternal affection.

One by one, they went through the files, with Huntly pulling a name from the stack as if selecting a card from a deck and Vinnie explaining their strategy for the gentleman. At first, his interest in their scheming had been a sort of appalled fascination, but the more he heard, the more he appreciated their level of detail and clever planning. As he'd noted earlier, it was a challenging game to figure out how all the puzzle pieces fit together.

Before Huntly knew it, an hour had passed, and although he wondered what could possibly take the duchess so long to find his report—perhaps she was compiling it—he appreciated having the time alone with her sister. Somehow, they had managed to restore their easy rapport of the shoe factory outing and he was grateful that Vinnie felt comfortable with him.

That he could not feel comfortable in her presence was a fact established long before this visit, but her recent speech had made an already challenging situation exceedingly difficult. Her honesty astounded him, the way she simply revealed how she was feeling without taking refuge behind white lies or polite whiskers, and he pictured her again in Mr. Brill's office—not the irresistible temptress with the heaving breasts but the brave girl accepting responsibility for her actions (which weren't really her actions). And to call herself docile! It was patently absurd, for Miss Lavinia Harlow did not shrink from anything.

How, he thought as he pulled the last dossier from the pile, could he expect her to shrink from this?

"Mr. Luther Townshend," he said with satisfaction. "I've been waiting all afternoon to discover how you learned of his plagiarism. You and Emma are clearly exhaustive in your research, but that seems like a particularly small needle in an exceptionally large haystack."

"Oh, we did not do all of this," Vinnie said with a laugh. "Emma has a team."

The marquess shook his head. "Why am I not surprised?"

"It is led by the redoubtable Mr. Squibbs, who is the finest lockpick in all of London," she said, sitting on the arm of a commodious leather wingchair. "She sought him out when she wanted to learn how to break into Sir Windbourne's residence."

Surprised, Huntly looked at her sharply. "Your fiancé?"

Vinnie's face turned ashen, and she looked down at her fingers, suddenly avoiding his eyes. "Yes, um, my sister's behavior is not always easy to explain. But suffice to say, she is an excellent judge of character and Mr. Squibbs is her best discovery by far. He is the one who oversaw the team that gathered most of the information. And they did it with remarkable speed."

Hating to see her so anxious and pale, he sought to bring back the amiable companion. "I like your sister."

Some of the color returned to her face, and she smiled faintly. "Me, too."

"I mean to say, I like her for Trent. They seem particularly well suited."

Now the smile was brilliant. "They are."

Realizing he could stand there looking at her all day—and that *that* was truly the untenable position he was in—he tore his eyes away and said, "So Mr. Townshend."

"He was a special case. I actually contributed the information, but it's not as impressive as you think," she added quickly. "The book he plagiarized was written by the vicar in my village, a wonderful, kindly old gentleman who noticed my love of horticulture and nurtured it. He was like a father to me, for my own parents were largely absent. Now that we are grown, my mother attends to us more regularly, but my father remains largely indifferent. He didn't even come to London for Emma's ball, preferring to remain at Viscount Inchape's estate in Tunbridge Wells for a seemingly endless hunting party. Mr. Broughton taught me everything he knew about flowers, which was compiled in a beautiful volume called *Beautiful Wild Flowers of the English Isles*. As soon as I read the first chapter of *Botanicus,* I knew Townshend had stolen most of the material from Mr. Broughton and was deeply offended on his behalf. That is why we are not complying with Trent's request not to use blackmail, with his consent, of course. He agrees the circumstance merits it. However, I will readily admit that in this case I'm settling an old score and if you feel outraged on behalf of your fellow society member, it will be perfectly justified. I'm happy to sit here while you ring a peal over my head."

"Oddly, I find his treatment is the only one I don't object to," he confessed with a sigh, then looked at the desk covered once again with scattered dossiers. So much information, he thought. So much maneuvering. He could not conceive how any of it would turn out. He did not suppose the play he'd set in motion with his careless action could come to any good, but he was done trying to stop it. As Vinnie had said, an invitation had been issued in her name and she alone reserved the right to accept or decline. Neither he nor the dowager was entitled to dictate her response.

The clock on the wall struck three o'clock, and Huntly, realizing just how long he had been there, announced that he should be going. At that moment, the door opened and Emma entered, carrying a tray of tea cakes.

"Look what I found," she announced as she placed the tray on the table in front of the settee. "The dowager was trying to hoard them, but I know where Mrs. Crenshaw keeps the stash. Sit down, please, and I'll arrange for tea."

Without further urging, Vinnie deposited herself on the settee and helped herself to a cake. Huntly, judging the distance from one end of the sofa to the other insufficient, sat in an armchair. Then he watched in amusement as Emma stuck her head outside the doorway and called for the butler.

Caruthers promptly appeared. "May I compliment your grace on successfully crossing the threshold?"

Emma laughed and darted a look that was at once amused and confused to her sister and Huntly, as if to marvel at the odd things servants sometimes say. "It's what I do, Caruthers. Crossing thresholds. Crossing lines. Now, we would really appreciate a pot of tea. Could you please arrange that?"

Caruthers promised to return shortly, and Emma, taking a tea cake for herself, sat down on the settee next to her sister. "I must apologize, Lord Huntly, for being unable to find your dossier. I swear to you that we did compile one, as I'd hate for you to think we are so confident of your vote, we won't try to coerce you. I simply must have misplaced it. I can't imagine where."

"Maybe Alex took it," Vinnie suggested. "He removed his own."

"You compiled a dossier on your husband?" Huntly asked, as amused as he was horrified.

Emma shrugged. "Not intentionally. There was a breakdown in communication between me and my team. Anyway, since I can't seem to find it, why don't you fill us in personally on all the pertinent facts. Remember, we are looking for weaknesses to exploit, so kindly start with your worst failings and work your way up."

Huntly, who had been on the verge of making his excuses, found this request to be so outrageous he had no choice but to comply. "I assure you, my worst traits are dreadfully dull, such as failing to join the captain of the *Triton* for meals because I was too engrossed in my work."

"Don't be modest. I'm sure you have some remarkably

interesting ones, too," she said confidently. "Regardless, every bit helps. Please continue. And don't forget to take a tea cake."

Although he'd had one foot out the door, Huntly consented to stay for a tea cake, and while he ate, he related several tales about life onboard ship. He tried to take his leave again a few minutes later when Tupper brought the tea, for he still had so much to do. Out of five assistant interviews scheduled for the day, he had conducted only two. But Emma insisted he have one cup and he got so much pleasure from hearing Vinnie laugh at his stories that he couldn't refuse. He accepted the one cup and then another, and calling himself a fool, he had a third.

No assistants were hired that day.

CHAPTER TEN

Upon discovering she was the subject of a caricature by the famous Martin Holyroodhouse, Vinnie's first thought was that she was now part of an exclusive club whose exalted membership included Lady Caroline Lamb, Napoleon, Prinny, Beau Brummel, several dozen politicians and Emma.

Her sister's response was not as sanguine, and her angry invectives, which she shouted as she strode from one end of the drawing room to the other, could be heard in the square outside.

"Please have a little respect for my ears, Emma," the dowager said from a chair next to the window. "Although I am aging as fast I can, my hearing remains deplorably strong."

Emma, who was not inclined to comply with any requests when in a rage, actually broke off mid-swear and apologized. "I'm sorry, ma'am. I know I'm not helping, but I can't stand inactivity. I need to do something. Can I not just go down to St. James's and buy out the stock?"

"That's a wonderful idea, my dear," the dowager said kindly. "Your purchasing every print Miss Biddle made won't convince that wretched woman at all to produce more."

Emma sighed and, with a cry of defeat, threw herself onto the sofa, where her sister was sitting silently, her hands clasped stiffly in her lap. Vinnie did not know what to say because she couldn't figure out how she felt. She was horrified by the picture, of course, which depicted all the members of the British Horticultural Society as potted flowers lined up on a windowsill, each of their distinctly recognizable faces surrounded by petals. Standing in front of them was a lampoon of Vinnie holding the Marquess of Huntly flower in her hand. "Plucked!" read the caption.

Her mortification was eased, however, by the illustrious company she was in, and she reviewed the list at regular intervals to bolster her courage.

She was grateful—so absurdly very grateful—for the dowager's mild response, for she had strongly opposed Vinnie's application for exactly this reason and had every right to offer recriminations, especially as she'd exposed the duke to the same indignity. But Trent's mother didn't seem to mind that her only son had been turned into a pink daisy and displayed in the window of 227 St. James.

As surprised as she was by the dowager's calm, she was even more taken aback by her sister's agitation. The Harlow Hoyden had been gracing Miss Biddle's front window for years—as well as Mrs. Humphrey's and Mr. Poolshank's—and she never once flinched at the farcical representations of her exploits. Indeed, she rarely deigned to acknowledge them, knowing that the more attention a picture received, the more encouraged the artist would be. The single worst thing a subject of a caricature could do was complain about the attention. King George himself once took issue with the work of Mr. Gillray, and the unrepentant cartoonist turned around and satirized the monarch's comment in yet another drawing.

Emma understood the futility—at least when it pertained to herself. When it had to do with her defenseless older sister, she railed against the injustice and consigned half the *ton* to hell.

Vinnie was trying not to be offended by this double standard, which, she felt, implied that she was too weak to handle what had been a regular occurrence for the indomitable Miss Harlow. It was true she had little experience with notoriety and she had spent a significant part of her life avoiding unwarranted attention, but that didn't mean she would crumble at the first stroke of an unkind pen.

The door opened and suddenly Louisa appeared on the threshold, her face a mask of distressed concern. "I came as soon as I heard," she announced with all the drama she could muster on such short notice. Then she fell to her knees beside her mother's chair and clutched her hand comfortingly. "You poor, poor dear. How are you holding up?"

Her mother smoothly extricated her hand, stood up and ordered her daughter to stop being so absurd. "Pull yourself together, Louisa, while I have Tupper bring you some tea. It's only a silly drawing. I don't understand why everyone is having agitated fits. Indeed, if you ask me some of those long-in-the-tooth gentlemen should be flattered to be considered among the tulips of the *ton*."

Louisa, who refused to believe her mission of mercy was not vitally necessary, spoke soothingly as if being careful not to alarm a bedlamite. "Of course, Mother, there's no reason to be upset. All is well. Please let me get the tea. You sit down by the window. Look how pretty the sky is."

Although Emma was not the intended target of Louisa's heavy-handed consolation—and a good thing, too, for she would not take as kindly as the dowager to having her shoulders clasped—she recognized in herself a similar strain of insulting histrionics and immediately changed her tone. She straightened up properly in her seat, stopped fidgeting and announced she would love a cup of tea.

"Then I propose we all resume our schedules for the day, for there is no point in our gathering in a single room as if keeping vigil," she said reasonably. "I have an appointment with the modiste at one, then I'm meeting Philip in Hyde Park. Do consider coming, Vinnie. He has acquired a new invention that he is calling a hobble-horse. It's a wooden horse with two wheels that you propel forward with your feet. From what I understand, it's meant to be used on flat terrain, but Philip is determined to try it down a hill."

"Then he will be hobbled for sure," remarked the dowager, who was still trying to overcome her daughter's officious concern. Having liberated her shoulders, she sought refuge behind a wingback chair, which was almost as tall as she. Louisa took her mother's behavior as proof of her frailty—needing a chair for support!—and redoubled her efforts.

Emma enjoyed the display immensely and was disappointed when Louisa went off to locate smelling salts as a precautionary measure.

"Shall I barricade the door, ma'am?" Emma asked as soon as her sister-in-law had left. "I have an infallible system."

Although the dowager was sorely tempted, she knew better than to encourage Emma in her antics. Furthermore, she was still peeved at her recent locked-door stunt, for she had quickly figured out that the game had been rigged against her. "I agree with your suggestion that we proceed with our day as if nothing untoward has happened because, if you will recall, that was my original suggestion. It is always distressing to see representations of oneself, but you mustn't let it upset you. I assure you, your elbows are not that pointy."

Both Harlow girls, who had never thought twice about their elbows, examined their arms while the dowager hid a smile.

Tupper brought the tea and Vinnie accepted a cup, but she did not participate in Emma and the dowager's discussion about Philip's recent acquisition. Although she did not know how to account for Emma's altered attitude, she was grateful for it. An infuriated Harlow Hoyden was a terrifying force, and Vinnie hated to think of what act of reprisal she might devise for poor Mr. Holyroodhouse.

Vinnie herself wasn't entirely above thoughts of revenge. She loathed the clever caricaturist for the skilled way he neatly summed up a complicated situation with a single image, making them all look like fools. The drawing of her was particularly unflattering, with her jabby elbows, bulbous nose, pointy chin, smug smile and eyebrows so heavily drawn she looked like a witch out of a child's fairy story. But the true victim of the piece was Huntly. Ruthlessly pulled from his pot, he was literally in the hands of a hideous woman, a hen-pecked milksop with no recourse. The caption said it all: He was plucked. Having created the unpleasant circumstance, it was now beyond his control and he could do nothing but submit to the mockery of the *ton*.

Although she knew it was just a drawing, Vinnie found it intolerable to see Huntly portrayed as weak and helpless when he was in fact the very opposite. No weak and helpless man would survive nearly two years at sea, collecting hundreds of specimens from dozens of tiny islands inhabited by dangerous fauna and most likely ill-bred cannibals. The Marquess of Huntly was strong and capable, and he didn't deserve the ridicule.

Vinnie, who thought her sister's agitation in defense of her was insulting, discovered she was too angry on Huntly's behalf to sit still. She ordered herself to calm down and finish her tea, but she simply could not stand it a moment more and jumped to her feet.

The dowager, finding her actions jarring, exhorted her to move with more delicacy. As Vinnie murmured an apology, Louisa returned to announce the completion of her five-point plan for Overcoming a Caricature Scandal. She held her list up triumphantly, and just as Emma grabbed it from her hand, Vinnie snuck out of the drawing room to pay a visit to Huntly. She was putting on her pelisse when she heard Emma exclaim, "Disavow all familiarity with the participants! Am I to pretend I don't know my own sister? Or husband, for that matter?"

Smiling faintly, Vinnie quietly let herself out the front door and quickly traversed the few blocks to the marquess's house. It had been five days since she'd seen him—five days since he'd come upon them in the study plotting the downfall of his fellow society members. She'd expected to hear from him in the interval, during which she and Emma had continued to negotiate deals for votes, but he had not been in contact. As she had expected further coercion, especially after he understood the thoroughness of their plan, she didn't know what to make of his silence. It seemed to imply a certain disgust of her and the enterprise in which she was engaged, but that was not the impression he'd given the other day. Indeed, upon taking his leave after several cups of tea, he'd appeared to be wryly amused by her endeavors.

Having left the house on impulse, Vinnie did not think to bring a maid, and standing alone on Huntly's doorstep, about to request entry into a bachelor's residence, she suddenly felt like a jabby-elbowed fishwife. Abruptly, she turned to leave and found herself face-to-face with the man himself.

His cheerful greeting died on his lips as he observed her look of distress. "Is something wrong, Miss Harlow?" he asked.

Vinnie, who had caught the easy smile before it faded, was surprised to find him in such good humor and could only conclude that he did not yet know of Mr. Holyroodhouse's drawing. It seemed unlikely that he could have passed an entire morning in ignorance—she had learned of the truth from a note delivered to the dowager only minutes after breakfast had been served—yet she could not conceive how any man who had seen himself depicted as an enfeebled flower could not be out of sorts.

"May I have a word, my lord?" she asked, looking around anxiously. If standing on the marquess's doorstep by herself had made her feel like the brazen harpy in the illustration, it was nothing compared with the uncomfortable sensation of standing on the marquess's doorstep *with* the marquess. She resisted the urge to curl her back and hide behind his broad shoulders.

He immediately agreed and upon entering the house, requested that tea be delivered to the drawing room at once. Then he paused and said, "No, Fleming, bring it to my study. Miss Harlow is as gifted a horticulturalist as her brother-in-law and would enjoy looking at some of my samples."

Vinnie, who found the heavy burden of her guilt already almost too much to carry, visibly shrunk under the weight of this kind tribute. "I really don't think—"

But Huntly wasn't listening to her attempt to demur, for he was asking his butler to retrieve a magnifying glass from the desk in his bedroom. Then he led her down the hall to his study, a bright room with red silk drapes, a large desk and several hefty crates aligned against the long wall.

"Please sit down and tell me what's on your mind," he said, indicating a cream-colored chair on the near side of the desk.

Grateful to have a large piece of oak furniture between them, Vinnie complied with his request and was dismayed when the marquess sat in the matching chair beside her, rather than the imposing wingback on the other side of the desk.

Sitting stiffly, although the chair was actually quite comfortable, she said quickly and with no preamble, "I am withdrawing my application for membership."

As soon as the words were out, Vinnie felt some of the tension leave her. She had known from the moment Tupper had returned from Miss Biddle's shop with the print—no, even earlier than that, when her grace read aloud Lady Courtland's description—that she had to withdraw. She was no milksop herself and as long as the scandal remained focused on her, she had no trouble ignoring her critics or outlasting the naysayers. She had found the challenge invigorating and enjoyed every minute she'd spent scheming with Emma over the dossiers.

There had been only one moment previously when she had thought about withdrawing—the other day when Huntly had called and Emma left them alone with the files. How happy she had been to see him striding into the room! Even after the awful turn he had done with the Brill factory tour, she'd felt her heart leap with excitement with his unexpected arrival. And because of it, she had carelessly revealed that Emma had broken into her fiancé's apartment. It was a stupid gaffe to make and attributable to the level of comfort she felt in the company of the marquess. If she'd felt more self-conscious around him, she would never have been so thoughtless. But it wasn't the slip that bothered Vinnie and made her rethink her admission into the society; it was the realization that she wanted to keep sliding. In that moment, she'd wanted to tell him everything about her relationship with Windbourne.

Such a confession would have been fatal, for she knew how terribly the entire episode—duped into an engagement by a traitorous spy whom she killed and then pretended to mourn for the sake of respectability—reflected on her. If Mr. Holyroodhouse's illustration made her look monstrous, it was nothing compared to what her own story would do to her.

Craving his good opinion, Vinnie could not risk losing it. She had his respect and knew the exact moment she'd earned it: in the distillation lab when Mr. Brill complimented her on her idea for how to improve the elasticity of India-rubber molecules. Huntly had turned and stared at her with such a glint in his eye. If she hadn't known better, she would have called it pride, but that was far too unlikely so it had to be respect.

That afternoon in Emma's study, appalled by her own admission and terrified by how easily she could give it all away, she'd thought about ending her candidacy right then and there. She couldn't bring herself to do it because she knew it also mean ending their association, something she was curiously unwilling to do.

But now she had done it, and the other Harlow girl's turn as a hoyden was over. She breathed deeply and felt the sigh almost pour out of her. Withdrawing was the right thing to do, for now Mr. Holyroodhouse and his ilk could turn their poisoned pens elsewhere.

"No," Huntly said.

Vinnie had been so wrapped up in her thoughts, she assumed she'd missed an entire conversation. "Excuse me?"

"No, you are not withdrawing your application for membership," he said firmly.

Although she could not imagine what brought about

this change of heart, it did not matter. "I am."

"You're not."

Vinnie tilted her head down, straightened her shoulders and folded her hands in her lap. Then, as if all that stood between her statement and the marquess's acceptance was bad posture, she said, "I am withdrawing."

Huntly crossed his legs. "You are not withdrawing."

"You don't seem to understand," she said carefully enunciating every word just in case unclear speech was the problem. "I'm withdrawing my candidacy. As of this moment, I'm no longer applying for membership to your society."

"And you don't seem to understand," he said with the same precision, "that you're not. You are going to go forward with your application. In fact, your treatise is due in three days and your presentation is scheduled for one week from tomorrow."

Vinnie jerked her head back, then shook it. "No."

"Yes."

Feeling as if she had stumbled into a play being performed by French-speaking actors, she paused for a moment to evaluate the situation. By all accounts, she was who she thought she was, Miss Lavinia Harlow; the gentleman across from her was the Marquess of Huntly; and they were both seated in the marquess's study. She was, after weeks of resisting, finally giving in to his demand that she withdraw. Huntly should say thank you and bid her good day.

Why wasn't he saying thank you and bidding her good day?

She recalled then that he didn't have all the available information necessary for making the right decision. "My lord, although I appreciate this unprecedented and inexplicable show of support—and please believe I am grateful for it—there seems to be a circumstance of which you are not aware."

"Plucked!" he said.

He said it so emphatically, Vinnie jumped. "You know."

"That I've been plucked?" he asked with a smile. "For a while now, yes."

Vinnie was confused by his amusement. "Then you must see that I can't continue."

"No, Miss Harlow, what I see is that you must continue," he said softly with that strange glint in his eyes. It was respect, Vinnie told herself. It couldn't be anything else.

Vinnie paused, took a deep breath, calmly ordered her thoughts and said without a hint of agitation, "My lord, for several weeks you have been trying to get me to withdraw, and now I am complying with your request. Can you please explain to me why you've changed your mind?"

Mimicking her overly serene pose, he said, "I'm happy to, Miss Harlow. It is true that previously I opposed your application to the society and had devoted a good deal of energy in the past two weeks to trying to change your mind. I can understand why you might find my change of heart confusing, especially in the light of Mr. Holyroodhouse's masterpiece, but it is because of Mr. Holyroodhouse's masterpiece that I did change my mind."

"You are teasing me," Vinnie said, unable to find any other explanation. "You know that illustration is horrid and that I have no choice but to withdraw to avoid more humiliation for all parties involved, so you are pretending that you don't want me to as a joke. You are getting back at me for causing you all this distress."

"The only distress you have caused me is the possibility that you might truly think so little of me as to believe that," he said with a seriousness she'd never heard from him before.

"I'm sorry," she said quickly, for *she* hated the thought of distressing *him*. "I'm afraid it has been a rather trying day. Of course I don't believe that."

He smiled. "Miss Harlow, if you had complied with my request any time in the past few weeks, I would have been relieved and grateful. That's the honest truth, as they say. But it is one thing for you to follow the advice of someone who is genuinely concerned about your welfare and the welfare of an institution he has belonged to for almost a decade. There is no shame in that. It is another thing entirely to cave to pressure from a toad-eating dandiprat with a pen. That is a mortification to which I cannot lend my countenance. Now," he said, in a more businesslike tone, "you asked me once if I would review your treatise and offer advice on how you may improve it. I'm afraid I was remiss in responding to your request at the time, but I would like to remedy that now. Please forward me a copy."

Vinnie felt like her head was spinning, so abrupt and complete was the marquess's change of heart. She couldn't accept his offer. He was only one of twenty-six members and surely the remaining twenty-five, excluding Alex, of course, wished she'd cave to pressure posthaste. But she would treasure it always. "I will ruin your club," she said sadly, thinking of the damage the illustration had already done. If she continued in her quest, more ridicule and mockery would inevitably follow.

Unswayed by her concern, he simply shook his head. "If a slip of a girl can ruin my club, then it was a paltry thing to begin with and I say good riddance."

Not knowing what to do with such outstanding graciousness, for she had never experienced anything like it before, Vinnie sought to make light of it. "Admit it. The only reason you want me to apply is because I said I won't. You're trying to thwart me."

"Not just you," the marquess said with a smile, remembering their previous conversation as clearly as she. "Mr. Holyroodhouse, too. And any number of bettors who are aligned against you at Brooks's. I can't decide who I'd like to thwart more."

Accepting defeat reluctantly, Vinnie offered a compromise, "I will cease my coercive tactics."

The marquess managed to look disappointed. "Not the plagiarizing Mr. Townshend, as well! It's a pleasure watching him squirm on your hook."

Despite her agitation, Vinnie laughed. "I have corrupted you."

Huntly leaned forward so that his knees were almost

touching Vinnie's and said in a suddenly low voice, "*Please corrupt me.*"

His look was so intense, his unsettling aquamarine eyes so bright, that Vinnie immediately flushed to the tips of her ears and hastily jumped to her feet, suddenly aware of the impropriety of her rash visit. "I see you have a lot of work to do, so I will let you get back to it."

The marquess stood as well. "I don't deserve such kindness. Please stay for tea. We haven't even touched it."

Stay for tea? Vinnie thought wildly, as emotion coursed through her. She couldn't possibly remain alone with him in his study for the length of an entire cup of tea. The idea was far too dangerous. Without question, she was at risk of revealing all her deep, dark secrets, but that concern paled in comparison to the peril posed by the revelation that had just struck her: It had *not* been the moment—in Mr. Brill's office, the compulsion that moved her to kiss him, the once-in-a-lifetime confluence of forces. No, it was not the remarkable convergence of events that had compelled her; it was Huntly himself.

"Thank you," she said firmly, if a little desperately, "but I really should go."

"Are you sure I cannot tempt you with exotic flora from far-off lands?" he asked cajolingly. "The crates in this room are filled with specimens waiting to be cataloged, for I have yet to hire an assistant. You would be doing me a huge favor if you could name one or two. I fear I'm running out of ideas and might start naming a few after myself, which is a practice I heartily disapprove of."

At this stunning offer, Vinnie felt something inside her twist painfully, for she would love nothing more than to bestow a name on a rare and wonderful flower. In the whole of her life, she never imagined getting such an opportunity, and everything inside her demanded that she say yes—yes, please, I would be honored and grateful and humbled and thrilled. But how could she stay with this new awareness throbbing inside her? And his offer only made it worse, for it revealed a generosity of spirit that exacerbated the compulsion.

She had to leave now.

Ruthlessly tamping down agonizing regret, she said calmly, "I am sure, my lord, but thank you for the generous offer."

"So you are just going to cruelly abandon me to my work?" he asked with an eyebrow raised.

He looked so endearing standing there in the middle of his study with all the trunks and crates, a forlorn explorer amidst the abundance of his adventures. "Yes, my lord."

"Fair enough," he said. "I'll have Fleming show you out."

"Please don't bother. I can find the front door myself."

Huntly nodded. "And you'll send me your treatise?"

In order to facilitate her leaving, she agreed to have it brought over right away, but in fact she knew she needed to write several more drafts before it was ready for perusal. There were sections she was pleased with—sections that had a lot of energy and focus—but overall the paper was too dry and academic. Maybe she would rework the introductory passage to start with the Stolen Trent, which was the orchid she'd made by hybridizing the *Rhyncholaelia digbyana* Emma had stolen from the duke with her own *Altensteinia nubigena*, to demonstrate the collaborative nature of horticulture. Or was that point of view too personal and— God forbid—too sentimental?

Vinnie kept her mind stubbornly focused on the question the whole way home, and when she finished the introduction to her satisfaction, she moved on to the next section. She spent the rest of the day and much of the night revising her treatise, and by the time she stopped, somewhere a little north of midnight, she was too exhausted to think of anything save sleep.

But in the morning, when she woke up, the first thing she thought of was the Marquess of Huntly's aquamarine eyes begging her to corrupt him.

Damn it.

CHAPTER ELEVEN

Huntly had been so determined not to seek out the Duke of Trent that when he finally found him—playing hazard at the Elder Davis on King Street—he was angry at the both of them.

"You're not at Mrs. Pleydell's musicale," he said accusingly as he came to stand behind him at the crowded baize table.

Trent kept his eyes trained firmly on his cousin Philip, who was shaking a pair of dice in his right hand. "No, I'm not."

"Neither are you at Covent Gardens."

Philip blew on the dice twice, jiggled them once more and tossed them onto the table. The crowd cheered as the main of six was established. "Likewise correct," the duke said.

"Nor are you at Lady Malmesbury's rout or Viscount Onslow's card party or any of your clubs," he said crossly.

Trent looked at his friend with an impatient glare and said, "No, I am here. My greenhead cousin has decided it was time he learned how to callously lose his quarterly income just like every other young pup in town, so I am here, at this hazard table, keeping an eye on him, a task that was already a dead bore before you started this tedious conversation."

The crowd grumbled, indicating that Philip had thrown out, and the duke turned back to the table in time to watch his cousin handing the dice to Lord Fellingham. He waited to see if his cousin made any side bets and was relieved when he walked away from the table.

Not put off by his friend's show of temper, Huntly persisted. "We need to talk."

Trent took a step back to make room for another misguided hopeful. "Now is not a good time," he said, wondering what game Philip would play next. He'd already been dunned at faro and vingt-et-un. Fortunately, the lad seemed to have little tolerance for losing and kept moving on in hopes of finding the game at which he could prevail. As the duke knew this was very unlikely to happen, he assumed they would be leaving soon.

"Now is the perfect time," Huntly said forcefully, clutching Trent by the elbow.

At the rough handling, temper flashed across the duke's face, but when he looked into his friend's eyes, he saw something like desperation and said, "All right. Let me talk to Philip."

No sooner had Trent made that statement than his cousin came over to announce that he was leaving with his friend Major Timothy Powis of the 10th Hussars. "Wants to show off his velocipede. I don't think it will be more impressive than my hobbled-horse because it's French and the Frenchies don't know how to build anything, but I don't want to be rude. Besides, this place is as boring as a yard of tin."

As Philip walked away, Huntly said with some of his old composure, "I've never known you to cub-sit before."

"And I hope you never will again," Trent assured him. "Emma is fond of the pup—he helped her out of a scrape a while ago—and she insisted I come. Actually, she insisted *she* come, but I thought it was wiser if I took the helm. Otherwise, we would no doubt have two new Mr. Holyroodhouse prints in the family. Now that we've gotten rid of the cawker, let's go to my club for a glass of port and you can tell me what has you in a high dudgeon."

Huntly gratefully followed him to the door, but as soon as they were outside, he said, "We don't have time for your club. We're going to the Rusty Plinth, where I'm sure you can get port, though, admittedly, it might do more harm than good."

The duke halted. "The Rusty Plinth? Is that a new hell?"

Impatient, the marquess gave Trent's shoulder a gentle push. He'd spent the last week resisting the urge to investigate Vinnie's fiancé—six bloody days of fighting a single overwhelming compulsion—and now that he'd given in to it, he was eager to start. "It's a tavern on the docks where we have an appointment—or, rather, did, several hours ago. I've had the devil's own time tracking you down, your grace. Next time, go to Mrs. Pleydell's musicale."

"Felix, I would swear you were tap-hackled, but I can't detect a whiff of alcohol on you," the duke said.

"I am not the least disguised, though I did have half an ale at the Rusty Plinth, so I am a little bit crooked. We'll take your coach," he said and gave Trent's driver the direction.

Curious now, the duke climbed into his carriage and waited for Huntly to settle across from him before asking why they were going to a tavern on the docks.

"I am trying to commission a dossier on Sir Waldo Windbourne from Mr. Squibbs, and he will agree to accept the assignment only with the consent of you or your wife," he stated boldly. "As I assumed you did not want me to take your wife to a taproom on the docks, I've requested your presence. If I am wrong, please tell me and I will drop you at your club while I pick up Emma, who is, by the way, at Mrs. Pleydell's musicale, exactly as she's supposed to be."

Although this was an extraordinary speech to be sure, the only thing that truly surprised the duke was that his wife stayed at Mrs. Pleydell's musicale for more than five minutes. Having heard her daughter perform on an earlier occasion, he knew how quickly her voice made one's ears bleed.

That Huntly wanted to know more about Vinnie's recently deceased fiancé was only to be expected, as it was probably most disconcerting to find oneself enamored of a lady who was in mourning for someone else. Trent knew that if he had been in the same situation with Emma, he would have been jealous of the dead man and annoyed at himself for being jealous of a dead man and angry that he could do nothing about either. For this reason, Huntly's interest in Windbourne was understandable and not at all remarkable. What was remarkable was the route he had taken in asking Mr. Squibbs to compile a dossier. That development was certainly surprising, and he appreciated the clever lockpick's caution in requiring his permission first.

Of course, the duke would not give it. It was not that he thought his oldest friend was unworthy of knowing the truth, for he trusted Huntly as he trusted himself. In fact, nothing would delight him more than to share the whole story, as it would give him an opportunity to boast of Emma's bravery and quick thinking and striking resourcefulness. Nobody was better at getting out of a scrape than his wife—though, to be fair, nobody was better at getting into one, too.

But the entire tale hinged on Vinnie and Trent knew what difficult waters those were to navigate. As she refused to talk about it, he could not pinpoint how she felt about the debacle that was her engagement, though he suspected she still felt the humiliation of being a dupe. It was natural to blame one's self for being taken in too easily, but it required a particular kind of resolution to remain indifferent to a person bent on earning your good opinion. He knew this from personal experience, as he himself had fallen prey to determined flattery when he was a callow youth like Philip.

Even if her ego had not succumbed to that shameful sting, there was still the matter of her fiancé's bloody death at her hand. Vinnie claimed to feel no remorse and he sincerely hoped it was true, for Sir Windbourne had been a villain who had betrayed every kindness of king and country and had compelled Vinnie to take his life in order to save her own.

But there, too, he knew the issue was not that simple and could well imagine how challenging it was to reconcile the cold, hard necessity of ending a life with the soul-crushing reality of taking one. The process could not be without its emotional ramifications, and he worried that in refusing to acknowledge them, Vinnie had made them worse.

Being forced to pretend to mourn for the man she killed did not improve circumstances, for it required her to publicly pay tribute to a human being she thoroughly despised. Nor did lying sit comfortably with her. An essentially honest person, she chafed at the pretense of false grief and longed to shout the truth from the rooftops.

Emma, feeling similarly stifled by the lie, had made up that absurd story about Sir Windbourne and the corset, which gave vent to her spleen but had the unfortunate effect of making Vinnie the target of speculation and ridicule. She went from being the almost-widow of an obscure baron to the almost-widow of that comically vain man who squeezed himself to death.

It was an intolerable situation for everyone, but giving Mr. Squibbs permission to dig up the entire story would not alleviate it. No, the only thing that would help was Vinnie finding the courage to confide all to Huntly. If she could not, then the two would never have a future together.

That Huntly and Vinnie should have a future together was something he was now willing to concede. When Emma had originally suggested a match on the flimsy pretext of Vinnie's dislike, he'd thought his wife was building castles out of clouds. But then the marquess called Vinnie difficult and he realized his friend was similarly afflicted. Now he could only conclude that his friend was top over tails, for why else would any sane-thinking man venture out to a shoe factory in the wilds of Acton Vale?

Having survived a courtship of the Harlow Hoyden, Trent knew the many twisted turns the path of true love could take and was fully sympathetic to his friend's plight. But that didn't mean he couldn't needle him a bit.

"Before I consider your request, please explain to me your interest in Sir Windbourne," Trent said.

Huntly, who had not intended to request anything, glared balefully at the duke and growled angrily.

"I'm sorry, I did not hear that clearly," Trent said.

Knowing he was on the ropes, the marquess clenched his fists restlessly and repeated himself. "The puzzle."

The duke had no idea what this meant, but he recognized the dodge of a man in love and respected the effort. "The puzzle?"

"Yes," he said impatiently. "Several things in regard to Miss Harlow's engagement do not fit together, and I would like to solve the puzzle."

"To what end?"

The marquess sighed loudly. Damn Alex and his sudden curiosity! Once Huntly had come home from a night of carousing with eight green lines drawn on each of his cheeks and Trent didn't say a word. Now he was asking more questions than a Bow Street Runner. It was insupportable! "My own edification," he said mildly.

"Well, then, for your own edification, I can assure you that the facts of Miss Harlow's engagement fit together perfectly. Do not tease yourself further."

If anything, Huntly's baleful glare grew more malevolent. "If you truly believe that, Trent, then you are a fool. Miss Harlow is one of the most honest, intelligent and sincere people I've ever met, and by all reports her fiancé was a pompous windbag who loved the sound of his own voice and was so vain he crushed himself to death with his own corset. The story of his demise is so preposterous, I cannot credit it. Are we really to believe a grown man would behave so outrageously? Then there's the matter of the duchess, your wife, breaking into the apartments of her own sister's fiancé. What cause could she have for taking such an extraordinary measure? Clearly, there's something havey-cavey afoot and I mean to discover what it is. If you are not willing to concede the validity of my questions, please be kind enough to give me permission to pursue them with some-one who will."

The only thing Trent was willing to concede was that Huntly's pretext of knowledge for knowledge's sake was the most preposterous thing he'd ever heard. "If you have ques-tions, you owe Vinnie the courtesy of answering them her-self. Snooping behind a person's back has never been known to further a relationship."

Huntly, who did not consider it snooping—such an in-trusive word—to commission a dossier, professed not to understand why his friend would describe his intermittent interaction with Miss Harlow as something so constant as a relationship. "As I said, my interest is merely in solving the puzzle she presents."

Trent hid a smile as the coach came to a stop. "Of course. I meant to say that snooping has never been known to further the completion of a puzzle. I suggest you consult Vinnie."

As he had never doubted the outcome of the conversa-tion, Huntly could scarcely believe what he was hearing, and he fixed the duke with another angry glare just as the door to the coach opened. "Are you denying my request?"

"Yes, and I expect Emma will do the same should you decide to return to Mrs. Pleydell's musicale to ask her. If you do, I caution you to bring cotton for your ears. Her daugh-ter singing an Italian aria sounds oddly like two tomcats fighting in an alley, which, for all I know, might be your taste in music, in which case, forgo the cotton," Trent said unhelpfully. "Alternatively, you could decide to stay and we can have that port you promised me."

Determined to argue his case further, Huntly followed the duke out of the carriage and spun around in surprise as he spotted the famous bow window of White's. "Why are we not at the docks?"

"Barkley and I have a system by which he looks to me whenever someone orders him to drive to a dangerous part of the city in the dark of night and I countermand it with a shake of my head," the duke explained, leading his friend toward the door. "It's a very subtle gesture so I'm not surprised you missed it."

Although Huntly was exceedingly annoyed at having his will thwarted a second time, he recognized the futility of arguing with the duke, who was always resolute in his decisions. He had fleetingly considered following his advice and seeking out the duchess, but he knew gaining her consent was even unlikelier, for Miss Harlow's sister would most definitely apply the term *snooping* to the benign act of puzzle solving.

Huntly hoped to continue his conversation with the duke in a quiet corner—futility had never deterred him before—but White's was crowded with familiar faces and they had to stop several times to greet friends. Even after a week, Mr. Holyroodhouse's masterpiece was still a favorite topic of conversation, and they both accepted the gentle ribbing of their peers without flinching. Huntly, in particular, refused to be goaded by their teasing, for what he had told Vinnie was the truth: He would not let a mushroomy upstart with a pen have any effect on his behavior.

Although he had decided before the publication of the offensive drawing that he would cease trying to change Miss Harlow's mind, he'd been shocked to hear himself decline her offer to withdraw. Only minutes before he'd discovered her on his doorstep, he had been seething at the insult dealt to the British Horticultural Society and cursing her stubbornness in creating an impossible situation. He willingly accepted his own culpability in the affair—plucked indeed!—but what man could be held accountable for the irrational response of an unreasonable woman?

The Miss Harlow who showed up at his town house that day had been an entirely reasonable creature. Understanding fully the awkward position in which she had put them all, she behaved properly and honorably by offering to remove herself. It was something she should have done weeks before, but no matter. She had finally done it—and with all the bravery he had come to expect from her.

And then he had turned her down.

How that came about, he still wasn't sure. Just that morning, he had been sitting at his desk wishing she would withdraw and then a few hours later she was sitting at his desk actually withdrawing and then just as unexpectedly he was sitting at the same desk saying no. The only explanation he could offer was inadequate, for it extended from some vague discomfort he'd felt in listening to her speech. He knew she was trying to restore dignity to all of them with her act, but all he saw was her shrinking—she, who never shrank. It offended him more than the drawing.

For days, he'd tried to understand his own behavior and yet all he kept coming back to was Miss Harlow's comment that her sister broke into Sir Windbourne's apartments. It was, as far as he could tell, the sole inconsistency in her story and the only indication that perhaps her beloved fiancé wasn't the paragon she'd made him out to be.

In seeking out Mr. Squibbs, he hoped to discover—

The truth was, he didn't know what he hoped to discover. All he wanted was a better handle on the situation. What he had told Trent was true, for Miss Lavinia Harlow was in fact a mystery to him, but the true puzzle was why he cared to solve it. There was something about her that pulled at him, something that had compelled him to offer her the most lavish gift he had—the opportunity to name a flower—in an attempt to get her to stay in his study for just a few minutes more.

Felix Horatio Dryden was a man accustomed to knowing his own mind, and he did not appreciate acting in ways inexplicable to himself. Unable to understand his own feelings, he decided action must be taken, and being a man of science, he knew acquiring knowledge was the best way to gain insight into an incomprehensible phenomenon. A dossier on Mr. Windbourne was the logical place to start.

He had not anticipated Mr. Squibbs, a remarkable gentleman indeed, taking an avuncular interest in the Harlow sisters and refusing to act without approval. He'd assume a

London lockpick would be up for sale to the highest bidder, and to discover instead a moral backbone that refused to bend to monetary inducement frustrated him to no end. Nor did he expect Trent to deny him, which, he admitted now, was naïve, for naturally the duke was protective of both his wife and her family. What he proposed was intrusive, he could see that now, and he should have approached the delicate manner in a less direct way to gain his friend's approval.

Huntly silently admitted that he hadn't been acting like himself lately, and as soon as he and Trent sat down in comfortable armchairs in the cardroom, he said, "Miss Harlow came to withdraw her application and I refused."

Trent waited for the server to deliver their port, then nodded approvingly. "If she had made the offer to me, I would have done the same thing."

The marquess laughed faintly. "Yes, but you don't want her to withdraw, while I, the architect of this mad charade, do."

"Then why did you refuse?"

Realizing that saying it aloud had made it no easier to understand, Huntly shrugged. "I don't know. I suppose the caricature seemed like bullying, and as a gentleman, I find that sort of behavior offensive."

Trent nodded as if this explanation was sufficient and in many ways it was, for he felt confident he understood what motivated his friend better than he did. The duke had heard all about Huntly's recent visit from Emma, who had stationed herself outside the study door for the entire hour she was ostensibly looking for the marquess's dossier. She claimed it was for the sake of propriety, as if that obscure notion had ever penetrated her brain, but her real purpose was to spy and her so-called fact-finding mission discovered an encouraging rapport between the subjects.

"He teased her and she teased him," Emma had reported, "and every so often there was an extended pause during which I could only imagine they were staring deeply into each other's eyes. I'm also happy to report that he still hasn't found an assistant to help with his book. Vinnie will be perfect for the job. We must get her to apply."

Before Huntly could try to explain himself further, Mr. Luther Townshend interrupted their tête-à-tête to thank the marquess for removing the threat of Miss Harlow. "I had a note from her last week assuring me that she had no intention of using the scurrilous information and encouraging me to vote on her membership according to my conscience. I don't know how you convinced her that her blackmail scheme was not only immoral but an affront to all womanhood, but I'm grateful for your success."

As he had actually done the opposite, Huntly wasn't sure how to respond and settled on demurring, which was only the truth. "Miss Harlow withstood my arguments and changed her mind for reasons of her own."

"Knowing the woman, I highly doubt that," Townshend said with a sly wink, "but I respect your modesty. In any case, the matter has been resolved to my satisfaction, which I never doubted. Had you not succeeded in reasoning with the hussy, I would have come to an agreement of my own with her using secret information that I had gathered, for she is not the only one who can compile dossiers."

Although the idea of Townshend acquiring secret information about Vinnie would ordinarily catch Huntly's attention, he was too incensed by his description of her to pay it proper heed. His hand constricted tightly around the glass of port as he forced himself to remain seated. It would not do to cause a scene in White's, for that would only draw further unwanted attention to Miss Harlow. "I must remind you that the lady in question is the duke's sister-in-law," he said in icy tones, "and he might not relish hearing her described in such terms."

Trent wiped an imaginary white fleck from the shoulder of his topcoat and said with quiet menace, "I do not."

Townshend flinched as he recalled Trent's reputation as a skilled pugilist, but he was far too sensible to be intimidated by the younger man. The duke could hardly strike him in the cardroom of the gentlemen's club and would certainly not ambush him in a dark alley. That sort of behavior was beneath the both of them. For this reason, he stood his ground, acknowledging the relationship with a stiff bow to the duke. "With all due respect, your grace, you are aware of the family into which you married."

Far from riling the duke further, this comment seemed to lighten his mood. "Indeed, I am," he said with a faint smile.

As he had not intended to amuse the duke with his intentionally provoking comment, Townshend was at a loss as to how to respond. Deciding he must have made his point so well that Trent could do naught but concede, he chose to walk away while he was still a point up. "I will leave you to your port now. I'm glad we had this conversation, and I look forward to seeing you tomorrow at Miss Harlow's presentation. I'm sure it will be fascinating."

Naturally, he said the word *fascinating* with a highly meaningful emphasis that implied it would be anything but fascinating.

"I'm sure it will," agreed Huntly, who didn't doubt that the evening would very interesting, regardless of the quality of Miss Harlow's presentation.

As soon as Townshend was out of earshot, Trent leaned forward and said, "It's not sporting of me to say, but I was actually quite pleased when Vinnie revealed the plagiarism charge to me. Townshend has always been too high in the instep for my comfort, and I liked the idea of his self-esteem being punctured."

Huntly sipped his port. "I never particularly minded his superciliousness, but in recent weeks, I've begun to find myself annoyed by it. In fact, I tried to encourage Miss Harlow to continue applying pressure to him, but she insisted on stopping all her machinations in the wake of the cartoon. That was, I believe, the compromise we struck, as she is unlikely to gain admittance without using coercion in one form or another."

"So it is as good as withdrawing," the duke observed.

"Exactly," Huntly said and thought about the events that would unfold the next night in the lecture hall of the British Horticultural Society. Despite the bravado he showed Townshend, the marquess felt a sense of dread every time he imagined Miss Harlow standing at the podium in the vast room filled with men who had gathered to mock and ridicule her. He wished with everything he was that he could save her from that.

"Does she have your vote?" Huntly asked.

"Yes," Trent said simply. "Does she have yours?"

"She does," Huntly said with an abrupt nod, "though I don't know if that is doing her a favor."

The duke considered him silently for several moments as he drank his port, and finishing the glass, indicated with a wave that he'd like another one. He understood how Huntly felt because he felt it, too. He knew their fellow members for the tough-minded, proud men they were, and not a single one of them would consider admitting a female into their club as an equal. Without a gentle finger pressed on the scale to tip it her way, he didn't doubt Vinnie would be rejected, and if it were up to him to decide, she would bow out of the presentation.

It was to the good, then, that it wasn't his decision to make, for if he had learned one thing from loving Emma, it was that you couldn't stop a person from being who she was. All you could do was stop yourself from being with her.

Trent didn't actually know what Felix would do when he discovered the truth about Vinnie. He had a strong suspicion in which direction he would fall, but it was impossible to know someone else's heart and mind completely. But he knew enough of his friend's to take the risk, so while the waiter refilled his glass, he told the marquess one more time to ask Vinnie about Sir Windbourne.

CHAPTER TWELVE

It was a revelation for Vinnie to discover that the fearless Harlow Hoyden was a complete coward when it came to watching her sister take a risk. She was one hundred percent behind Vinnie's application, and she knew she would make a staggering presentation that would leave the members of the British Horticultural Society stunned. But she couldn't seem to sit still in anticipation of the event. The entire day, she jittered and hovered and fussed and at one point she even said she wished she could simply fall asleep at that very moment and wake up when the whole ordeal was over.

Vinnie, who had spent her entire life jittering and hovering and fussing and wishing she could breeze past the more-tense moments of Emma's life in an unconscious fog (a certain trip to Dover in the company of a murderer sprang to mind), was torn between amusement and affront at this unexpected development. As the older sibling, it naturally fell to her to protect her younger sister, a responsibility, she felt, that did not go both ways. In contrast, Emma had always considered the nine minutes that separated them an accident of birth, not an allocation of roles, and found her sibling's point of view to be as limiting as it was offensive.

An enthusiastic debate followed, which, during its full

hour, provided much fodder for the fascinated servants, and when the duke looked into the study midway through to see Emma rattling off a list of occasions in which she had protected her older sister from harm or censure, Vinnie caught his eye and winked. She was doing what she always did—in this case, protecting her little sister from worrying about her.

When Emma finally figured out what was going on, she halted in midsentence and then cited the current argument as proof of Vinnie's appalling behavior in their current argument about Vinnie's appalling behavior. Instantly contrite, Vinnie apologized for coddling her sister to an excessive degree, which Emma took as further proof of excessive coddling.

In the end, Vinnie was relieved to have spent one full hour when she wasn't compulsively practicing her presentation in her head. As soon as she and Emma resolved their dispute, the compulsion resumed and she discovered that the more she reviewed it, the more mistakes she made. Seeking a distraction, she tried to get the dowager to chastise her again for inappropriately applying for membership, but her grace, being of the what's-done-is-done school, insisted on supporting her decision by thoughtfully lecturing her on how to improve her speech. In total, she provided twelve tips, which ranged from actually helpful ("Do not grasp the podium so tightly that your knuckles turn a frightful shade of white") to discouraging ("A woman should never raise her voice above a whisper").

Desperate, Vinnie considered challenging Trent to a boxing match in hopes that he would knock her out for a few hours.

Eventually, however, the tense, interminable day ended, and Vinnie, riding silently with Trent and Emma in the coach, found herself wondering why she had wished the hours away. If only it were morning again and she was trying to eat a plate of greasy kippers.

When they arrived, Emma, who was not invited to attend the presentation, announced she would spend the whole evening waiting in the coach. Vinnie exhorted her not to be absurd but gave up trying to convince her sister to be rational when Sarah arrived in her own carriage to keep Emma company.

"Save your persuasion skills for those who really need persuading," her sister-in-law said.

Vinnie sighed and told Emma not to throw objects at or call names to or in any other way harass arriving members of the organization. Her sister blinked at her with her famous who-me expression. Vinnie wasn't fooled but nor was she worried with Sarah there to restrain her more crude impulses, and as she entered the venerable building, she felt oddly calm.

Her calm carried her through introductions with several imposing figures, her only contact with whom had been polite notes promising the fulfillment of long-deferred goals in exchange for their support, and a conversation with Mr. Berry in which he quickly ran through a list of society protocols that all aspirants had to follow. Her composure deserted her, however, as soon as she stepped into the lecture hall, an immense rotunda beneath a towering dome supported by a dozen columns in the Corinthian style. There were two sections of tiered leather-bound seats and a standing-room-only gallery high overhead. The room was magnificent, the site of soaring oratory and of the birth of great ideas, and, seeing it, Vinnie felt small and insignificant. Any confidence she had was crushed by the massive and ornate space, and she stood on the threshold, gawking like a chewbacon, as Mr. Berry urged her forward. Reluctantly, she stepped inside.

Mr. Berry continued his narration as he led her to the podium and indicated where she should place her notes. "The acoustics are very good, and we've never had a single complaint about the speaker not being heard properly," he assured her before adding with an accusatory note, "However, we've never had a female speaker before so I don't know how that may affect matters."

His tone clearly implied that any problems she encountered were of her own making, and as such, she would have to devise a solution, as he had neither the experience nor the inclination to solve them himself.

Feeling quite alone, she stared up at the beautiful dome. Her heart, which had been steady only a few minutes before, now beat with the insistence of a team of horses racing across a field, and she felt her breath growing shallow. If she could not bring herself to breathe properly, she would faint and that must not happen. She knew she was no groundbreaking reformer blazing a trail of vindication for all women everywhere, but she was enough of a pioneer to realize fainting at this moment would be a betrayal of her entire sex.

She needed to think of something else, and, turning to ask Mr. Berry about the rotunda's architecture, discovered the clerk had beaten a hasty retreat at the first opportunity. She barely caught a glimpse of his departing back as the door closed behind him.

"Coward," she muttered, not sure if she was talking about herself or the clerk. All she knew for certain was that the case was dire. Being literally abandoned by Mr. Berry, who, admittedly, had not been a particularly staunch ally to begin with, intensified her anxiety, and she very much feared she might actually collapse on the spot. If she was fortunate enough to fall forward, the podium should break her fall.

Unable to bear being alone in that magnificent empty room a moment longer, she resolved to find Alex, who had left her in the unreliable care of Mr. Berry, and ask him about the architecture or the acoustics or the weather—anything to keep her mind focused on something other than her own impending disaster. Before she could take a single step, the door opened again to admit Huntly.

"This is your official seven-minute warning," he said. "The room will open in two minutes, and you will be expected to begin five minutes later. Most speakers find it calming to sit in one of the chairs behind the podium while the rows are filling up, although tonight's assembly will be much more intimate than our usual events. Trent wanted to come in to give you the customary seven-minute warning, but I asked him to please let me, as the fact that you're here to receive this warning at all is my fault and I feel I must take this opportunity to apologize one last time for the unconscionable disservice I have done you."

The marquess spoke quickly and at length, and his sentences all seemed to run together, as if he wasn't clear where one ended and the other began. Listening to him chatter, Vinnie realized he was as anxious as she was about her presentation. It was everywhere about him—in the tight pull of his voice, in the rambling way he talked, in the fearful spark in his astonishing aquamarine eyes. The famously composed marquess who had calmly and infuriatingly claimed responsibility for his own unfortunate soaking was nowhere in evidence.

Nonplussed, Vinnie stared at him as everything fell into place. All at once, she understood why she had been unsettled by him and angered by him and flustered and confused and entertained and compelled.

It had always been there, just beneath the surface, but she had been too overwhelmed by her response to him to notice, and it was only now that she could feel worry for her flickering off him like candlelight that she could understand her own feelings.

The realization that she loved him was staggering and terrifying, but it was wonderful, too, for after the debacle of her engagement she had given up on ever finding someone she could trust and respect, let alone love.

Yet even as she delighted in the relief that Windbourne had not damaged her heart beyond repair, she conceded that he had permanently damaged her prospects. A murderer and a liar with no conscience or allegiance to the country that bore him, he had remade her in his own image, forcing her to brutally end his life and then lie about it to the entire world.

Nothing could come of anything—her feelings for the marquess, his feelings for her—if she didn't tell him the truth. Giving another person the power to break her heart was the one thing that scared Vinnie more than making her presentation. It was the one thing grander than this rotunda and its glorious dome and its graceful columns and its two tiers of elegant seats. It was also the one thing that had terrified the Harlow Hoyden and turned the urbane Duke of Trent into a callow youth.

With a heart swooning with hope and fear and the understanding that she was about to do a remarkably reckless thing but determined not to let that cower her, for she was also about to give a lecture on drainage systems from a podium never before visited by a woman to an audience of cynical men who disapproved of her and the outcome of that was already too unpredictable to bear, so why not take this risk, too, she said, "I killed my fiancé. He was a spy and a traitor and he had tried to kill Emma once, and just as I was saving her from his next attempt, he swung around with a fish knife that he intended to drive into my stomach, so I shot him."

Vinnie spoke quickly but calmly with a comforting sense of detachment as if she were watching herself speak from the gallery above. She saw astonishment blaze into Huntly's eyes, dispelling the anxiety, but whatever else he might feel—and what that would be, she couldn't imagine—she did not have a chance to find out, for as soon as she said the word *shot,* the doors to the lecture hall opened and a booming voice announced that the program would begin in five minutes. In walked the twenty-five other members of the British Horticultural Society and Mr. Berry and the esteemed clerk's wife, whose gracious presence would lend the all-male proceedings the hint of propriety they needed.

Suddenly, the conversation of serious men filled the room, and Vinnie jumped back, afraid that Huntly might try to address her remarkable confession surrounded by his colleagues. She settled into one of the chairs behind the podium, folded her hands, turned her head down and waited patiently for the program to start. Silently, she reviewed her presentation, grateful to have something to take her mind off Huntly. She didn't know where he was or what he was doing, for she'd resolved not to look at him again until her lecture was over. The task ahead of her was sufficiently daunting without adding the further challenge of trying to decipher the marquess's emotions.

The room grew silent as Trent approached the podium to begin the proceedings. "As you know, it is customary for the sponsoring member of the society to introduce the candidate, but as we are making many breaks with tradition this evening, I requested the privilege, which the Marquess of Huntly graciously acceded," the duke said smoothly. If he had any concerns about her performance, he did not show it. "I wanted to introduce Miss Lavinia Harlow, not because she is my sister-in-law but because she is among the most resourceful and dedicated horticulturalists I've ever had the pleasure to meet. She has a vast knowledge of drainage systems, which, I'm convinced, exceeds even that of the great England landscape artist Capability Brown. Miss Harlow is also in the process of inventing an elasticized watering hose employing Mr. Samuel Brill's method for waterproofing leather shoes. I'm sure it sounds outlandish, but I've witnessed her progress over recent months and promise you that any day now each of you will be employing her invention in your gardens and conservatories."

If Vinnie had expected to be heartened by the duke's admiring speech, she was disappointed to discover it had the opposite effect, for the woman he described sounded at once insufferably proficient and intolerably unfeminine. The members of the British Horticultural Society were far too conservative to find such a combination admirable or even bearable.

It doesn't matter, she thought defiantly, for there's nothing I can do about it now. Then she smothered a smile as she realized there had been nothing she could do about it before either. She could not have changed her sex to appease the society even if she had desired to.

"I could stand up here all evening singing the praises of Miss Harlow," Trent continued, "but I know that would embarrass her, for she is as modest as she is skilled. For that reason, I will content myself with asking you to please join me in welcoming Miss Lavinia Harlow to the podium."

Taking one final deep breath, Vinnie stood up and walked over to Trent. Mr. Berry's list of protocols, though extensive, did not address how a female speaker should greet her brother-in-law, and she decided to hold out her hand for shaking as she had seen her sister do time and again. It was a bold, masculine gesture, but she figured it was too late to pretend to possess a proper womanly fragility, for a properly fragile woman would not have been there in the first place.

Trent gave her hand a firm shake, then bent over it as if bowing and said softly in her ear, "Please note the spot of green over Mr. Townshend's left ear. Though he does not know it, a piece of spinach has attached itself to his person."

The absurdity of the statement and the wink that accompanied it brought a smile to her face, and it was with that perfectly composed expression that she took the podium and thanked the honored members of the British Horticultural Society for inviting her to speak.

"My topic this evening is drainage," she stated forthrightly with a glance at her notes. She tilted her head down not because she needed to review the material, which she had all but memorized, but because she couldn't bear to look at the intimidating crowd before her. "Achieving the ideal system of drains had long bedeviled me in the conservatory in my family's ancestral home and again in my brother's town house. As all horticulturalists know, ensuring that one's plants receive the proper amount of water is vital to the successful propagation of any species. Through a series of experimentations, many of which failed, I arrived at a successful method of drainage for both locations."

Vinnie paused as she turned the page and forced herself to look up, for burying her nose in the podium seemed cowardly. She was far too nervous to make out individual faces, let alone a leaf of spinach over Mr. Townshend's left ear, and all she saw was a group of men politely paying attention. She knew full well their courtesy did not stem from respect for her person but rather for themselves and their esteemed institution, but she didn't mind. Her goal for the evening was singular and simple, for all she hoped to accomplish was to express her ideas cogently without embarrassing herself. As she spoke about the various trials and failures that had led to the perfecting of her own drainage systems, she realized she would meet that objective. She knew her material well and could articulate it in language that was both elegant and basic.

All the material she covered in her lecture was gathered in her pamphlet, "A Horticulturalist's Rudimentary Guide to the Implementation of Drainage Systems," which the British Horticultural Society itself had published. Although their own organization had issued the booklet, none of the members had actually read it, and now that they heard the information it contained, they were surprised to find it helpful. Far from providing rudimentary tips to amateur gardeners, the pamphlet offered highly advanced, relevant advice, and when Vinnie opened her guide to show a graph charting moisture levels, Lord Peter Waldegrave raised a hand to request a personal copy so that he may see the illustration better. Several other members echoed the appeal, and she waited patiently as Mr. Berry handed out twenty-six copies of her book, its widest distribution by far.

Vinnie resumed her lecture a few minutes later, picking up the discussion of moisture levels exactly where she left off, but she had to stop again almost immediately when Lord Richard Marlton asked her to clarify what she meant by soil density.

"Soil density is a term I created to describe how compact the soil is," she explained, instructing her audience to turn to page fourteen, where they would find a chart of varying soil densities.

Additional questions followed as the society members digested her ideas and delved deeper into her concepts, and by the time she finished her presentation an hour later, she felt more like an Oxford don leading a seminar than a supplicant seeking acceptance.

The ovation Vinnie received was significantly more enthusiastic than the polite smattering of applause she'd anticipated, and, flushing with delight, she bowed her head as she thanked them for their time and consideration. Without question, she was the modest person Trent had described in his introduction, but who, she wondered, could meet such overwhelming approval head on? It felt too brash or brazen.

Overcoming her natural reticence, she graciously accepted the well wishes of the many members who approached her to congratulate her on such an edifying lecture. Although she was no longer in danger of fainting, she was still grateful for the extra support the podium provided.

"Admirably done, Miss Harlow," the Earl of Moray said as he bowed over her hand. He was a tall, lithe man whose elegant waistcoat did not seem to suffer from having been produced by the second-best tailor in London. "Admirably done indeed."

"Thank you, my lord," she said, sparing him barely a glance as her eyes swept the room for a glimpse of the marquess. The lecture had ended more than fifteen minutes ago, and she had yet to catch sight of him. She had spied him once during her lecture—he was seated to the left in the second row behind Sir Charles Barton—but looking directly at him had caused her to lose her train of thought so she immediately glanced away.

"I found the lecture to be remarkably informative," the earl added with an eager smile, "and hope I may call on you to seek further edification."

Assuring the earl that she was more than happy to provide all the edification he needed, she turned to respond to another comment from Sir Barton and suddenly Huntly was there, not next to her, not close enough to touch, but within her sights and only a few feet away. Their eyes met, and Vinnie's heart hitched as she recalled their last exchange, her reckless confession, the way she had all but laid her heart at his feet. She opened her mouth as if to say something to him, then immediately closed it because she didn't know what she intended to say. Her mind was blank, cleared of all thought by the indecent brightness that glowed in his magnificent blue-green eyes.

She felt the breathless vertigo of an hour before return and struggled to reply intelligibly to Moray's next comment—something about promising to call on her at the earliest convenience.

"Yes, of course, please," she said absently, bestowing a brief look at him before darting her eyes back to Huntly. He was no longer there. She looked and looked, even standing on her tippy-toes and stretching her neck, but she could not find him. In the space of mere seconds, he'd removed himself entirely from her vicinity.

She refused to be troubled by the marquess's abrupt departure, for it could mean one of a hundred things, such as he was thirsty or was called away by an associate, and she determinedly put it out of her mind as Lord Marlton asked her to elaborate on soil porosity, another one of her concepts. While she explained aeration, Trent appeared beside her and gave her hand a crushing squeeze, which she correctly interpreted as the silent version of a triumphant scream. Without pausing in her speech, she turned her head slightly and thanked him with a smile. Marlton, who was reading the glossary in the appendix, did not notice either gesture, nor did Sir Percival Lonsdale, who was looking at the pamphlet over his shoulder.

Eventually, the crowd dispersed as the members of the club retired to the dining room to have supper, and Mr. Berry, who had been eager to disavow all knowledge of her only two hours before, took the opportunity to reiterate how pleased he was with the depth and usefulness of the pamphlet. As he himself had commissioned the work, Vinnie once again found the untempered surprise in his tone puzzling, but she was nonetheless grateful for his enthusiasm.

From a seat in the penultimate row, Mrs. Berry coughed discreetly, and her husband, instantly heeding the signal, broke off his conversation to beg her forgiveness for keeping her so late. Vinnie was fairly certain the apology was directed at her, but she couldn't quite overcome the feeling that it was actually intended for his wife, who clearly did not find society business as engrossing as Mr. Berry.

Mindful of the service the woman had done her, Vinnie thanked her for kindly chaperoning the event.

"I don't mind doing it once," Mrs. Berry said with a hint of peevishness that clearly indicated she would not make it a regular habit should Vinnie have the impudence to actually become a member.

As that was unlikely to happen, despite that evening's success, Vinnie assured the clerk's wife she would not be called upon to make the sacrifice again. Mrs. Berry harrumphed in response.

With an anxious glance at his wife, Mr. Berry offered to accompany Miss Harlow to her carriage, a suggestion for which she was grateful, as it had been a long, exhausting day and she was ready to go home. Another few minutes, and she might fall actually asleep on her feet. The thought was amusing because several times during the event she had imagined herself lying on the floor, and she glanced down, wondering if there was something inevitable about the black marble tiles.

As he guided Vinnie through the building, he reviewed the voting protocol as a courtesy, for, as he mentioned, all society protocols were thoroughly explained to her upon arrival. She did not doubt his veracity, but she had been too anxious to listen his protocols before the presentation and she was too exhausted to hear them now.

"Our process is more highly evolved than other clubs such as White's or Brooks's," he stated proudly, "for the blackball system is a blunt instrument and the society prefers an apparatus that is more finely tuned. As such, no one individual member gets to decide the fate of a candidate. He must build a coalition of like-minded peers that equals or exceeds twenty percent of the membership, or, as it stand now, six men. If the naysayers fall short of their goal by five percent or less, they are given an opportunity to present their case to the membership in hopes of changing one or two minds. If that happens, recount protocol takes over."

Mr. Berry continued to explain the procedures governing the election of new members until they reached the entry hall, and Vinnie, who found the process overly involved and complex, was almost grateful that she would never have to follow the rules herself.

True to her word, Emma was exactly where she said she would be, and when Vinnie opened the door to the carriage, she found her brother, Roger, had joined them. The coach had been turned into an intimate cardroom, with brandy for the gentlemen and ratafia for the ladies and loo at ha'penny a point. Emma had just declared herself winner of the trick when she noticed Vinnie's face, which was pale from exhaustion, and she dropped the cards as she reached for her sister.

"Oh, you poor dear, you look as if you've been pulled behind a horse for a week," Emma said, wrapping her arms around Vinnie as she made room for her on the bench. Sarah caught the wineglass before it spilled and placed it in a basket on the floor. "Are you hungry? Do you want to eat? Mrs. Chater prepared some meat pies and pickled vegetables."

The carriage door closed and a few moments later, the vehicle lurched forward. Vinnie rested her head against the cushion, closed her eyes and said, "I would love something to eat, yes. I'm famished."

Sarah carefully withdrew the meat pies from the basket and held them up. "I have ham or sausage."

With her eyes still closed, Vinnie requested the former and gratefully received the ham. Her brother tried to take the other pie, but his wife tsked in disapproval and reminded him he'd had a proper dinner at his club. She then offered to prepare him a plate of pickled asparagus, to which he responded with a request for additional brandy. Emma said she would like asparagus *and* brandy, causing Sarah to tsk again.

After listening to their chatter, which continued for several minutes, Vinnie asked if anyone cared to know how her presentation went.

Emma gave her sister's shoulder an affectionate squeeze and said, "We know it went beautifully and that you were a triumph."

Confused, Vinnie opened her eyes. "Did Alex give you a report?"

Emma shook her head.

"Then how do you know that?" Vinnie asked.

"Because we know you," Emma said simply, humbling Vinnie with her unequivocal faith. "Now you just sit back and regain your energy. Don't forget there's a sausage pie here with your name on it, assuming we can keep Roger's grubby hands off it."

"You mean hand," her brother said, raising his lone surviving arm. He had lost the other one in a riding accident caused by the traitorous Sir Windbourne. Although he found many tasks difficult to perform without the appendage and had moments when he was cross and blue-deviled, he was, for the most part, grateful to be alive and good-natured about his condition.

"Duly noted," Emma said, "but don't think gaining my sympathy will obtain you the sausage roll, for I am resolute."

"As am I," Sarah said.

Laughing at the absurdity, for her brother frequently made elaborate plays for sympathy to no avail, Vinnie sat back, per her sister's orders, and took another bite of the ham pie. Although the pastry was large and filling, her appetite was too ferocious to be appeased by only one and she decided that she would have the sausage pie, as well. She also stole a stalk of asparagus from Emma's plate, and not thirty seconds later, received her own portion of pickled vegetables from Sarah.

"Do not mistake our savoir faire for indifference," Emma said. "We are all on pins and needles to hear about your evening and are making a supreme effort to let you revive before pestering you with hundreds of questions. I, personally, have twenty-five recorded in a notebook to ensure I don't forget a single one. Additionally, I know the dowager is just as eager to hear how your presentation went, although she would claim only mild interest if pressed."

Vinnie appreciated their forbearance and realized that the meat pies had in fact proved restorative, for she felt some of her excitement return. By the time the party was settled in the Grosvenor Square drawing room, she had recovered her strength entirely and was able to give an energetic, comprehensive account of the event, starting with a detailed description of the great rotunda, with its swoon-inducing dome and dependable podium, which, in her retelling, was cast as her staunchest ally in the room. She told them about Mr. Berry's protocols and Trent's kind introduction and the moment—the perfectly wonderful, ground-breaking moment—when Lord Peter Waldegrave raised his hand to request a copy of her pamphlet. Emma squealed with delight and Sarah clapped her hands and even the dowager smiled with approval.

And the leaf of spinach! How could she tell them *all* about the presentation without remembering to mention the leaf of spinach that was still hanging above Mr. Townshend's left ear when he came to begrudgingly congratulate her for a "not entirely uninformative" lecture. "It must reveal a flaw in your character," Vinnie observed earnestly, "when none of your friends or colleagues will tell you about the vegetation in your coiffure."

The narration went on for hours, supplemented by a cold collation of lamb cutlets and peas, and by the time Sarah and Roger took their leave at one o'clock, Vinnie was once again exhausted. The day, with its endless cycles of highs and lows, had finally taken its toll, and she could barely keep her head up as Emma walked her to her room. She was so tired, she could not tell if the kiss the dowager had bestowed on her cheek, along with the words *well done,* was real or imagined, and when Emma changed her into her nightgown, she provided so little assistance, her sister accused her of being like a jelly tower from one of Mrs. Raffald's cookery books.

It was only after Emma had tucked the blanket around her, blew out the candles and closed the door gently behind her that Vinnie realized she hadn't said a word about Huntly. Somehow, in all the excitement about her presentation, she'd failed to tell Emma about the other hugely important event that had occurred, and thinking that was an oversight too great to let stand, she resolved to tell her about it right then. Over and over again, she thought about getting up, but she could not make her legs move, and as she drifted into sleep a few moments later, she wondered how two such remarkable things could have happened in a single night.

CHAPTER THIRTEEN

The Duke of Trent did not think it was coy to insist upon waiting for the subject of the previous night's vote to appear before discussing the results of the aforementioned ballot, no matter how often his wife leveled the charge at him.

"I appreciate that you don't want to *tell* me the results," Emma said fairly, "so why don't we do this: You point your thumb up to the ceiling if it's positive or down to the floor if it's negative, like the crowd deciding the fate of a gladiator in ancient Rome."

Feeling this sly evasion did not warrant a response, Trent took a sip of tea and asked Tupper if the eggs were done yet.

"I'll check with the kitchens immediately, your grace," the footman said.

Emma examined her husband thoughtfully for a few minutes, trying to decipher from his movements and temperament which way the vote had gone but both were too placid and consistent to provide insights. "All right, then. Perhaps a pointed thumb up or down is too much of a commitment for you or perhaps you feel that gladiator fights are too barbaric for the breakfast table. I understand entirely, so I have another proposition. If the vote was positive, you will pass me the butter. If it was negative, you will not pass me the butter. Now, will you or won't you pass me the butter?"

Before the duke could even not *not* respond to his wife's ridiculous suggestion, Tupper, who had just that moment returned to report on the eggs, heard the duchess's request for butter and passed the dish to her himself. Feeling pleased with his own level of service, the footman leaned back on his heels and told his grace to expect the eggs directly.

"Very good," Trent said, smiling at how thoroughly and unintentionally Emma's scheme had been thwarted.

"Honestly, I don't know why you are being so coy about this," Emma said exasperated. "Vinnie would want me to know as soon as possible."

This line of reasoning had no more success than any of her previous arguments. "I cannot attest to Vinnie's preferences, only my own, and that is that Vinnie should hear the results of the vote first," he said firmly, glancing up when Jepson entered with the platter of eggs.

Deciding to attack the problem from another angle, Emma pushed back her chair to stand up, and the duke, who knew exactly her intentions, sternly told her not to wake up her sister.

"Standing outside someone's door isn't waking her up," she muttered as Tupper insisted on helping her push her chair back in. She thanked him with an absent smile and assented to Jepson's offer of eggs.

"It is when you throw a ball against her door," Trent said.

Emma rolled her eyes at the absurd suggestion. "I wasn't going to throw a ball."

"A shoe, then," her husband said.

Emma conceded the truth of this comment with a shrug.

Vinnie, who had not needed a shoe or a ball to be thrown against her door to rouse her from bed, only the memory of her confession to Huntly, found something very comforting about arriving to the breakfast table amid a heated debate between her sister and Trent. It made the day seem as unextraordinary as any other. In fact, however, it was the most significant day of her entire life, for now or in a few minutes or a few hours—definitely sometime before supper—she would discover how the Marquess of Huntly felt about her.

If only she hadn't jumped yesterday when that booming voice announced the imminent start of the program, if only she had kept her eyes trained on his, then she would know what lay on the other side of his astonished look: horror or joy.

In the giddy aftermath of her presentation, she had felt certain it would be joy, for she could think of no other way to interpret the look he had given her—that searing, intense, heart-in-his-eyes look that arrowed straight to her heart. Surely, that said more than any hastily conceived sentence ever could. In the cold light of day, however, as she struggled to hold on to that look, and as she tried to understand why he had suddenly disappeared and as each minute ticked by without word from him, she became less and less certain.

A man needed time to think, she told herself reasonably, and her announcement had contained some rather remarkable information, which would require a man to think even more. It wasn't merely that she'd revealed herself to be a killer, a fact that would no doubt require some adjustment on the part of a suitor, but she also divulged that their whole relationship had been a lie. For the entire time Huntly had known her, she had professed to being a woman in mourning, and he had treated her as one. Now he had to amend that image of her. No doubt he was reviewing every conversation they had had in light of this new development to figure out if it had any bearing on the way he felt.

It was not unreasonable for Huntly to discover that it did have some bearing on the way he felt. If that happened, she would not blame him.

But even as she thought those words to herself, she knew she would blame him. It wasn't fair or reasonable, but a woman with a broken heart was allowed to carry a grudge.

Well aware that none of these thoughts were helpful—and that thinking them would not help pass the time—Vinnie strode into the breakfast parlor with a bright smile on her face. To her surprise, the smile was actually sincere, for as soon as she saw Alex, she realized she had not thanked him yet for saving her last night, as his comment about the leaf of spinach in Townshend's hair had done nothing less.

Seeing the grin, Trent stood up and wrapped her in a hug. "Watching last night, I could not have been any prouder," he said, tightening his arms, "and yet somehow, this morning, greeting you as a fellow member, I'm prouder still."

Emma shrieked in excitement, leaped to her feet and pulled her sister into a hug so enthusiastic it knocked them both to the ground. For Vinnie, the idea of being accepted was so outside the realm of possibility that she couldn't understand what was happening. Splayed on the rug, she stared up at Trent, imploring him with her eyes to make sense of it.

Her sister, having little patience with stunned shock, immediately called for Tupper to bring a bottle of champagne to the table for a proper celebration.

Since Emma seemed content to sit on the floor all day, Trent helped his struggling sister-in-law to her feet and said it plainly: "You have been accepted into the British Horticultural Society. You did it, Vinnie."

As if unable to believe it, she shook her head and accepted the chair Alex held out of her. "How is that possible?" she asked.

Trent grinned as he offered a hand to his wife, who echoed the question. "Your Amazing Brill Method Improvised Elasticized Hose," he said.

"My what?" Vinnie asked.

"Your hose," he said again, "the one you've been working on for months. That hose is how you gained entry. Everyone was very impressed with your drainage systems and by sunset today, dozens of your pamphlets will be distributed to estate managers all across the country, but it was your hose that did it."

As delighted as she was by her manual's success, she couldn't fathom what her imperfect invention had to do with anything. "But I didn't talk about my hose."

"True," conceded Trent, "but I did."

This announcement did little to clarify matters for her. "I appreciate that you are enthusiastic about the project, but it seems unlikely to me that the other members of the society care by what device water is delivered to their plants."

"They don't," he agreed. "But the members of the Society for the Advancement of Horticultural Knowledge care greatly and are working on their own elasticized hose. When I informed my fellow members of that fact and assured them that yours was only days away from completion, they decided it was well worth having a woman among their ranks if they could lord her invention over the rival organization. Indeed, the fact that the elasticized hose was invented by a female is the best part of the prospective lording, for it means a lone woman could do better and faster what all the great minds of the Society for the Advancement of Horticultural Knowledge could not."

Vinnie found this all too remarkable to digest and stared at Trent in wonder.

"How did you know the Society for the Advancement of Horticultural Knowledge was developing its own hose?" Emma asked.

Trent blinked at her several times in imitation of his wife's own famous innocent look. "I might have commissioned a dossier from Mr. Squibbs."

Delighted, Emma squealed again and reached across the table for her husband's hand. "Last night, when I heard about the spinach in Townshend's hair, I could not have been any prouder," she said, "and somehow, this morning, hearing that you commissioned your own report, I'm prouder still."

"Thank you, imp," he said sincerely. "That means a lot."

Overwhelmed, Vinnie said softly, "You did this for me?"

Trent shook his head. "No, for me."

Before she could give voice to her full gratitude, Tupper returned with a bottle of champagne and filled three glasses. "Could you please locate her grace and inform her we are raising a celebratory glass if she would like to join us. And please don't forget to open another bottle for everyone downstairs," Emma said generously. As soon as he was gone, she turned to Trent. "Would it be too much to give the servants the day off?"

"Just a little," the duke said.

While they waited for the dowager, Emma asked, "What was the final tally?"

"Twenty-one to five."

Emma immediately insisted on hearing the names of the naysayers, but Trent swore he was not at liberty to say. "It's against protocol, but even so I wouldn't divulge the information. The men have a right to their own opinion, and I won't have you torturing them because it disagrees with yours."

As this statement was too close to the truth, Emma didn't even try to deny it. Instead, she said, "*Torture* is such a strong word."

Although the specifics of Mr. Berry's explanation escaped her, Vinnie had a vague recollection that five votes required a revote and asked Trent about it.

The duke smiled. "You are referring to the recount protocol, and, yes, we had several recounts as the no votes tried to convince at least one yes vote to change his mind. At one point, the no coalition actually accomplished that, but the vote swung back in the other direction during the confirmation recount protocol. Trust me, Vinnie, you don't want to hear the specifics, for they are extremely tedious. The voting went on until three in the morning. I was never so glad of anything as when Mr. Berry invoked the sudden death recount protocol."

Emma, who couldn't bear the thought of being kept completely in the dark, said, "Just tell me this at least: Did Huntly vote yes?"

At the mention of the marquess, Vinnie felt the blood drain from her face and the champagne glass slide out of her suddenly boneless fingers, causing a spill. Trent immediately grabbed a cloth from the sideboard to soak it up while Emma rushed to her sister's side.

"Are you all right?" she asked, pressing one hand against Vinnie's forehead. "You don't have a fever. You are probably still exhausted from all the excitement."

Vinnie took exception to the implication that she was overwrought or that her nerves were frail and assured Emma she was fine. Her sister leaned back, examining her thoughtfully, but before she could make further comment, the dowager arrived to lament Vinnie's success with so much good cheer that one could only assume she didn't mean it.

After breakfast, Emma tried to convince the newest member of the British Horticultural Society to go shopping for stationery that boldly declared that accomplishment. "Perhaps with a lovely floral border. Or is that too obvious? Oh, I know, let's pick out new curtains for the society's reading room. That will terrify your new associates."

Vinnie smiled at the suggestion but didn't think terrifying her new associates was the best way to start off her tenure. More to the point, she didn't want to leave the house in case the marquess called. She didn't explain that to Emma—suddenly, the thought of confessing her confession, of saying the words out loud, was intolerable—and instead employed several reasonable excuses to get out of the outing. When her sister denied them all, she resorted to citing her frail nerves, a pretext Emma accepted with insulting speed.

Once in her room, Vinnie tried to occupy her mind with various activities. She picked up the gothic novel her sister had lent her months ago, but when the young man who was really a young lady turned out to be an emissary of Satan, she threw it across the room in disgust. Next, she took out a clean sheet of white paper and wrote "A Horti-culturalist's Advanced Guide to the Implementation of

Drainage Systems" along the top. For months, she'd been meaning to record her thoughts for a follow-up manual, but now that she had a quill in hand, she couldn't recall a single idea. She scratched out the pamphlet's title and wrote, "Miss Lavinia Harlow, Member, British Horticultural Society." After staring at her name for ten minutes, she realized that wasn't a satisfying activity, crumpled up the sheet and threw it across the room, where it landed several feet short of the offending novel.

Nothing held her attention, and after three hours of intermittently pacing the floor with increasingly agitated steps—now it was one o'clock, now it was two—she could no longer bear the silence of her bedroom. She fled to the conservatory to modify her latest formulation for her invention. It was not merely that she craved the distraction of an engrossing project, which the watering hose usually was, but that the task itself made her feel closer to Huntly. Just the simple act of reviewing the formula that she'd gotten on their trip to Brill & Company's factory gave her the sense that he was nearby and that he was thinking of her.

She needed to feel that way because as the day dragged on, the truth slowly started to sink in: He was not coming. If he returned her regard, he would have called upon her by now, for he would have found the separation as unbearable as she. The fact that he hadn't sent a note either indicated something particularly damning to Vinnie, for if there was one thing she knew about the Marquess of Huntly, it was that his manners were impeccable. If he was uncertain about how he felt or indifferent to her in the wake of her confession, he would have forwarded an explanation at once to put her out of her misery. The only excuse for the extended silence was she repulsed him beyond all bounds of courtesy. He was too appalled to even write a polite missive.

Vinnie had finally presented him with the one disconcerting event for which he had no response at all. Despite his excellent breeding, he could not claim responsibility and apologize for her murderous bent.

She found this revelation to be profoundly upsetting, and even as she continued to work on her project, tears ran down her cheeks, making it impossible to see if she was spreading the new formulation evenly along the hose. She knew she should stop, but the only thing saving her from the utter devastation of her feelings was a useful activity. The task itself was irrelevant, and when she turned on the water to test the new hose, the fact that it actually held together made her cry even harder.

There Vinnie stood in the middle of the duke's beautiful conservatory, weeping as if there was nothing good left in the world, while shards of sunlight glistened off water streaming from her absolutely perfect elasticized hose. She had done it. After five months, ten prototypes, six ruined gowns and one chemical burn on her left hand, she had finally invented the Amazing Brill Method Improvised Elasticized Hose.

This moment should be sweet, she thought, as a fresh wave of sadness overcame her, and the fact that it wasn't made her angry with Huntly for ruining it and furious with herself for letting him and irate with Windbourne—yes, Windbourne, for it always came back to that bloody, awful, evil man—for turning her into this person whom Huntly could not love.

Utterly devastated at last, Vinnie slowly sunk to the floor and curled up into a ball. Still holding the hose, she kept her hand steady so that water wouldn't flood the room, for even in her misery she remained mindful of the duke's pristine tile floor—an act of consideration that would seem to indicate to Vinnie that she was at least a little lovable, though she knew for a fact she was not.

She stayed crumpled on the floor crying until Caruthers interrupted to tell her she had a visitor. At once, she leaped to her feet, the hose flailing in every direction as water surged through it, and ran out of the room. Without pausing to straighten her hair or dry her eyes or neaten her dress or clean her face, she ran down the hall and past the stairs and tore into the drawing room, her eyes wild as she looked for Huntly.

She came to an abrupt stop in the middle of the room.

It was not Huntly.

It was Mr. Townshend.

Mr. Townshend?

Her surprise was such that she didn't feel disappointed or even renewed devastation, just confusion. "Mr. Townshend?" she asked, as if seeking confirmation.

"Miss Harlow," he said with an agreeable smile. "I see I've taken you away from some important task, for you are quite rumpled."

Vinnie knew very well that *rumpled* did not begin to describe how incredibly disheveled she was. There was not a single thing about her appearance that was appropriate for greeting a caller in the drawing room, but there was nothing she could do it about it now, so she sat down. "I was working on my hose project."

"Ah, yes, your amazing invention. You will be able to get back to it very shortly, for I won't keep you long," he announced, leaning against the mantelpiece despite her entreaty to take a seat. "First, I would like to congratulate you on your presentation last night and your acceptance into the society. Both are significant achievements, and you should be very proud."

Given Vinnie's low estimation of Mr. Townshend's character, she was entirely taken aback by this show of graciousness. "Thank you."

"In my experience, I find it's the attainment of one's objective that has value," he said, "not the objective itself. Oftentimes, the goal is insignificant and what we cherish is the knowledge that we are able to accomplish our goal. Do you not find this to be so?"

With a slow tilt of her head, Vinnie nodded, not because she agreed with him but because he seemed to want her to agree with him very badly and she hated to be rude. In truth, she didn't entirely understand what he was trying to say about goals and objectives.

"I'm glad we are on the same page, my dear, for it means you won't mind declining your membership to the society," he said brusquely. "Do send the note immediately. Mr. Berry is expecting it." Then, as if that concluded their business, he straightened his shoulders and walked toward the door.

She found his overbearing confidence to be as unsettling as it was absurd. "I will not be declining," she said firmly.

"Unless you want all of England to know you killed your fiancé and then pretended to mourn his death, you will," he said, his tone mild but the gleam in his eyes clearly triumphant. "I have the better hand, Miss Harlow. Murder trumps plagiarism, so be a good girl and submit to the superior maneuvering."

As he spoke, Vinnie felt a calmness wash over her and it seemed amazing to her that just a few minutes before she'd been weeping like a babe over the Marquess of Huntly, that she'd actually curled herself into a ball because the pain of losing him was so great she couldn't stand.

Losing him—as if she'd ever had him.

She was shocked to discover that he cared so little for her that he could heartlessly broadcast her deepest, darkest secret to the world. Even if he didn't love her, she would have thought he had more integrity than that. He had certainly seemed like a man of honor, insisting that she could not withdraw her application to appease bullies and gossips. But what did she really know of men's integrity or how they behaved? The only man who'd ever professed to love her had tried to puncture her stomach with a fish knife. Perhaps all men were this dishonorable. Perhaps they all thought nothing of betrayal. Perhaps they didn't even consider it betrayal when it involved a mere woman.

Huntly had betrayed her before—that perfect visit to Mr. Brill's factory, supposedly arranged to make amends for wrongs done to her person but in actuality calculated to make her submit to his will. Even that betrayal wasn't without precedent, for he had put her up for membership as an act of petty revenge. Surely that wasn't the action of an honorable man.

That the marquess was responsible for this current misery, she didn't doubt. Vinnie was a practical young woman and the facts were plain: Only six other people on the face of the earth knew the truth—she, Emma, Alex, Roger, Sarah and Mr. Garrison, Roger's boss in the Home Office—and they had known it for several months. More than that, they had nothing to gain from the true story getting out. Indeed, it would hurt each of them, Garrison most of all. Only one of the seven learned of it the night before: Huntly.

What the marquess had to gain from telling Townshend was unclear, for if he'd wanted to coerce her into not joining the society, he could have done it himself. It was possible that he hadn't meant to reveal her secret to the deputy director of Kew Gardens, that the truth somehow slipped out while they were discussing her pamphlet or vintages of claret. Maybe he didn't realize how Townshend planned to use the information. Maybe he knew and approved but couldn't bring himself to be present.

All this was possible, thought Vinnie, though none of it was likely, and she was too clever to take comfort in unlikely stories.

Taking her silence as assent, Townshend nodded his approval. "I knew you would see reason. Now don't keep Mr. Berry waiting too long."

As Townshend reached for the door, Vinnie said, "You had a leaf of spinach in your hair last night."

Confused, he paused and turned to look at her.

"Just above your ear," she explained, standing up to walk over to him. "It's no longer there so I have to assume at some point you noticed it yourself and removed it. Trent pointed it out to me as he was leaving the podium, and the information was well timed because up until that moment, I thought I was going to have a paroxysm, I was so nervous. I honestly believed I might faint or otherwise humiliate myself."

As she spoke, Townshend's face reddened and his fingers grasped the doorknob so tightly his knuckles turned white. Emboldened, Vinnie took another step forward.

"But then Trent told me about the leaf of spinach," she continued, her tone as matter-of-fact as his, even as she warmed to her subject, "and I learned that out in that audience was an absurd human being who thought he was surrounded by friends and yet not a single one preferred telling him about a leaf of spinach in his hair to laughing at him behind his back. That, I realized, was more humiliating than anything I could do and I calmed down. So thank you, Mr. Townshend, for helping me attain my objective, for I could not have done it without you. And I will write that note to Mr. Berry immediately because there is nothing more repugnant to me than being a member of an organization that would accept you." She opened the drawing room door as he stood gaping at her, paralyzed by rage. "Now, good day, sir."

Vinnie stiffened her shoulders in anticipation of an attack when he opened his mouth to speak, but he immediately closed it again and swept out of the room with an ineffectual grunt. Then he stomped through the hall, out the front door and down the stairs to the street, where his horse waited for him. Anger undermined his usual coordination, and it took him three clumsy tries to climb onto the back of the patient animal. She stood in the doorway until he disappeared down the square, then grabbed her pelisse and stepped outside. She saw Emma on the sidewalk in front of the house, as she had just arrived home with several books from Hatchard's.

Vinnie nodded in greeting but did not break stride.

Surprised, her sister called after her to ask where she was going without her maid.

"To strangle the Marquess of Huntly," she announced.

Emma smiled. "Very good. I'll hold supper until you get back."

Vinnie did not bother to say thank you.

CHAPTER FOURTEEN

As he stood in the drawing room of Viscount Inchape's family seat near Tunbridge Well waiting for Miss Harlow's father to appear, the Marquess of Huntly conceded that perhaps setting out on a five-hour dash immediately after the meeting concluded to request her hand in marriage had not been the best plan. Not only was he covered in travel dust, but he was still wearing his dark-blue tailcoat with pewter buttons and white breeches from the night before. He looked absurd standing in the bright light of day in his evening clothes.

He hoped the man wouldn't hold his impatience against him.

From everything Trent had said about Mr. Edward Harlow, he didn't think it would be a problem, for the man showed little interest in any of his children. Unlike his wife, he had not bothered to return to London for the ball the dowager threw to celebrate his daughter's marriage. He much preferred hunting with cronies and gambling with friends and dallying with dancers.

Trent himself had not asked Emma's father formally for her hand. Instead, he contented himself with the nearest Harlow at the time, which happened to be Vinnie. Later, he sent a formal letter introducing himself and requesting they meet to discuss marriage contracts. Harlow responded with a brief note welcoming him to the family and suggesting he work out the details with his son, Roger.

Despite the duke's inauspicious experience with the patriarch, the marquess could not bring himself to skirt tradition by asking her brother or—God forbid—Emma for permission. It must be her father, for following proper etiquette was the only way to demonstrate just how highly he honored her.

Now, however, he wondered if changing into proper clothes for traveling might have been a better way of honoring her. He'd considered going home first, but detouring to Berkeley Square had seemed like an intolerable waste of time.

Indeed, the entire evening had seemed like an intolerable waste of time. All those votes and counts and recounts and sudden deaths and sudden redeaths—the meeting had gone on forever. Even when the rest of Townshend's coalition had been ready to concede simply to bring the endless proceedings to an end, the stubborn deputy director of Kew had stood firm, insisting to anyone who would listen that a woman, no matter how well versed in drainage pipes, did not belong in the British Horticultural Society. It was an affront to everything in which they believed.

At first, it had appeared as if Townshend's opinion would hold sway but then Trent—good old clever Trent—played the rivalry card, announcing that Vinnie's hose invention was a thousand times more ingenious than a similar device on which the Society for the Advancement of Horticultural Knowledge was working. Furthermore, hers was nearly complete, whereas the other organization's still needed months of work.

Trent's announcement was the deciding factor for many of their fellow members, but it took another three excruciating hours to convince Townshend that his fight was futile.

To be fair, the entire day had been excruciating for the marquess, not just the extended battle over Vinnie's acceptance. From the moment he'd woken up, he'd worried about her, imagining her in a state of anxiety so intense she couldn't string two words together, let alone make a coherent presentation, and then he had caught sight of her in the lecture hall, her face so pale under the high dome, almost as if she were about to faint. Seeing that look made his heart ache, and he realized he'd never been more nervous in his entire life, not even when the *Triton* hit a storm off the coast of Tonga and took on water. Thinking he might die paled in comparison to worrying about her.

And then for her to calmly explain that she had killed her fiancé!

Felix Horatio Dryden, Marquess of Huntly, could not conceive of a stranger moment in his entire life. In the space of a few seconds, he'd gone from worrying that a woman whom he admired might humiliate herself to realizing the woman he loved had a whole heart to realizing the woman he loved had been through a horrifying experience to worrying again that the woman he loved was too frail to make her presentation.

Through it all in that moment—the woman he loved.

It was just as Trent said: The truth didn't mean anything if it didn't come from Vinnie.

While she spoke, he tried to pay attention, but it was too hard to focus on the present when his mind was so busy reviewing the past and planning for the future. He recalled all those moments when he'd believed Vinnie was mourning her fiancé, most of which he'd created by trying to use Windbourne's memory to manipulate her behavior, and felt a combination of disgust and relief. Disgust, yes, for how often he'd cruelly reminded her of that murderous bastard. But relief, such overwhelming relief, that he wasn't competing with a dead man, that a long-lost love didn't permanently hold a piece of her heart.

If it was selfish of him to feel that way, so be it.

He didn't feel too badly about listening to her presentation with only half an ear, for as soon as she started talking, he knew she would succeed beyond his wildest expectations. Far from the faint, pale creature standing under the dome, the woman speaking at the podium was his Vinnie, the brave, wonderful girl who calmly took responsibility for her actions and brooked no interference.

And because it was his Vinnie, wading through the sea of well wishers after the performance to congratulate her had been the most excruciating thing of all. When he'd finally gotten near, when his eyes had finally caught hers in a heart-stopping look, he realized being close to her was even worse. Better to withdraw and wait until he could have all of her, not just a scrap.

It was then that he'd decided to seek out her father's permission as soon as the meeting was over.

So he had and now he was stuck cooling his heels in Viscount Inchape's drawing room, waiting for Mr. Edward Harlow to return from the morning hunt. He'd been assured by the butler that the party would be back at any moment, as breakfast had been requested for ten o'clock and it was a quarter to now. Fifteen minutes was not long to wait, but he begrudged every second away from Vinnie. Furthermore, he still had a five-hour ride back to London, during which he would have to change horses and eat, and he couldn't possibly propose in these clothes. No, he'd have to go home to bathe and change and find his mother's ring.

Eons would pass before he saw Vinnie again.

To his relief, the door opened not ten minutes later and in walked a tall man with gray hair cut à la Brutus and blue eyes. He bore little physical resemblance to either the Harlow twins or their brother, but he saw Vinnie in his direct, forthright gaze. "Good morning, my lord, I understand you are here to see me."

Despite the duke's promise of paternal indifference, Huntly suddenly felt himself grow anxious. "I am, sir, yes," he said and introduced himself. "I'm an intimate of the Duke of Trent's and as such have gotten to know your daughters. They are lovely."

Harlow's brow furrowed at this seeming non sequitur, but he sat down and gestured that the marquess do the same. "I trust you are not here because Emma has slighted you or discomforted you or in some other way caused you harm. Though she remains a hoyden, she is no longer a minor and as such no longer my responsibility. If you have a problem, I suggest you apply to your friend the duke."

"I assure you, sir, Emma has not caused me any harm," he said, surprised to find himself offended on the young lady's behalf. "I think she's delightful, and even if I did not, I would certainly not run to you with tales."

The gentleman smiled faintly. "That is to your credit. I'm sorry to report that other young men have not shown your forbearance."

"I'm here about your other daughter."

"My other daughter?" Harlow repeated, as if not entirely certain there was another Harlow girl. "You mean Lavinia?"

"Yes, Lavinia."

Harlow raised his eyebrows at this unexpected news. "Well, I must tell you, the same rules apply. She is of age and whatever Vinnie has done to offend you—though what she could have done to have offend you is a mystery—must be taken up with her."

"She has not offended me at all," Huntly said smoothly, more than confident after this brief exchange that his request would not be denied. "I would like to marry her and am here to request her hand."

Instantly, Harlow's expression cleared. "Is that all? Yes, you have my permission," he said, standing up and offering to shake the marquess's hand again. "I trust we are done here?"

As the meeting had gone more and less as the duke had described, Huntly said, "Yes, sir. Shall I take up the matter of contracts with your son?"

"A capital idea. I'm returning to my room to rest, but the others are about to sit down for breakfast. I'm sure the viscount won't mind if you join them," Harlow said, making the offer with what his future son-in-law would describe as indifferent graciousness. The gentleman, though polite, did not seem at all interested in getting to know the man her daughter was about the marry, a development that disappointed, if didn't surprise, the marquess. If his own parents were alive, he imagined they would be eager to meet Vinnie.

"I appreciate the offer, sir, but I see no reason to linger when I have much to settle in London," he said with a bow. "I will give your regards to your daughters."

If Harlow thought this was another capital idea, he didn't say so, for he was already halfway out of the room when Huntly spoke.

The ride back to town went more smoothly than the ride out, half of which was passed in the dark. He drove quickly, stopping once to change horses at the Black Bull and have a midday meal, and returned to Berkeley Square a little after four o'clock. Since nobody had known where he had gone, his entire staff was relieved to see him arrive home only slightly worse for wear, except his valet, to whose keen eye Huntly looked considerably worse for wear. Upon removing the formerly pristine white waistcoat, Petrie shook his head sorrowfully and immediately put the offending garment in the trash receptacle, from which it was promptly removed by the housekeeper, who felt there was never a sufficient number of rags to be had.

Although making the trip to Tunbridge Wells and back within thirteen hours had been uncomfortable and inconvenient, the marquess, relaxing finally in a warm bath, was remarkably glad he had done it. He had complied with acceptable protocol and could proceed as he wished with nothing in his way.

As eager as he was to make his proposal—what an inadequate word *eager* was to describe the unbearable impatience he felt!—Huntly requested a quick snack be served in the study, for he was clever enough not to ask for a woman's hand on an empty stomach.

He was just about to start eating a joint of roast beef when the door to his study flew open and in stormed Vinnie, who slammed the door with a resounding crack in a nonplussed Fleming's face. Surprised by her appearance—both the suddenness of it and the remarkable way she looked, for not only was her dress stained and torn, including a long rip at the hem, but the color in her face was inordinately high. Obviously, she had been working on her invention, and his first thought—after, of course, thinking how wonderful it was that she was there when he'd just been wanting her there—was that she had finally mastered the formulation. But then he noticed her eyes, not the red rims or the puffiness, though his quick gaze observed those elements as well, but the fierce anger in them, the spitting fire, as if she loathed him entirely and couldn't wait to explain why.

Transfixed by her rage, he stayed planted to the spot as she raised her hand and slapped him across the cheek.

"I withdrew!" Vinnie screamed, her anger an almost palpable thing. She took several steps back, as if being close enough to strike him was too near. "I stood in this very room, and I withdrew. But you said no, you bastard. You said no, and now you seek to destroy me and all you had to do was let me withdraw a week ago. You are a vile, bloody coward and I despise you."

Huntly did not know what was happening. As when he'd walked into the conservatory all those weeks ago expecting to admire the duke's orchids and instead found himself met by a wall of water, he couldn't conceive what was going on. Now, like then, the world suddenly stopped making sense.

Last time, he'd apologized. Confronted with an inexplicable situation, incapable of grasping the larger picture, he'd sought refuge in familiar courtesies and accepted blame for something with which he had nothing to do.

He could not go that route again. How could he treat her like a polite stranger when he loved her more than anything else in the world? So, despite his instincts and despite a sick dread that her hatred was unalterable, he took several steps forward, looked her in the eye and said with just as much vehemence as she, "I love you." He waited a moment, then said it again. "I love you. I love you. I"—pause—"love"—pause again—"you. I would *never* do anything to destroy you, for that would mean destroying myself. I love you."

Vinnie launched herself at him. He could think of no other word to describe the way she propelled herself into his arms, the whole length of her body suddenly pressed against the whole length of his.

He was still unable to comprehend what was happening to him. That Vinnie would wrap her arms around his neck, that she would run her hands through his hair, that she would press her lips against his in frantic need made no more sense than her seething anger. Lack of sleep played a part, he knew, for it weakened his ability to reason as surely as it did his self-control, but even if this bewilderment was a permanent condition, he didn't care. He was a man of science who believed the world was ultimately a knowable place with enough investigation, but he would happily live in a state of absolute confusion if he could do so with her.

As mystified as he was as to why it was happening, he certainly knew *what* was happening, and he returned her kiss with equal fervor, pulling her body tightly against his as if trying to absorb it into his own.

His befuddled mind retained enough sense to realize this wasn't the sort of activity one did in the middle of the study on a desk with a joint of beef and a bottle of claret, so he lifted her up and carried her to the thick rug in front of the fireplace. The blaze crackled as he lowered her gently, and he kneeled across from her, kissing her softly, deeply, heartrendingly. He pulled back to look into her eyes, and when she leaned forward to capture his lips again, he raised her head until her gaze locked with his. "I love you. I love you."

With her eyes intently focused on his, Vinnie clutched his shirt in both hands and pulled it over his head in one fluid movement. His breath hitched as she laid first her hands on his chest, then her lips. As incredible as his need was, as unbearably intense his craving, it paled in comparison with the gratitude he felt at her simple touch. He had known this would happen—from the moment when she'd launched herself forward it had been inevitable—but he'd never imagined how humbled it would make him feel to know this incredible, brave girl wanted him.

His gaze just as unwavering as hers, his movements considerably less smooth, he removed her tattered dress and stared at her gorgeous form in the flickering light of the fire, unable to believe how perfect she was. With a touch that was almost deferential, he cupped her breast and bestowed a butterfly-soft kiss on her nipple. She moaned in pleasure and tried to pull him closer. He resisted, determined not to rush a single moment of this remarkable experience. He pressed his lips against her other breast, teasing the nipple until she cried out his name. It was the first thing she'd said since calling him a vile coward, and he relished the desire in her voice, the longing, the yearning. Dizzy with it, he trailed his hand down her chest, across her stomach and over the mount of her womanhood until he could feel the soft folds of her flesh quivering with need. Gently, he brushed a finger over her nub of desire, and feeling her writhe, brushed it again and again and again until she cried out with pleasure and sighed his name. Then he captured her lips again in a searing kiss as her hands caressed his body—his arms, his chest, his back—until they came to an unbearable boundary. Without breaking contact, he shifted his hips and as soon as she removed his trousers, her hands resumed their heady stroking.

Her fingers, tentative at first but with growing certainty, touched his manhood, and he had to close his eyes to absorb the pleasure. He didn't know how long he would be able to hold on and yet he knew he would hold on forever if that was what she wanted. Whatever she wanted was hers, and when her smooth movements became frantic, he decided she wanted more.

With a hypnotic kiss, he pressed her back gently against the rug, positioned himself over her and looked down. Staring into her stunning blue eyes, he wondered why he had ever thought the world didn't make sense. The world made perfect sense, and when the haze of desire lifted from her gaze, he said with the certainty of the ages, "I love you." Then he shifted his hips forward, entering her body gradually and gently, attuned to her every response—her every moan, her every shudder, her every tremor. He kept his movements slow and smooth, savoring everything about her: the silken feel of her thighs, the soft breath of her sighs, the tight clutch of her arms as she held him against her. The feel of her hips as they moved under him was like a drug pulling him deeper and deeper into a swirling abyss, and when he finally heard her cry out in release, he felt himself dissolve into the encompassing blackness.

Vinnie was satisfied—oh, was she satisfied. Having whipped into the room, hurling accusation, her anger a snarling beast she could barely keep on a leash, she had expected an argument, a shouting match, disgust, hatred, disdain, even indifference, but she had never imagined she'd see terror flash in his remarkably beautiful eyes. It was terror, pure and simple, unadulterated by logic or reason or understanding. Huntly had no idea why she was raving about and was terrified she would never stop.

It was that terror, more than the declaration of love, that had propelled her into his arms. At the sight of it, all the emotions of the day—happiness, excitement, anxiety, grief, shock, fury—coalesced into a single compulsion to touch him. And it wasn't enough to touch him once, to banish the terror and then step back. No, she had to keep on touching him until all of him was revealed, until there wasn't a single unlit corner for him to hide in. Felix Dryden, Marquess of Huntly, was hers now because she knew him completely.

Yes, she was very satisfied indeed.

Vinnie didn't know how Townshend had pulled off his trick, but it seemed likelier to her that the prime minister himself had revealed the truth than the man sweetly kissing her neck.

Luxuriating in the feel of him, she stretched lazily and marveled at the absurd unpredictability of the world—that she could wind up ravished in his study after an afternoon of weeping uncontrollably in her conservatory.

Suddenly, she recalled that afternoon's endeavors. "I perfected the hose," she said, her oddly husky voiced tinged with excitement.

Huntly raised his head from its comfortable perch at the nape of her neck, and it was only when she saw the amusement gleaming in his gorgeous eyes that she realized her first words should have probably have been more loverlike.

"I'd thought that was why you had come," he said, lightly running a hand over her cheek, as if compelled beyond himself to touch her again and again. "I saw your stained work dress and flushed face and thought you'd been in such a rush to tell me, you didn't bother to change. Congratulations. Congratulations, as well, on your acceptance into the British Horticultural Society. You have done the impossible, my love, and I'm extremely proud of you. Proud of myself, too," he added with a cheeky grin, "for thinking of it in the first place."

Vinnie laughed and allowed that he deserved some of the credit. Then she raised the other unloverlike subject that was on her mind. "We need to alert the home secretary that he has a traitor in his office, for there's no other way to account for Townshend using the truth about Windbourne to coerce me into turning down my acceptance."

"Ah, so that is the charge of which I stand accused," Huntly said softly, looking Vinnie in the eyes and adding soberly, "I did not tell him."

Grinning with an audacious wickedness she hadn't known she was capable of, she said, "I thought I'd made a fairly convincing display of my belief in your innocence, but if you are still in doubt, my lord, I'm happy to prove it again."

Unable to resist the invitation in her eyes, he pressed her firmly against the rug as his hands encircled her breasts. He kissed her deeply, one, two, three times, and then, just when it seemed as if she would indeed have the pleasure of proving it again, he groaned loudly, rolled onto his side and reached for his clothes. He glared at her as he tugged on his shirt and trousers. "You have the disconcerting ability, as no one else in the world, of making me lose all sense of propriety," he growled. "I don't know how you do it, and I can't say I like it very much." He marched over to his desk, tugged open a drawer, pulled out a small box and then slammed the drawer shut. "We need to discuss Townshend and your membership, which you are not declining to appease that weaselly cur, and we absolutely need to dispense with the traitor in the Home Office but first—" He broke off his tirade to toss the contents of the box at her on the rug. "First let the record show that I tried to do it properly. I even got your father's permission. But that's all ruined now, so you might as well put that on your finger and we shall call it a day."

Vinnie picked up the ring—a delicate affair with rubies and diamonds—and watched it glimmer and sparkle in the firelight, as transfixed by its beauty as she was her own emotions.

The compact between them had already been made. The moment he had said he loved her, this agreement had been forged, so, yes, she was happy to put on the ring and call it a day.

And yet she was deeply moved by the churlishness of his proposal, for what woman wouldn't want to know that she made her lover behave uncharacteristically? It was only right, she thought, as he had the exact same effect on her: how else to explain the practical Miss Lavinia Harlow lying naked on a rug before a crackling fire in a gentleman's study? Her own sense of propriety had been so lost, it hadn't even occurred to her to lock the door. She was as exposed and vulnerable as any woman could possibly be and she didn't care, which merely confirmed what she had suspected several times in the last few weeks: She was every bit a Harlow hoyden.

As she made no move to put on the ring, Huntly dropped to his knees and slid it on for her finger. Then he laid his forehead against hers and said, "I love you."

This time, she responded appropriately. "I love you, too."

Hearing the words, which, of course, he'd known in his heart for almost twenty-four hours, so moved the marquess that Vinnie found herself once again lying beneath him. She was happy to stay there for the rest of the night, if not the rest of her life, but he rolled off her again, this time with a sigh and a deeply felt goddamn it. He pulled down his shirt, which Vinnie had tried to slide over his head without his noticing. She had come very close.

When he finished tucking in his shirt, Huntly raised her into a sitting position and tugged on her walking gown.

"You look like a street urchin," he announced, rubbing his thumb against a black smudge on her cheek, "for which we must be grateful, as none of my staff would suspect me of behaving in such a reprehensible manner with a grubby ragamuffin."

As much as she shared his respect for decorum, she found his devotion to it at that particular moment to be extremely inconvenient. She had a problem with it at other times, as well, and didn't hesitate to say so while he fastened the buttons on her dress. "I appreciate your attempt to do things properly, but the next time an emotionally wrought woman tells you she killed her fiancé, I would recommend against a sojourn in Tunbridge Wells and advise an immediate visit to the overwrought young lady so that she doesn't spend the entire day thinking you despise her."

Startled, Huntly turned her around to look at him.

"What did you think I would do today?" she asked with a faint smile. "I mean, other than work on my invention. I expected you every moment, and when you didn't come, it broke my heart."

The stricken expression on his face broke her heart all over again, but she couldn't stop herself from speaking the truth. The only way to put her past behind her was to share it with her future. "I don't regret shooting Windbourne," she announced matter-of-factly. "I am far too sensible to regret taking a necessary action. If I hadn't killed him, he would have surely killed me and very likely Emma. I do not worry about my immortal soul, for I cannot believe God would punish me for acting in self-defense, nor do I lay awake at night tortured by my conscience. In more than six months, I never once regretted it and yet this afternoon, when I realized you weren't coming, I felt unbearable remorse because I assumed you couldn't love a murderer."

He gripped her shoulders and growled, "You are not a murderer."

She smiled gratefully at his defense of her. "It doesn't matter now."

Unsatisfied, he shook her gently. "Of course it matters, for you are not a murderer. What you are is the bravest woman I've ever met, and I'm humbled that you would trust me with your heart after such an inconceivable betrayal."

Humbled herself by his remarkable statement—he had to be the only human being in the world to think the sensible Miss Lavinia Harlow brave—she felt tears rise in her throat and pushed them back. She would not be one of those silly women who were so overwhelmed by their own happiness they could not help but cry. Instead, she sought to lighten the mood with a glance at his desk. "Was that a joint of roast beef I saw when I came in?"

Taken aback by the change in subject, Huntly could only nod.

Vinnie stood up. "Do you mind if I partake? I'm suddenly ravenous."

A proper place setting had been laid for the marquess, but she picked up the joint with her fingers and took a generous bite. Having spent the day first in anxious impatience and then in inconsolable disappointment, she was in fact starving and couldn't remember a cold slab of beef ever tasting so delicious. She tore off a piece and held it out to Huntly, "Here," she said.

He obligingly—and eagerly—tasted the meat from her fingers and pulled back reluctantly when the activity that immediately followed threatened to get out of hand. He took several deep, calming breaths, then tried to straighten her hair. "It's too incriminatingly disheveled for me to summon Fleming," he explained.

For some reason, his administrations made her giggle and as much as she tried to keep her head straight to assist him in his endeavor, she couldn't stop seeking out his gaze, for she loved seeing the glint of laughter in his gorgeous eyes.

When he finally had her curls in a semblance of order, he rang the bell for his butler and requested as elaborate a meal as possible in the shortest amount of time. Fleming agreed with all due urgency, then tarried for several minutes as he offered Huntly his congratulations.

"My valet will also be profoundly relieved," Huntly said when his butler finally left. "He's out of sorts with me for not showing sufficient concern over my appearance in my pursuit of your father's blessing. He tolerated my lackadaisical standards when we were at sea but now that we have returned to civilization, I must exert myself to live up to his."

Vinnie was amused to find an ally in her disapproval of the Tunbridge Wells scheme and promptly said so, which had the immediate effect of putting the marquess on the defensive, for having never proposed before, how could he know better? They debated the matter for some time—would a note to her residence ("Off on absurd errand society deems necessary, will return presently") really have been so difficult to arrange?—and they didn't notice twenty minutes had passed until Fleming returned with two footmen carrying platters of food.

They talked easily as they ate, reviewing past events from a new perspective. Huntly apologized for turning the trip to Mr. Brill's factory into a cold-blooded bargain. "That was never my intention," he said. "I swear when I arrived at your house that morning, my purpose was to make amends.

Then we kissed and my wits deserted me and all I could think about was putting distance between us before I lost control of my actions again."

Gratified by this confession, Vinnie happily volunteered that she had been so confounded by his beautiful green-blue eyes she had spoken absolute nonsense on their first meeting. She still didn't know from whence she got the name Mrs. Wellburger. Recalling the incident, Huntly cheerfully confessed that he'd thought her certifiably insane and was deeply disturbed by the prospect of his friend being married to a bedlamite.

"I will say now how greatly relieved I was—though for a different reason than at this moment—to discover Trent had married the other Harlow Hoyden," he added with a glint in his eye.

Vinnie found the idea of being mistaken for the new duchess to be hilarious and launched into the tale of Emma and the duke's courtship, leaving nothing out, not even her sister's absurd plan to have Trent seduce her, which did not reflect well on either of them. Naturally, she told him of the mad dash to the coast in successive carriages—Windbourne followed by Emma and Philip followed by Vinnie and Trent—and of the baron's treachery. Although she still felt like the most insensible fool in all the kingdom not to recognize the insincerity of her fiancé's regard, the sting was gone, for it no longer mattered. She would suffer the indignities of a dozen Windbournes if it meant she could have one Huntly in the end.

In the same way, she no longer resented the endless months devoted to false mourning. It had been painful indeed to demonstrate so much respect for so unworthy an object, but it salved her feelings considerably to imagine that putrid little toad burning in eternal hellfire with his fist clenched in rage at her happiness with the marquess, whose superior social standing would further rankle his greedy little soul.

Huntly listened to her account with a mixture of fascination, outrage, amusement, admiration, surprise and anger, and although he tried to keep his questions to a minimum, he couldn't help interrupting from time to time. When she explained how awkward Emma had made things by spreading that ludicrous tale of Windbourne's death, he said on a note of triumph, "I knew that story had to be the invention of a perverse mind from the very moment I heard it."

Vinnie wholeheartedly agreed to the perversity of her sister's mind and admitted she had been trying for months to come up with a satisfying scheme to repay Emma for the indignity of a corseted fiancé. Her future bridegroom, who was not only sympathetic to her plight but amused by the challenge, promptly volunteered to help her in that endeavor. Vinnie eschewed the schoolboy pranks that readily sprang to mind as being too well suited to their victim, as Emma would be delighted by a frog in her shoe and would no doubt adopt it as a pet. To be truly effective, she observed, the plan had to be something her sister would find unpleasant, at which point the marquess suggested they recruit the dowager to dragoon Emma into planning a rout or, even better, a musicale. Vinnie loved the idea so much, she started to clap and when, a half hour later, the object of their plot entered the room with her husband, they were discussing dates for her downfall.

"Don't fear. I have routed the villain and all is well," Emma announced as she strode into the room, not at all disconcerted to find her sister sitting indecently close to the marquess on the settee by the fire—which was just as well, for Vinnie was disconcerted enough for the two of them. Keenly aware of the impropriety of the situation, she jumped in alarm, darted to her feet and scooted around the settee so that it stood as a barrier between her and Huntly. Her surprised betrothed rose as well.

"What she means to say is, we've come to put Vinnie's mind at ease, but I see you've already done that," the duke said with a sly grin at his friend. "I believe congratulations are in order. I couldn't be happier for the both of you."

Huntly gratefully accepted his friend's felicitations and

embraced him warmly, while Emma watched with an uncertain expression that was clearly exaggerated.

"Is it official? May I congratulate her now?" she asked her husband before turning to her sister to explain, "I'm under strict orders not to embarrass you with my expectations, as I had assumed there was only one way a threat of strangulation could end—an engagement, of course, being it. Did you even try to strangle him or did you jump immediately to the proposal?"

Vinnie blushed becomingly as she recalled the activity to which she and Huntly had immediately jumped, but if her sister noticed the color sweeping her cheeks, she didn't comment. Instead, she wrapped her arms around her and said how truly happy and delighted she was.

Her response was the exact opposite of her reaction last time, when Emma had greeted the announcement of her sister's engagement with a tight smile, a weak hug and a few muttered words, which may have been *how nice*. Emma's family had attributed her underwhelming response to a fear of losing her close connection to her twin to the even closer connection of a husband, but it turned out that she merely saw Windbourne more clearly than everyone else.

Neither sister made mention of the earlier episode, but they were both thinking about it, and when Emma whispered, "He's perfect for you," Vinnie realized how much she needed her blessing. Her relationship with Windbourne would never have worked for that reason alone.

The duke insisted Emma relinquish Vinnie so that he may congratulate her properly, and as soon as she was free, he wrapped her in a tight hug.

Softly and with the same heartfelt sincerity with which Trent had once thanked her for bringing him and Emma together, Vinnie said, "Thank you, my dear friend."

Her brother-in-law declined to take any credit for the match, not even for the service of introducing her to his friend, and insisted he was grateful to her, for he knew if she didn't help Huntly catalog the hundreds of specimens he'd brought back from the South Seas, he himself would somehow be coerced into doing it. Vinnie found the prospect of examining and classifying new species of flowers so incredibly satisfying, her level of contentment, already impossibly high, inched impossibly higher.

It was, she announced, fair compensation for giving up her membership to the British Horticultural Society.

At once, several voices objected, the loudest of which belonged to the marquess, who proposed a dawn appointment with Townshend to resolve the problem once and for all. Vinnie, who found her fiancé's valiant proposition as noble as it was ridiculous, kindly declined his offer and suggested they devote their energy to the more worthy matter of discovering the traitor in the home secretary's office.

Huntly caviled at the idea that any matter was more worthy than she and countered that knuckling under to a plagiarizing bounder offended every sensibility. He could not let the insult stand!

Vinnie once again appreciated the sentiment for all its gallantry but pointed out, as the insult had not been dealt to him, it wasn't for him to decide whether it stood or fell.

The marquess, speaking as a member of the British Horticultural Society, which had had eleven tedious votes on the matter the night before, insisted that it *was* for him to decide, as her membership had been approved in a fully democratic process and he would not let the will of the people be overthrown by one petty tyrant who didn't have the sense to do research for his own book. He then tried to enlist the duke's support for this line of reasoning, but Trent simply smiled and shook his head. Next, Huntly turned to Emma, in whom he felt sure he had an ally, and urged her to convince her sister to take a more aggressive stance.

Emma nodded enthusiastically. "As anyone who knows me is aware, I'm always happy to urge Vinnie to take a more aggressive stance regardless of the situation, which is why I was delighted when she announced she was coming here to strangle you. But in this instance, it's not necessary.

As I said when we arrived, the villain has been routed. Townshend has not only been made to name the source of his information in Lord Sidmouth's office but to resign his membership as well."

Vinnie, who knew her sister's methods well enough not to question them, cheered gratefully and suggested they celebrate with dessert, which had not been included in the elaborate meal Fleming had served. "Bread and butter pudding would not be amiss."

Not as familiar with Emma's ways, despite an afternoon perusing her dossiers, Huntly looked at her in surprise. "How did you arrange that?"

Emma shrugged with what her sister knew to be false modesty and explained, "I assure you, my methods in this instance are far from remarkable and would have no doubt occurred to you or Vinnie had your brains not been addled by love. As my sister rightly pointed out, the person who provided Townshend with the details of the Windbourne case was acting illegally, for the file contained information known to only a select few. It therefore required very little effort to convince Townshend that simply being in possession of those facts made him a traitor to the Crown. The prospect of spending twenty years in Newgate—or did I threaten him with beheading?—went a long way in loosening his tongue. Once I had the name of the culprit, who, by the way, turned out to be the cousin of the secretary's wife, I promised I would keep my silence if he resigned his membership. I also assured him that if any hint of the Windbourne affair got out, I would assume he was the source and report him immediately to the prince. I assure you, he was sufficiently cowered by the threat. I don't believe he will give us any more trouble, though I do think asking Mr. Squibbs to do additional research on the man would be a wise countermeasure, as it is always better to have more information on one's quarry than less. Now, I think a little sweet treat is a wonderful idea. May I request Shrewsbury cakes?"

"That would be lovely indeed," said Vinnie, who looked

pointedly at their host. She might be marrying into the household, but she couldn't very well start ordering the servants around.

The marquess, who was not done interrogating her sister, either did not notice the hint or refused to take it. "But how did you know about Townshend's ultimatum? I only just discovered it from Vinnie."

"That actually required a bit of deduction," Emma admitted, sitting on the settee recently vacated by her sister, "which was sparked by Trent's cousin Philip, whose nose for gossip and talent for spreading it equals Lady Jersey. He had heard from Denbigh, who had heard from Finch-Hatton, who had heard from Moray, who had heard from Mr. Berry himself that Townshend had instructed him to burn Miss Harlow's membership file, as she had decided to pass on the pleasure. I could not let such a provocative statement go unheeded and sought out Townshend in his home. A complete cad, he was only too happy to inform me he'd beaten Vinnie at her own game and would publish even more scandalous information about her if she did not withdraw her acceptance. Obviously, that could mean only one thing, as Vinnie has no other sins. Though, to be clear," she added forcefully with a sharp look at Huntly to make sure he agreed, "killing a murderer bent on taking your life is not a sin."

"We are entirely clear," Huntly assured Emma, who dipped her head in approval. "I won't pretend I'm not disappointed to be deprived of the opportunity to plant him a facer, but you have resolved the matter satisfactorily and for that I'm grateful."

Now the duke laughed. "A familiar sentiment I myself voiced."

Sympathetic to their feelings, Emma offered what little consolation she could. "I realize it's not the same thing, but Philip, who accompanied me to Townshend's house, gave the gentleman a slight elbow shove on our way out, which had the fortunate effect of sending him careening into the fireplace. It was not lit at the time," she added apologetical-ly, "but he did get a significant amount of coal on his person when he landed in the hearth. He was sputtering in anger as we showed ourselves out."

Vinnie giggled at the image of the dictatorial deputy di-rector of Kew Gardens covered in ash like a chimney sweep. Feeling very pleased with her sister, she sat down next to her on the settee and generously offered up the sec-retary's cousin as potential quarry to her fiancé. "If your pugilistic tendencies are still not appeased, I mean. Addi-tionally, a visit to Lord Sidmouth is in order to warn him of the vulnerabilities in his filing system."

Trent quickly assured her that a letter had already been sent.

"And that, I believe, concludes this episode quite nicely," Emma said with satisfaction. "Now, did I hear someone say jam tartlets?"

"No, imp," said her husband, "that was the echo cham-ber in your head. We should be leaving as you have the thea-ter this evening—and make no mistake, I take great delight in saying this—with Lady Bolingbroke and her daughter."

Emma winced as if in pain.

Huntly looked from Vinnie to her sister. "I thought you abandoned all manipulative schemes and decided to do the honorable thing."

"We did," said Vinnie, dimpling, "but Lady Boling-broke seems to feel the honorable thing consists of our keeping our word to bring her daughter into fashion. She would not accept no for an answer, despite our very reason-able arguments, so Emma is taking her to *The Merchant of Venice* tonight and for a ride in the park tomorrow."

Her twin narrowed her eyes. "You mean *we* are taking her to *The Merchant of Venice* tonight. I only committed to the event for your sake, so romantic bliss or not, you are com-ing with me." She stood up and walked over to her future brother-in-law. "I honestly can't tell you how happy I am to welcome you to the family. I think you will make Vinnie a wonderful husband, and that truly delights me. However, in the interest of full disclosure, I must advise you against taking Vinnie away on a high-seas adventure for several years. I do not know what scheme I will come up with to prevent the voyage, but it will be complex, effective and, I'm reasonably sure, quite unpleasant for you."

"Emma!" Vinnie said sharply.

The marquess, whose future plans did not at the moment include a second journey, though he would not rule it out completely, leaned down to give his best friend's wife a kiss on the cheek. "I consider myself duly warned," he said good-naturedly.

Emma looked at the duke with a wry smile. "He doesn't believe me."

Trent shrugged. "Well, you are fairly unbelievable, my love."

Vinnie stood up as well. "I will go to the theater tonight and to the park tomorrow, and I reserve the right to go on a high-seas adventure if I so chose."

"Just because you are my sister does not mean you are immune to my scheming," Emma said sternly, which made Vinnie laugh. Obviously, she was not immune, for was that not where it had all started: with Emma's scheme to break up her engagement with Windbourne. Nothing had ever benefitted the Harlow sisters more.

"You should head home. I'll be along presently," Vinnie said with a sidelong glance at her betrothed.

Intercepting the look, which belied the promptness of the word *presently*, Trent said, "You have five minutes. We'll wait in the carriage."

Now she directed a sullen glance at his grace. "I gave you fifteen minutes," she grumbled, referring to the interval she'd allowed him to remain alone in a room with Emma to make his proposal.

"Clearly, I'm the better chaperone," he stated, pressing his hand to the small of his wife's back to guide her to the door. "I trust we will see you tomorrow, Felix, and every day thereafter. You are welcome to come as early as you like, for I know my mother will be eager to offer her felicitations as well. She will also plan the wedding for you, so unless you want to wait six months for a fashionable affair at St. George's, I suggest you apply for a special license at once. The timing, no doubt, will cause the highest sticklers to raise their brows, but I'm sure you'll agree it's better to suffer their disapproval than to wait."

Huntly heartily fell in with this plan, and as soon as the door closed behind Emma and the duke, he turned to Vinnie to discuss their nuptials. She nodded politely at what seemed to her to be unimportant details, then interrupted when a thought occurred to her.

"My hose!" she said excitedly. "You must come very early tomorrow so I can demonstrate how beautifully my hose works."

"And that, my love," he said, laughing as he pressed her against the door and kissed her so gently, her knees went weak, "is where I"—another kiss, another weakened joint—"came in."

As breathless as she was, Vinnie managed to say with some asperity, "Yes, and I forgive you."

He kissed her eyes, her cheeks, the tip of her nose, the line of her jaw. "Forgive me?" he asked as he pulled back slightly to look at her with eyes hazy with desire.

"For coming into the conservatory with your appallingly impeccable manners and your stunning aquamarine eyes just as my hose was exploding and making me feel foolish and inadequate. For that," she explained, "I forgive you."

Huntly pressed his body against hers, and Vinnie felt herself throb with expectation and need. "I can't let you do that," he explained in a husky voice. "No, a man of my appallingly impeccable manners must first make amends." So saying, he ran his hands along her thighs, over her hips and up her torso to her breasts as he pleaded with her to please let him make amends. His lips, trailing a line of kisses from her collarbone to her chin, spread the fire to an unbearable degree. Then, with his eyes focused on hers, he said please one more time and captured her lips in a kiss so intoxicating, it had her begging for forgiveness, too.

And with that, the sensible Miss Lavinia Harlow lost her senses completely.

ABOUT THE AUTHOR

Lynn Messina is author of ten novels, including the best-selling *Fashionistas*, which has been translated into sixteen languages. Her essays have appeared in *Self, American Baby* and the *New York Times* Modern Love column, and she's a regular contributor to the *Times* Motherlode blog. She lives in New York City with her husband and sons.